TOLEDANO

It onsiderable shock to Simon Good on
hi se from prison to find his reception
c(ree includes Mr Justice Meddlisome
– ꞁe ꞁnan directly responsible for his
te ꞁry removal from society. He learns
fr ꞁe Judge, whose good name is being
tꞁ ꞁed, that a flabby but enthusiastic
m ꞁerꞁrook, Mario Toledano, is out to kill
hꞁꞁn. Good's anxiety to find the motive for
this a parently pointless vendetta and his
atte t, for once honourable, to destroy the
eviꞁꞁꞁce of a youthful indiscretion on the
pꞁꞁ ꞁ ꞁ the Judge, lead him into a series of
extrꞁ ꞁdinary events...

TOLEDANO

TOLEDANO

by

George Davis

Dales Large Print Books
Long Preston, North Yorkshire,
BD23 4ND, England.

British Library Cataloguing in Publication Data.

Davis, George
    Toledano.

    A catalogue record of this book is
    available from the British Library

    ISBN   978-1-84262-806-5 pbk

First published in Great Britain in 1962 by
Chapman & Hall Limited

Dales Large Print is an imprint of Library Magna Books Ltd.

Printed and bound in Great Britain by
T.J. (International) Ltd., Cornwall, PL28 8RW

Contents

The characters and companies
in this story
are entirely fictitious

CHAPTER 1

Up Against Two Brick Walls

Mr Hammersley held on grimly to the gunwale and his spectacles, feeling slightly sick, straining his eyes through the salty, stinging spume into the blackness of the night, dulled by the savage blow he had received, shivering with wet and cold and shock, a little afraid, and yet determined to bring the man, now poised in the prow ready to jump, to his senses if he possibly could.

A dim echo of Quenella Mansfield's sudden cry – 'Stop him, Charles!' – sighed through his befuddled brain like the dying wail of a siren. Siren? Sirens were mythical creatures, half women, half birds, sailors' dreams, and he was no sailor. But Quenella Mansfield was a particular friend of Simon Good, and if Quenny shouted 'Stop him!', stop him he would. How well he remembered his first encounter in the Temple with this curious mixture of a man!

With a savage crunch, the boat thrust itself against the sloping shingle bank, urged forward by the rolling breakers and a propeller

11

which now began to thrash the air as the greedy undertow sucked and writhed back into the maw of the next great roller. Thank heaven the violent storm which had lambasted that part of the coast of Portugal for the past twenty-four hours was blowing itself out.

The man in the prow leapt on to the beach as an angry wave snarled out of the night and broke completely over the helpless shell, twisting it sideways, hustling it forwards, and tearing it back again as the water receded.

Screwing up his courage, Hammersley climbed on a thwart, steadied himself, and followed with a valiant jump into the surf, landing knee-deep in a rushing, tumbling undertow which sought to drag him into the breakers and destroy him.

'Come back, you fool!' he yelled, but the screeching wind only tossed his words back at him. Next moment he was floundering chest-high in a fierce breath-taking maelstrom as the next roller rushed madly up the shingle. 'If ever I get out of this lot alive I'll run away and join a circus,' he found himself thinking inconsequentially.

Willy-nilly, he was tossed forward like a cork in the sudden lifting upsurge, and he did all he could to assist this movement as he realised in a panic he was in grave danger of drowning, that he'd be lucky if he made the beach. Within sight of success he found his legs sucked away from under him, he found himself fighting and gulping for air, swallowing six of the Seven Seas in the process, the tangy salt water turning his stomach to the point of nausea. As he recollected it, the nearest landfall he was likely to encounter in the direction he was then travelling was Flores in the Azores, some nine hundred miles to the west, and it was therefore imperative that he made Portugal, nine yards to the east. Several of the less laudable incidents in his life reeled themselves off before him, and he wondered if this was *it*.

He was flung suddenly against a smooth, partly submerged rock, and to this he clutched grimly with every ounce of his strength as the sea and shingle rushed madly back over him. For a brief moment the whipped-up frenzy relented, and Hammersley, obeying a primeval instinct which told him it was now or never, scrabbled his way in the dark to the edge of the foreshore and emerged from the foam, feeling like nothing on earth, or at best, a cross between Aphrodite and the Sword Excalibur.

With a sob he stumbled up the shingle beach, gulping in great lungfuls of air, fumbling for his glasses, which, by a miracle and a rubber band wound round one ear, were still hanging on precariously, rubbing the lenses between thumb and forefinger to

13

restore visibility, knuckling his eyes to rid them of the salty spume which all but blinded him.

Thus Charles Hammersley set foot in Portugal on that storm-swept autumn night, and he would have preferred one of the more conventional routes recommended by Thos. Cook.

In his predicament he had lost his quarry. The elemental blackness was terrifying. Out of the tail of his eye he was suddenly conscious of a streak of fire hurtling up into the heavens, and before his mind could analyse it, the whole stretch of beach was lit up by a gently-falling ball of green light. Instinctively, Hammersley froze, as did the man scrambling up the beach thirty yards ahead, each obeying a drill instilled by numbers long ago, a drill which said 'When the Very light bursts, freeze'; even now the reflex action was as much a habit as reaching for a cigarette when somebody else lights up.

He squinted ahead into the eerie light which gave everything a curiously static appearance, and spotted the crouching man over to his right.

'Come back, you fool!' he yelled again, giving chase. 'You'll never get away with it!'

Abandoning caution, the other scuttered away towards a great outcrop of rock at the foot of a gaunt cliff which was thrown into sharp relief by the cold light of the flare. Hewn into the outcrop was a steep flight of granite steps leading to the top of a jetty which stuck out into the sea like a crooked arm, a jetty which was partly man-made and partly formed by a tumble of rocks from the cliff above. As the unholy light faded, Hammersley caught a glimpse of the cottages clustered snugly beyond the seaweed-covered wall, had a momentary impression of box-like villas clinging in terraces to the cliff beyond, saw the dim form crunching urgently over to the foot of the steps. For the briefest of fleeting moments he thought there were two figures, close together, but he dismissed the idea as being a trick of halation due to his salted-up spectacles.

An acute wave of nausea swept over him as the brine got to work on his stomach. There was a sudden stab of red on his right, coming from the direction of the steps, something he didn't understand, something his mind couldn't cope with at that moment. Again it came, and a bullet whined away over his head into the night. In alarm, he realised what it was. Bless my soul, the fool was firing, he hoped not at him. How he hated violence; and how he welcomed the sudden darkness which fell again, a darkness a thousand times more intense.

Chokingly, and with one hand on his stomach, he went forward again. He'd done all that was humanly possible for Quenny Mansfield, for Simon Good, but now he feared that it was too late, that he'd failed. A sudden steep shelf in the beach caught him unawares. He stumbled and fell flat on his face. He felt very ill. He felt very alone. He vomited violently and lay there shivering...

Somewhere or other he'd read that every seventh wave was a monster. The daddy of them all suddenly ripsnorted out of the breakers, rushed with gathering fury up the shingle, reached out and tried to claim him. He seemed to be enveloped in a luxuriousness beyond compare, was conscious of warmth where there should have been coldness, felt he was in that celestial twilight between wakefulness and sleep. As the water receded, leaving him uncovered, he went through the motions of tucking himself in. And then passed out.

This was definitely not his line.

The man now at the top of the treacherous steps stood for a moment in indecision, half wishing another Very signal would cast its lifeless illumination over the scene, so he could get his bearings. As if reading his thoughts, a thin trail of sparks streaked up into the night, and even before it burst into a green fire-ball he was flat on his face behind a low, tarry-smelling cabinet of fishing tackle on the far edge of the jetty.

As the evil, searching light hung there in the sky, he peered down across the tiny harbour at the jostling fishing boats and yachts straining to get away from their moorings, saw the giant black marker buoys heaving about like corks, spotted, in the tumble of white horses just beyond the harbour bar, the yacht *Kestrel* labouring in the heavy swell. Time was short. If things hadn't gone according to plan, and they got over the bar in one piece, they would soon be on his tracks, searching, searching, always searching. More than likely, he thought grimly, they'd end up at the bottom of the Bahia de Boa Fidelidade. The Bay of Good Faith. Some joke!

He screwed his head round and gazed intently at the houses across the harbour. A swinging inn-sign caught his attention, and his heart lifted. If only he could make it before they fired any more of those wretched lights. He committed to memory the obstacles along the jetty; and the green light had scarcely died before he was on his feet, running like greased lightning along the slippery stonework. He reached the foremost cottages, picked his way between two of them, found himself in the shelter of a narrow, ill-lit backstreet. Moving swiftly along it he came to where the inadequate main road out of Boa Fidelidade crossed over. It would be about a mile inland from here, he thought, where the road went through the narrow Marcelo Gorge, where the landslip had completely blocked the road. The rain-driven streets were empty; he worked his way along the backstreet to the far side of the harbour, and came out just short of the inn with the swinging sign, a sign which needed no words. It was just a picture of two keys crossed, executed in gold paint. The gold glinted in the inviting warm light which trickled through gaps in the curtains of the long bow window. The entrance to the place was in the lee of a side street, tucked well away from the bluster of the elements. A creaking, weather-beaten board over the portico said AS CHAVES CRUZADAS, and proclaimed that the Cross-Keys was a *pousada* – an inn with accommodation; he grimly hoped he would be accommodated.

Pausing for a moment in the deep, open doorway, he brushed away the rain from his face, ran his fingers through his hair, endeavoured to tidy his sodden, clinging clothing. Mechanically his eye took in an ancient Citroën lorry which almost blocked the entrance, registered in the dim light the giant lettering which proudly announced, amidst a welter of pasted hand-bills, GUIDO PEPPI – LE CIRQUE ET LA MÉNAGERIE LES PLUS GRANDS DU MONDE. It couldn't be a bigger circus than the one he was in already, he reflected mirthlessly.

He bent his ear for a moment to the chatter and laughter coming from behind the heavy protective curtain which hung on large wooden rings. It was a babel of many tongues, and he recognised Portuguese, French, Italian and English; Boa Fidelidade, although no bigger than a postage stamp, attracted many wealthy visitors, and it seemed that the landslip and storm had trapped them all in the Cross-Keys. Pulling aside the curtain, he found himself in the blue, fuggy atmosphere of a well-lit bar, surprisingly alive and full of people. The warmth of a blazing log fire, which crackled in a broad brick fireplace to his left, reached out and enveloped him like a heavenly dream, and for a moment his eyes were dazzled by the scintillating array of bottles, glasses and pewter on shelves backed by plate glass mirrors.

His acute awareness made him conscious that the conversation eased a little as he paused irresolutely there by the curtain, that although nobody actually turned round to stare at him, eyes were watching in the angled mirrors. A polite question-mark seemed to be thrown at him. Who is this wet, bedraggled stranger? What does he want? Where is he from? He turned and adjusted the curtain with a sharp flip, the wooden

19

rings racketing noisily along the rod. This action appeared as a rebuke to their guarded inquisitiveness, and was a signal for them to say to themselves: Let us not be rude; it is none of our concern; we are embarrassing a stranger rather than giving him a welcome; at least let us mind our own business. As if by magic, by the time he turned round and made for a vacant spot at the bar, converation was almost normal again, possibly a shade louder, a trifle forced, geared a fraction higher. Or perhaps at that moment he was hypersensitive to atmosphere and it was all a delusion.

The barman approached, polishing a glass with a white cloth, raising an eyebrow by way of invitation. He was well-built, looked as though he might have done some wrestling in his time, wore a spotless tussore jacket, was impassive, wall-eyed, suave, the sort of man you wouldn't trust with sixpence.

'Good evening, *senhor*,' he said, in a surprisingly gentle voice. 'What can I get you?'

'You can get me Mr Toledano.'

The chatter at the bar stopped as if someone had thrown a switch. The stranger had not spoken loudly, his voice had matched the barman's, but the effect was electrical. Apparently it wasn't considered etiquette to ask for Mr Toledano to be got. The barman became motionless, mentally sizing up the situation, wondering whether to feign ignorance and fail to comprehend the question, or whether to throw the man out. He saw the wintry, bitter gleam in the eyes across the bar, and lost some of his rugged benevolence.

'He's not available.'

'He's expecting me.'

'I'll see.' He turned and went up some stairs partially concealed by a tinkling bead curtain immediately behind him. Desultory snatches of conversation broke out in the bar until he returned. 'You're to go up,' he growled, holding aside the curtain to allow this quietly menacing customer to pass.

The other pushed by without a word. At the top of the stairs was a door from under which came a subdued line of light. Conscious that the radio down in the bar was now blaring at full strength, he thrust his way into the room, kicked the door shut behind him, and stood staring at the fleshy individual manicuring his fingernails at a desk in the corner; an individual who didn't bother to look up at the intrusion, who appeared not to have the slightest interest in anything but the all-absorbing half-moons and cuticles.

'Mr Toledano?'

'Could be,' agreed the adipose creature, without interest, buffing his nails on his coat lapel and holding them under the desk-light to get the effect. 'And who might you be?' he added indifferently.

'If you could be Mario Toledano, I might be Simon Good.'

The oily character at the desk became very still. His eyes flicked upwards for the first time. And the olive face assumed an intelligence out of keeping with the slab of flesh. He placed the elegant little nail file on the square of green baize on the desk, and carefully lined it up beside a gold pencil. 'I've been waiting a long time for this moment, my friend,' he said, and his voice was like velvet – with a two-edged knife wrapped up in it. 'How can I be sure you are Simon Good? You look different from how I remember you. That is only to be expected. Doubtless you don't remember me. I can't make up my mind whether you're an older man than I expected looking young, or a younger man looking old.'

'If you're prepared to strike an average, you're left with Simon Good,' said the other tersely. 'Put my appearance down to the ravages of time. And if you'd had the trouble I've had in getting here, you'd look like nothing on earth, too. You're no oil painting yourself.'

'They say the road through the gorge has been re-opened,' said the other, ignoring the jibe. 'What proof of identity have you to offer?'

'What proof have I that you are Mario Toledano?'

The fleshy face creased up into a replica of a smile, but there was no humour in the slaty eyes or in the sensuous mouth. 'If you get what you've come for, that is all the proof you require that I am Mario Toledano. Any other proof must come from you.'

'Does the name Peter Meek mean anything to you?'

'Indeed it does. And so it does, I imagine, to anyone else who read an account of that dual-named gentleman's trial for stealing electricity. So?'

'Does the name Charles Hammersley mean anything, then?'

'No. Should it?'

'I'm trying to establish identity.'

'I want proof, not names out of a hat.'

'Then I'll try you with some addresses.'

'By all means do.'

'Rotterdam, Oude Dijkstraat, 17b.'

The eyes set in the creases narrowed fractionally. 'Yes. And?'

'Krefeld. Johannestrasse, 34.'

Mario Toledano stared unwinkingly at the other for a long moment. 'What do you know about those addresses?'

'You'd be surprised.'

'Are you working for the British Government?'

The other laughed harshly. 'I don't like

work,' he said, 'and when I'm obliged to, I work on my own behalf.'

Mario Toledano chuckled throatily. 'You've almost convinced me,' he said. 'But if you are Simon Good, you have something for me.' He watched the weather-blasted man in front of him dig into his hip pocket for a grubby envelope, which he thrust down on the desk impatiently. Toledano examined it carefully, looking at the stamp and the postmark. He eased back the stamp, and revealed an initial. Unhurriedly he extracted from the envelope a folded sheet of paper, which he spread out flat on the desk. It was semi-glossy paper, and appeared to be a photostat copy of a document. Completely indifferent to the other's impatience, he held it in front of the desk-light, and found the water-mark for which he was looking. He looked up and smiled genially. 'Relax,' he said, 'you've come a long way, and you must be tired, but I just have to be certain. Suppose I tell you you haven't yet convinced me?' The smile was even warmer, but the tension mounted.

'Oh, you mean this,' grunted the other. He fished in his trouser pocket and produced something which looked like a coin with a piece of ribbon attached. 'The ribbon's lost its pristine beauty – it's been through hell and high water – but I expect it will serve your purpose.' He tossed it down on the desk.

An excited gleam came into Toledano's eye as he picked up the object and handled it, examining obverse and reverse and then the edge. 'Yes, I think this will serve my purpose,' he agreed. He opened a drawer at his side and took out a small leather box. Undoing the catch, he carefully placed the object inside. It fitted the indentations perfectly. 'Yes, very well indeed,' he said thoughtfully. Then, abruptly, 'You look worn out, you've been under a strain. In a few more moments you will be able to have a nice long undisturbed sleep. They seem to be making more noise than ever down in the bar, so I'll put you in a room at the back. I don't think you'll be disturbed.'

'It's not sleep I want – it's the original of that document. And now I've convinced you I'm Simon Good, or Peter Meek – whichever you prefer – perhaps you'll be gracious enough to show me any other pages you might possess. I'm intensely interested in historical papers.'

Mr Toledano looked wary. 'I didn't say you'd convinced me,' he said. 'I merely said I had to be certain.' He was playing for time, for just a few seconds while his hand went out to the open drawer. There was no doubt in his mind at all that this was Peter Meek, the man for whom he had been waiting so long. His hand reached the drawer.

'I've fulfilled my part of the bargain,'

growled the other impatiently, 'now fulfil yours.'

'If you say so,' agreed Toledano, and now all the sun of the Levant was in the smile. The tension in the room oozed away. He produced a gun and shot the man before him dead.

It was done so smoothly, quickly, that the other had no time to register surprise or fear. As he slumped slowly over the desk his eyes just showed fleeting sheer disbelief. A once powerful hand clutched at the loose square of green baize, clutched at anything to hold on to this world, but lost the battle. The nail file fell to the floor. For a man who had lived so recklessly it was an inglorious end.

Mario Toledano never did things by halves. His motto was that if you're going to shoot a man dead, shoot him very dead. Too many people came back, too many people 'did a Moriarty' ... and that could be awkward. His brother Emilio could never come back. Neither would Major Peter Meek. He fired two more rounds with cold precision. Shot him very dead... The whole thing was very distasteful.

He picked up the nail file and had another go at his cuticles.

All that had happened more than a week ago, and now Mr Toledano was a very worried man. Everything had gone so smoothly, without a hitch, without a hint of repercussion. His obligation to Mr Justice Meddlisome had been fulfilled and Peter Meek had paid the penalty. And now strange forces were at work which had shaken him rigid...

Some inexplicable forces are accepted without comprehension or apprehension. The earth went round the sun, the sun went round other suns, and possibly the universe went round other universes. But things which went round Mr Toledano, ordinary things surely capable of simple explanation, yet nevertheless inexplicable, upset him profoundly, as they would upset any intelligent, sensitive person.

Consider then the circumstances.

Mario Toledano had many sidelines, most of which were not praiseworthy. In the course of these pursuits he sometimes found it necessary to go to earth like the fox he was. Each of his foxholes had at least two exits, and this was not in case of fire. Mr Toledano could handle fire – he had played with it all his life – but he had a genuine horror of being trapped by the normal processes of the law.

The last bastion in his line of defences was the Hidden House. A word or two about the Hidden House...

In the dim and distant past when the now

flourishing mountain village of Pontemurio was no more than a tiny hamlet, there was a small parcel of stony land which nobody wanted because right in the middle of it was a towering rocky promontory known locally as Giant's Hammer. A poor smallholder from Alcobaca, who knew nothing of previous abortive attempts to extract crops from the arid soil which surrounded the outcrop, bought it and managed to extract a meagre existence and pay off the outrageous mortgage a couple of months before he died of overwork. In order to preserve what to him at least was valuable soil, the new owner had built his house back into the solid rockface of Giant's Hammer, using the excavated stone and rubble to wall off the tiny courtyard – big enough only to house the dog kennel – in front of the dwelling. As time went on, and his family grew larger and the needs for accommodation became correspondingly greater, the habitation went farther and farther back into the rock; and the wall grew longer, closely following the contour of the crag either side of the house, and finally became higher. This served two purposes, first to keep his young children off the reluctant crops, and secondly to extend his cultivation of peaches which thrived on the hot sunny side.

With the demise of its head, the family's limited fortunes dwindled. The land to the rear of Giant's Hammer was gradually sold as the village developed, and finally the plot in front of the high wall went in building lots at prices which would have surprised the original landowner. All that now remained of the initial parcel was the house in the rock with its tiny forecourt, approached from either side by the narrow passage formed by the rock-face and the blank, windowless backs of houses which, because of the inflated value of the building sites, were built right back against the wall. Indeed, the passage at either end where it debouched into the road was completely covered, as permission had been sought by the enterprising builder to build back over it to the face of Giant's Hammer. Thus the original house of dreams became the Hidden House.

In the fulness of time it fell into disuse as a habitation, became a storehouse, grew successively more depressing, was closed and shuttered, and the covered alley deteriorated into nothing more than a refuge for all the cats and mongrels in creation. Until Mr Toledano came upon it, and some said it was still used by a mongrel.

Although by now the alleyway was re-garded as a right of way for anyone foolish enough to venture along it, it was, of course, still included in the freehold of the Hidden House. Going to considerable trouble to trace the freeholder, Mr Toledano asked the price and paid cash without question. A stout, Spanish oak door was placed at each end of the passage, Mr Toledano's own builders moved in from Lisbon, and at great expense the house was secretly converted into a palace – fortress – with modern sanitation, refrigeration and even its own auxiliary power plant. And a magnificent built-in safe. *And* two exits. All very convenient.

The closing of the passageway caused considerable local feeling. It was actually a short cut between the two principal roads of the village, and although few used it everyone without exception felt Toledano was interfering with their civil liberty. They soon became used to the idea, however. In fact, the new owner was very rarely in residence, and even when he was, few saw either his coming or going for he varied his form of exit between the two doors, and it was impossible fully to tell his movements. The massive American deep-freeze in the kitchen held six months' supply of food.

The blurry image of Mr Toledano soon became a myth in the minds of the populace, and he would not have wished otherwise, for the Hidden House was his last bastion, wherein he could slink in the dead of night, and vanish from the face of the earth. The circumstances had now arisen when it was necessary for him to do just that. There were now intensive international police inquiries afoot, and he wanted time to sort out his documents and collect his ill-gotten wealth in the shape of diamonds. It was time he moved on – South America? Peru? Lima was colourful. They said the Andes were full of beauty. Mr Toledano liked colourful places, people and things. But if he didn't carry out the operation with due speed he stood in grave danger of being overtaken by a relentless Nemesis.

He had reversed his car into the isolated lock-up garage he owned on the outskirts of the village, and, carefully securing the roll-back doors, had pocketed the key and made his way in the fast gathering twilight to where the road forked into the two principal streets of Pontemurio. The main street, comparatively well-lit, was to the left. He took the gloomy thoroughfare to the right, deciding to use the less conspicuous entrance to his refuge. Deep in thought, he made his way mechanically to where there should have been a Spanish oak door. And then he came up with a sickening jolt. For a moment he wondered if he'd taken the wrong turning. Something akin to fear fluttered through his being.

There was no Spanish oak door. The passageway was completely and solidly bricked in to match either side of the wall.

Disbelief, anger, fear, all jiggled along a pulse of baffled impotence as with the aid of his lighter he examined the workmanship. It was a skilled job. The edges were carefully bonded into the surrounding brickwork.

Snapping out the flame, he retraced his steps to the apex of the fork, and hurried along to the other entrance, nearly breaking into a trot in his anxiety.

Just beyond this entrance was an old-fashioned street-lamp set high on a wall-bracket, and normally this cast a black shadow where the door was recessed. He craned forward as he panicked along. *There was no black shadow.*

Breathlessly, he stared agape at the new whiteness of the trim brick wall which effectively sealed this entrance too.

The Hidden House was not only well and truly hidden. It was inaccessible.

Fear struck deeply. He glanced up and down the street. Most of the inhabitants were down at Guido Peppi's Circus, and what few people were in the street paid him scant attention. But every shadow was a menace. As he walked unsteadily back to his lock-up garage, ice-cold prickles crept out of his loins and spread up to the nape of his neck. He opened the roll-back doors sufficiently to enter, closed them behind him with a clang, and switched on a small electric heater in the wall. In spite of the mildness of the evening he found he was shivering. Subsiding into the front seat of the car, he lit a cigarette and tried to think.

Perhaps he shouldn't have killed Peter Meek... An alarming thought suddenly rip-jagged home. Perhaps he hadn't killed Peter Meek! He'd certainly killed somebody. The disturbing thought then was *who had he killed?* The man had produced proof of identity. And those addresses! How did he know those addresses? He cast his mind back. The Hidden House, Pontemurio, wasn't one of them. He drew heavily on his cigarette and found that his hand was trembling. And then something slid unasked into his turbulent brain.

The brickwork. There was something about the brickwork, something his eye had seen but his brain had only half registered. He sat there motionless, cigarette poised in mid air between two elegant fingers, his mind groping to fasten on to that mercuric, elusive something. A seeker after knowledge, at one stage in his full life he had studied building construction, and irritating fragments of learning slithered around in his mind like eels in a pot. And then suddenly all movement stopped and he was able to pin down the little bit he wanted.

With an exclamation he flipped away his cigarette, and was soon on his way back to the brick walls, examining first one and then hurrying round to the other. He snapped his fingers in self-approval. He was right. It was a small point, but he was right, and Mr Toledano liked to be right, even if he was wrong in being right.

It concerned the actual bricklaying, the style or method employed. One wall was laid using English bond, the other Flemish bond. It could mean something. Or nothing. He was inclined to think something. Just what, he couldn't imagine. Two people had done the job in a hurry? It must have been done in a hurry, because things were normal less than a fortnight ago when he'd concentrated most of his wealth there in the safe. But even if the walls had gone up in a hurry they wouldn't come down in a hurry. Whoever had done the job hadn't used mortar, they'd used a rich mixture of quick-drying cement, and it had set like granite.

He went back to his car and tried to organise his thoughts. He had the Addendum to Sea-Lion in the dispatch box he'd collected from Guido Peppi that very evening… Another flutter of alarm coursed through his veins, and he reached over quickly for the black box on the back seat. Fumbling with a key, he wrenched open the lid. Addendum to Sea-Lion wasn't there. The deeds of Giant's Hammer were. He sat there aghast, wrestling with this new twist.

A little over a week ago he had locked those deeds in the modern safe at the Hidden House, with the diamonds. And if the deeds had turned up where Addendum to Sea-Lion should have been, what had been the fate of the diamonds?

Guido Peppi would have a lot to answer for.

Mr Toledano checked his gun, and slipped back the safety catch. He would first have a word with Guido Peppi. And then he would see what could be done about effecting entry to his eyrie. He was surrounded by circumstances which trapped him *outside* his nest, was as doomed as an escaped cage-bird that couldn't get back into its cage.

He was up against a brick wall. Two brick walls...

CHAPTER 2

Justice Comes to Wormwood Scrubs

The immediate events leading up to Mario Toledano's abject dejection found their origins in the publicity surrounding what became known as the 'Ice-Shilling Trial'. It will be recalled that Major Peter Meek, who had received a posthumous decoration for bravery in the field during World War II, turned up years later at the Tyburn & New York Insurance Company under the name of Simon Good; and with the aid of some of his wartime cronies was amassing riches by a series of complicated insurance frauds, investing the proceeds in Tyburn & New York stock, a company in which he had every confidence. Roag's Syndicate (the nominee company concealing their identity) was doing very nicely, thank you, when Simon Good slipped up and was unfortunate enough to be caught out using an 'ice-shilling' in his electricity meter. True to the tenets of the Syndicate ('Roguery with caution – each for all and everyone for himself, Jack') his cronies – Hammersley, Blake, Dutchy and Rip Strookman – vanished into limbo, and Simon Good went down on the instruction of Mr Justice Middlisome for twelve months.

This period, reduced by the ruling of the Court of Criminal Appeal and with suitable reduction for good behaviour (Simon Good was a model prisoner) was now almost completed, and the Commander (Crime) New Scotland Yard, not from any motives of kindliness, thought it might be a good idea to see what happened when Simon Good was released from custody. He suggested as much to Superintendent Lingard.

Lingard had been the sixth man present when Roag's Syndicate was born under fire in World War II, the difference being that he had made it quite clear that he was on the other side of the fence and would do his utmost to bring any wrongdoer to justice. As has been related elsewhere, he achieved – so far as concerned Simon Good – the right results from the wrong circumstances.

'Simon Good leaves the Scrubs, tomorrow, Lingard. It might be interesting to see if anyone welcomes him back to the Great Outside. The Fraud Squad have been delving into his background. There seems to be a vague link with a financial group known as Roag's Syndicate. They now have a small office off Pall Mall, in Racquet Alley – I know, I know, it's most appropriate!'

'How *vague* is the link, sir?'

'Vague enough. You remember that man Blake you told me about? The one who used to work for Lumm's Safes before they were taken over, who now owns a string of restaurants, the Golden Porcupine, the Golden Touch, the Golden Handshake etc., etc. Well, the clerk-cum-accountant who does work for the Syndicate is a very smooth gentleman who divides his time between London and Brussels. Interpol very kindly supplied us with a little of *his* background. Believe it or not, they've traced him back to a hotel-restaurant in Brussels, in the Rue du Dépôt, known as the Golden Fleece.'

'Blake's?' breathed Lingard, his eyes gleaming.

'On the face of it, no. But Blake has been seen there. Mind you, so far as the Fraud Squad can ascertain, Roag's aren't doing anything financially illegal, they're merely investing money – there's nothing wrong in that of itself. But it would be interesting to know where the money's coming from.'

'I wonder if the Tyburn & New York will take Simon Good back?' mused Lingard.

'A little more time will tell,' said the Commander. 'And talking of insurance companies, someone's gone and mislaid himself at the Goodwill Insurance Company in St James's Street. Seems a curious sort of chap, been missing for some time now. Run along tomorrow morning and see what you make of it, will you? Only don't take any action in the matter without my express authority.'

'Another insurance company! Has the whole industry gone crazy? One thing, this joker's disappearance can't have anything to do with Simon Good's pack of rogues.'

'I wouldn't be too sure of that,' said the Commander gloomily. 'There are usually two jokers in every pack. Only ... only this one's what you might call a *serious* joker...'

Ambrose Meddlisome awoke from a restless, uneasy sleep, a sleep hag-ridden and wild with dreams, and it took him several seconds to remember where he was. The mists cleared slowly. He was at the Mendozas' house at Shere, where the night before he had attended – it must be confessed, somewhat unenthusiastically – a party, and his hosts had prevailed upon him to stay the night.

Mr Justice Meddlisome didn't like parties; he just didn't seem to fit in nowadays, he felt he was socially impossible. But the Mendozas meant something special to him.

There was a discreet tap on the door, and young Caroline Mendoza peeped in.

'So you are awake, Ambrose. I knocked before, but you didn't answer. I wasn't going to disturb you, but John said you wanted to get to town. I've brought you some tea and toast.'

He struggled up in bed and took the tray on his lap.

'Thank you, my dear. It was a delightful party last night. I enjoyed myself immensely.'

She looked at him quizzically. 'John and I thought you were rather quiet. Are you worried about something? Can we help? It must be pretty grim with your housekeeper ill – would you like to stay on here for a while?'

'Thank you all the same, my dear, no. I do have a problem, but I'm afraid it's one you can't help me with. Bless you for the kindly thought though, I do appreciate it. You both mean very much to me.'

Caroline Mendoza turned away abruptly. She went out to the landing again, and brought back a bowl of cut flowers.

'I know you like flowers, Ambrose. I picked them first thing. Wrong to have flowers in a bedroom, I know, but they do brighten up the place a bit. Your special variety.'

She pulled back the curtains and placed the bowl on the window sill, and he watched her trim figure as she left him to his tea. 'The bathroom's free and there's plenty of hot water when you want it,' she said, as she closed the door.

Brilliant morning sunshine struck a slant through the flowers left there for his well-being. The way he felt this morning they might just as well have been for his demise. He tried to shake off the last traces of his nightmare.

Most dreams vanish with sunshine and a cup of tea, but the image of the gross, unpleasant creature with the fleshy, sensuous face, who pursued him relentlessly through the night, threatening to expose the distant past, remained with him until after the second cup.

The morning sun was strong, but the name Toledano left icy fingermarks which didn't melt.

Whatever happened to him, nothing must spoil the lives of Caroline and John...

He groped under the pillow for his handkerchief, and patted his pyjama pocket to no avail. Must have left it in his suit, he thought idly. He clambered out of bed and went over to the wardrobe. One thing that had come out of last night's party was that his mind was now made up, he was very clear on that point. So far as he himself was concerned, Mario Toledano could roast in sulphur. If that gentleman thought he could intimidate an English judge on account of Addendum to Sea-Lion, he was very much mistaken. But if he intended, as he had threatened, to stretch out his tentacles farther afield, that was a different matter.

A few chance remarks old Mr Bulworthy (manager of the Goodwill Insurance Company) made the night before had stirred the bitter-sweet memories of youth, and had given Ambrose Meddlisome his restless night.

Coming in alone from the perfume-laden garden, more than a little nostalgic, a mixture of regrets and tenderness, he was gently inserting himself in the crush at the running buffet in the dining-room, when he had come up behind Bulworthy and a friend, and found to his embarrassment that they were discussing him.

'...Old Meddlisome's quiet tonight. Seems a bit withdrawn.'

'Probably got problems like the rest of us. Anyway, I suppose you get like that if you're a judge. You have to make your own decisions, and he's probably trying to make one now.'

'He's been avoiding people all the evening – except John and Caroline.'

'If this wasn't their party, you can take it from me he'd be at home with a dry-as-dust book and a glass of port.'

'Yes, the three of them certainly get on well together. Just as well, must be lonely with that old housekeeper of his. Pity he never married.'

'The way he fusses round Caroline,' said

old Bulworthy, 'you'd think she was his daughter...'

His daughter! If they only knew! He rummaged absent-mindedly through his suit pockets... If John gave him a lift to Hammersmith, he could take public transport to the White City, and walk from there... He appeared to have lost his handkerchief. He glanced down the neat deck of trays in the wardrobe, and his eye caught one labelled HANDKERCHIEFS. Caroline wouldn't mind if he borrowed one. He pulled the tray out on its runners, and took one from the tidy pile. Vaguely it occurred to him that the tray was a little heavy for its size, and he examined it curiously. There were some folded tray-cloths at the back, and he put his fingers amongst them. Some small object fell and rattled at the back of the tray, but he didn't pay particular attention to it because it was then that he saw the gun... An automatic, although he didn't know it. And a small box of ammunition.

And being a man of peace, of law and order, he wondered how you loaded the thing and fired it...

It was exactly eleven o'clock that same morning when Charles Hammersley arrived at the imposing main entrance to H.M. Prison at Wormwood Scrubs. He thought it would be only courteous to welcome his old O.C. back into Civvy Street and put him on the right road again, especially if he showed any signs of reform. The warm morning sun threw up the bright green foliage of the trees lining the forecourt, and all was right with the world. If only Hammersley knew what was to develop later, he would have steered clear of Wormwood Scrubs, for Hammersley was essentially a gentle creature who hated violence.

He gazed with mild interest at a well-dressed, elderly gentleman who was meandering slowly up and down by the private quarters flanking the courtyard. Something on his mind, thought Hammersley. Perhaps waiting for his brother to come out, one could never tell what private sorrows were masked by a cloak of apparent respectability. Ah, well! He passed through into the courtyard, and strolled along to the forbidding prison gates at the far end. Polishing his spectacles, he digested the large notice, in fading, painted letters, which told him of all the offences that well-meaning people outside could commit by attempting to introduce to people inside such comforts as letters, tobacco and files. He glanced round and caught the elderly gentleman's eye. 'Good morning, sir,' he beamed. 'It's good to be alive.'

'Indeed!' agreed Mr Justice Meddlisome.

'Especially this side of the wicket-gate.'

'It's a wicked world,' opined Hammersley tolerantly.

Nodding briefly, they parted and wandered away in opposite directions, only to come together again on the return journey. Hammersley foresaw that this was likely to cause some further minor embarrassment, and, ever thoughtful of others, moved away at right-angles, cutting short the outward leg of his journey to upset the rhythm so that they didn't come together again face to face. Mr Justice Meddlisome also did one or two neat turnings-on-the-march with the same thing in mind, and anyone watching them would have assumed they were working out some intricate manœuvre for the Royal Tournament.

It was four minutes past eleven by the clock over Hammersmith Hospital, while Hammersley was walking away towards the road and Mr Meddlisome was wheeling in towards the main doors, when the small wicket-gate opened and out stepped Simon Good, his suit creased from long storage. A prison officer took a quick peep at the outside world, apparently didn't care for what he saw, and shut the wicket with a bang.

The Judge approached Simon diffidently. 'Good morning, Meek,' he said doubtfully.

Simon Good stopped dead in his tracks. Recognition was not instantaneous. The

Judge looked different without a wig. 'My Lord! This is a pleasure! Or is it?'

'Please forget courtroom procedure and call me Meddlisome,' said the Judge sharply.

'By all means, if your Lordship pleases. And do call me Simon. Simon Good.'

'I prefer to call you by your correct name, and not by an adopted one not legalised by deed poll.'

'Isn't this rather like rubbing salt into a wound for a judge to come and meet his – victim?' asked Simon blandly. 'Or is it all part of the new Criminal Justice Act? A sort of get-together and make-it-up gesture?'

The Judge ignored this. 'This is an unusual hour to set you free, is it not?' he asked. 'I am, of course, more concerned with the organisation for getting people into, rather than out of, these establishments, but I thought they generally released prisoners early in the morning, about eight o'clock.'

'Oh, yes, I believe they do. In a way, it's rather like a hotel, you know, where the room has to be vacated by such and such an hour so the maids can change the linen. Except, of course, they haven't got maids here – at least, I didn't see any. Possibly only a two-star place. Actually I had one or two things I wanted to clear up in the library – get the new man settled in, and so forth. I asked the Governor if I could stay to lunch. He was awfully decent about it, but explained that I wasn't on the ration strength after eight o'clock. I rather liked the library job.'

'You earned full remission for good behaviour, of course?'

'An exemplary prisoner, my Lord – Mr Meddlisome. I was picked out for redband material immediately. I was even a Quasimodo.'

'A *what?*' exclaimed the Judge.

'A Quasimodo. The chapel redband. The trusted prisoner who is responsible for dusting out the prison chapel and arranging the flowers. Derived from Quasimodo in *The Hunchback of Notre-Dame.*'

'Congratulations,' said the Judge without enthusiasm. 'And may I also congratulate you on the way you handled your side of the Appeal? I could see you had advised your legal advisers.'

'Thank you. May I congratulate you on the way you handled your side, too? I'd completely overlooked the "contempt" angle.'

'To be truthful, so had I until you put me on my mettle in court. I learned quite a bit from you during the trial, and became infected with a glimmer of your speciousness. But for your flagrant contempt of court, I think you might have almost got away with it. Between you and me, apart from the contempt aspect, the sentence *was* a trifle stiff for the crime. However, bearing in mind the Appeal Court's reduced sentence, and your full remission which, of course, you've earned, I think you will agree you haven't done so badly.'

'I've had better holidays,' said Simon.

Mr Meddlisome gazed speculatively at him for a moment. 'I would say you *deserved* a full five years.'

'For using an "ice-shilling" in an emergency?' said Simon, in what appeared to be astonishment.

'You know full well what for,' said the Judge acidly. 'In any event, I'm by no means convinced there was in any sense an emergency.'

'What else was there then, apart from the shilling?'

'Suppose you tell me,' said the Judge.

'Some other time?' suggested Simon. 'I'm sure you will appreciate I've had a very trying morning, what with signing for my own property and one thing and another. Now I take it, Mr Meddlisome, you haven't come along here merely to say hello?'

Ambrose Meddlisome hesitated for a moment, and then made his decision.

'I've come,' he said, 'because I want your help.'

He had crossed his Rubicon.

To say that Simon Good was staggered would be an understatement. '*My* help?'

'Yes.'

'What's your trouble? Have you got yourself tangled with a striptease queen?'

'Don't be outrageous, Meek!'

'Well, we can't stand here talking – they'll think we're planning to break in. You have your car?'

'I came by public transport.'

'Come and sit in mine, then. I've had the Jaguar brought round, should be here by now. I told them to park it in the lane round the corner – not so ostentatious as just outside the main gates; most of the prison officers don't run to Jags, and I shouldn't like to upset them. Grand chaps.'

It was as he steered the Judge through the avenue of trees in the forecourt that he became conscious of Hammersley hovering in the background, the usually placid bespectacled face a masterpiece of agitated indecision.

'My dear Hammersley! How nice of you to come! What it is to have friends! Charles, meet a – business acquaintance of mine, Mr Meddlisome.'

'Pleased to meet you,' said Hammersley. 'Any friend of Mr Good's a friend of mine,' and he didn't notice the Judge's look of scepticism. 'The name sort of rings a bell. Your Jaguar's parked in the lane at the side, Mr Good,' he added.

'We were just about to go and sit in it,' said

49

Simon, leading the way. They got into the car, and Mr Meddlisome eyed Hammersley doubtfully.

'You can talk freely before one of my technical advisers,' said Simon, catching the look.

'What I have to say is for your ears only,' said the Judge.

'Let's have some real coffee first,' suggested Simon. 'Hammersley! You've brought some of my favourite cigarettes? Good! Where shall we go?'

'I know a little place in Holland Park Avenue,' said Hammersley. 'It has the unusual quality of looking like a coffee shop rather than an opium den in old Shanghai. Are you sure you wouldn't like something stronger?'

'I would prefer coffee,' said the Judge.

'A pity,' said Hammersley regretfully. 'I once promised to show Mr Good how to get a drink for nothing.'

'*You* were the friend who was going to show him?'

'Yes,' said Hammersley enthusiastically. 'He's told you about it, has he?' he added with pleasure.

'Mr Meek did mention the matter to me,' agreed Meddlisome, his mind slipping back through the epi-cyclic gears to Peter Meek's atrocious flippancy in the dock.

'Perhaps you'd prefer to have something at

my modest bachelor establishment at Richmond?' said Simon.

'Where the notorious "ice-shillings" were made?'

'Shilling. Singular. I said so at my trial, remember? By the way, you'll have to lend me one, Hammersley.'

'For the meter? I haven't got one,' said Hammersley firmly. 'Perhaps Mr Meddlisome can oblige.'

Simon Good was diffident. 'I hardly like to bother him.'

Meddlisome, J., fished one out of some small change. 'Here you are,' he said. 'I can't go wrong for a shilling.'

'Don't say that!' warned Simon sharply. 'You know what happened to me – although I suppose you'd have to come before a different judge.' And Mr Meddlisome's eye flickered, for he was not without humour.

'If it wouldn't matter either way to you,' he said dryly, 'I think I'd prefer Hammersley's coffee shop. You may keep the shilling, of course,' he added, and this time his voice was dehydrated.

Superintendent Lingard watched the cream-and-crimson Jaguar draw gently away and accelerate towards Wood Lane. He recognised Hammersley without much difficulty; to his trained mind Charles Hammersley was almost offensively in-

51

offensive, and there had to be a reason for anyone who was like that. But he failed completely to recognise Mr Justice Meddlisome. The absence of wig and gown made quite a difference...

Lingard signalled his car and proceeded to the Goodwill Insurance Company.

'Before we order,' said Hammersley a few minutes later in the coffee house of his choice, 'are you both certain you wouldn't like me to show you how to get a drink for nothing?'

'Some other time, perhaps?' urged Mr Meddlisome anxiously.

'It *can* be done,' insisted Hammersley, eager to make the point with someone who was obviously one of Simon's close friends. (Who else would refer to him as '*Mr Meek*'?) 'It's all a question of confidence.' He ordered a pot of coffee and did the honours. 'You must have confidence. If you've got confidence you can get away with murder – do you ever feel like getting away with murder, sir?'

The Judge was silent for a moment. A wintry look came into his eye as he thought of Mario Toledano. And the gun in the drawer. 'Sometimes I do,' he said quietly.

'For example,' prattled on Hammersley in full spate, 'I once knew a bloke who couldn't afford the exorbitant fares on the

Underground. So what did he do?'

'Walked?' said Simon without conviction.

'Dear me, no!' Hammersley was astonished at such naïvety.

'Took advantage of the cheaper rates afforded by season tickets?' suggested Mr Meddlisome without hope.

'You've done something like this yourself, sir?' asked Hammersley admiringly.

'I have a suspicion that I might not have,' replied the Judge grimly.

'Oh. Well, what he did was to stick two old season tickets together, face to face, so that virtually he had one season ticket with two backs.'

'Where did that get him?' asked Meddlisome curiously.

'Practically anywhere on the system. Provided the station had two ticket collectors at the exit.'

'Two collectors? Surely that rendered him even more liable to detection?' frowned Meddlisome.

'Oh, no, the scheme wouldn't work without two collectors. You see, he used to hold his ticket upright by the corner, and walk through between them. The idea is that each collector thinks the *other* is looking at the front of it.' Hammersley smiled reminiscently. 'That man had confidence if anyone did.'

'"Had?" Doesn't he do it now?'

'He – um – doesn't need a season ticket where he's living at present,' said Hammersley regretfully. 'He's got a different sort of season. And he's actually waiting for his ticket.'

'So it didn't get him very far after all.'

'You could put it like that, I suppose,' agreed Mr Hammersley. 'Nevertheless, confidence does count. I once bought up a surplus stock of army boots at a knock-out price. Ten thousand pairs, size elevens.'

'Elevens!' exclaimed the Judge. 'Weren't they difficult to dispose of?'

'They were, in a way. You see, when the cases were opened up, they were all *left* feet. Been wrongly packed at the supply depot. They forgot to tell me that. They never did trace what happened to the ten thousand right feet. Shipped to a one-legged army in South America, I shouldn't wonder. But I tackled my own problem with finesse and confidence. And disposed of them at a profit. Shall I tell you how?'

'Intrigued as I am,' demurred the Judge, 'I can't help feeling it would be wisest for me not to know. I came to talk to Meek, and time presses.'

'It makes a fascinating story,' said Hammersley regretfully, 'and one abounding with a confidence which illustrates my contention.' He frowned at Mr Meddlisome thoughtfully. 'You, sir, I assume you are a senior civil servant – executive grade. Connected with records, possibly. Or public relations, perhaps?'

'You could say all that again,' put in Simon, highly amused.

'I knew it!' cried Hammersley, stirring his coffee vigorously. 'There's something about your manner, sir, which tells me you have a flair for dealing with people. And in dealing with them you must be called upon to make decisions. And you must have confidence in the decision you make, otherwise neither you nor the person you're dealing with is satisfied.'

'Ninety per cent of the people I deal with aren't satisfied,' confessed the Judge.

'Some people are never satisfied,' tutted Hammersley. 'But that seems a very high proportion. What, might I ask, is your precise vocation?'

'I'm a judge.'

'Yes, well there you are then, a judge–'

Charles Hammersley was transfixed. A white-hot razzle-dazzle of light rose up and hit him between the eyes. He suddenly remembered an important engagement on the other side of London, and made to take his immediate leave.

Mr Meddlisome extended a restraining hand. 'Finish your coffee first,' he said. He very gently pushed Hammersley back into his seat...

CHAPTER 3

Shock After Shock

Hammersley subsided uneasily and took a gulp at the remains of his coffee.

'Relax, Hammersley. I merely want to ask Meek one or two questions.'

'I just can't wait,' said Simon.

'Do you know a man called Toledano?'

'No.'

'Think hard,' said the Judge.

'I don't have to,' said Simon. 'Either you know a man called Toledano or you don't. I don't. Why?'

'He says you killed his brother...'

Simon Good was thunderstruck.

'That almost amounts to slander,' he said at length, and this time really searched his memory for the name. 'I've a good mind to sue him. What is he? A purveyor of ice-cream?'

'No,' said the Judge grimly, 'a purveyor of death.'

'Oh dear,' said Mr Hammersley, 'more violence. I want no part of it. You may be a judge, Mr Meddlisome, but you're not going to get me mixed up with anything illegal.'

'You must have more confidence,' said the Judge. 'I'm surprised you didn't recognise me. Didn't you get a good seat at Meek's trial?'

'I wasn't there,' said Hammersley quickly. 'I was quite overcome when I read about it in the papers. If you'll pardon my saying so, I thought you were rather hard on Major Meek.'

'So did the Appeal Court.'

'You can count me in,' said Simon. 'More coffee, Charles?'

'Thank you, no. This is no place for me. I can't stand violence. A joke, yes, but not violence. It was the one thing that upset me about the war. I could have really enjoyed it but for that. I was quite happy as Major Meek's batman, making new friends, seeing new places, but when everyone started fighting each other it upset me no end.'

'War has its drawbacks,' agreed the Judge sardonically. 'I notice you call Meek by his correct name – although I don't know if he's entitled to the "Major" now.'

'He'll always be Major Meek to me,' said Hammersley. 'Can't see the point of changing names – it's the sort of thing a criminal does.'

'Yes,' said the Judge, in a strangulated voice. 'Tell me, Meek, how long have you been calling yourself Simon Good?'

'It came about during the war. I lost my memory when I was blown up in Northwest Europe. *I* came down, but the memory lingered on. I suppose when they found me I must have said "Good!", and they thought I was trying to give my name, number and rank. You know how these things work out.'

'Yes, very conveniently,' said the Judge, scarcely moving his lips.

Hammersley pushed back his seat and got up. He was regaining something of his normal composure. 'Well, if you'll both excuse me, I must be off. I have to make a mercy call on an old sergeant-major friend of mine who's done so much shouting he's deafened himself. He's receiving psychiatric treatment.'

'Psychiatric treatment?' repeated Mr Meddlisome. 'Why?'

'He can't hear anything he says, and he thinks he's only thought it. That makes him shout all the louder. Sad case. Well, it's been nice meeting you, my Lord, but I hope I shan't need your professional services. I bid you good day.'

He turned abruptly, and, deep in thought, left without paying.

The Judge's smile faded as Hammersley departed. The granite glitter was back in his eye. 'Give me a direct answer, Meek. Did you kill Toledano's brother?'

'If I say yes, where does that put me, my Lord?' asked Simon.

'Perhaps I should ask if you're certain you *haven't* killed his brother – knocked him down with your car, for example. Think deeply.'

Simon stirred his coffee thoughtfully. 'Mr Meddlisome. Unless one is killing brothers all the time one doesn't have to think deeply, one just knows. Either you've killed a man's brother or you haven't. I haven't. Even if his name is Toledano.'

The Judge's eyes fixed coldly on Simon Good. 'Unless you did it when you lost your memory in North-west Europe?'

'I'd say this Toledano is a raving lunatic.'

'That doesn't make him any the less dangerous.'

'It doesn't necessarily make him dangerous.'

'I said he was a purveyor of death.'

'So you did,' said Simon, endeavouring to get a little sugar out of a pot expressly designed to prevent just that. 'So he's a killer, is he? And who does he propose to kill next?'

'You,' said Mr Meddlisome...

Simon Good sat very still. The sugar container was poised upside down over his cup; it didn't matter, since nothing came out of it. It was of modern design. It kept the sugar dry, it kept the sugar clean; one could even see the sugar. But one couldn't get at it. It was really clever.

'I thought I'd let you know,' said the Judge.

'Nice of you, although I can't say you've made me the happiest man in the world. Might I enquire how you came by this information, or is it *sub judice?*'

'About ten days after you came up on trial before me I received a letter consisting of one short sentence in Portuguese. It was date-stamped Lisbon, and the sender omitted to put his address. My brother-in-law, who has a flair for European languages, translated it for me.'

'What did it say?' asked Simon curiously.

'It said *"Major Meek – why only twelve months?"* It was signed "Mario Toledano".'

'No friend of mine,' said Simon. 'How did you react?'

'I was pleased to think that someone had taken the trouble to write to me all the way from Lisbon, apparently supporting my original sentiments – especially as it arrived when I was beginning to have misgivings on the equity of the term I'd given you. We decided that Mr Toledano was an avid reader of English newspapers as it was doubtful if your case would find its way into the foreign press. I hope I haven't shattered your sensitive ego.'

'I am picking up the pieces. And so?'

'I forgot all about it. After your appeal, I was obliged to take a brief holiday. The publicity and anonymous letters (both for and against) all out of proportion to the merits of the case, took their toll, and I suppose I was on the verge of the mildest of breakdowns.'

'I'm sorry if you suffered on my account.'

'I suffered on my own account,' hastened the Judge. 'I think you're the only person who ever really got me rattled in court, and I made foolish admissions about my anger. You very cleverly seized on the point, Meek, and put me in the most unenviable position I'd ever been in in my unruffled career as a judge. And that was why I suffered – if suffered is the word – Meek. On *my* account. Not yours.'

'I am still picking up the pieces, my Lord.'

'Have you ever been to Portugal, Meek?'

'I've never been able to afford it,' said Simon with great simplicity.

'H'm! Well, that's where I went for my holiday – without thinking anything of the letter. My brother-in-law knows the country well – he was there during the war – and I suppose following the talk we had over the letter the idea must have been planted in my mind that it would be a good place to go to for a change. I caught a 'plane to Lisbon, spent a few days exploring the capital, and then went on to Estoril. Regrettably the publicity was still with me. At London Airport I was photographed boarding the 'plane, and when the English papers caught up with me in Lisbon, there I was on the front page featured as "Ice-Shilling Judge Leaves for Portugal". One of the less kind dailies saw fit to publish an atrocious picture of me with the caption, "The Ice-Man Go-eth."'

Simon Good grinned and immediately begged his Lordship's pardon.

'It wasn't amusing at the time, Meek. I thought all sorts of dire things about the newspaper concerned, but as it was a paper produced for the non-reading masses, I curbed my irritation. Time heals, and after a few days in Lisbon I could see the funny side of it. Unfortunately there was an important difference between those photographs of me published at the time of your Appeal and those taken at the airport.'

'You weren't wearing a wig. And that rendered you recognisable in Portugal by anyone who'd read an English paper. You were in fact recognised and suffered even more embarrassment.'

'Full marks. On my second morning in Estoril I was sitting under one of those gaily-coloured umbrellas on the terrace of my hotel, when a man strolled by looking for somewhere to sit. He caught my eye, and as most of the tables were crowded I invited him to sit with me. I realised afterwards he would have sat there anyway. He put down a carefully folded newspaper in such a position that I found myself staring at a picture of myself. If I wondered whether my expression had given me away, his opening remark swept away all doubt. "I wasn't certain, *senhor*, until I saw your look of dismay." His face crinkled in self-satisfaction, and I took an instant dislike to the man. "Allow me to introduce myself," he said. "My name is Mario Toledano."

"'I remember the name," I said, as casually as I could. "You wrote to me."

"'Yes," he said genially, "I wrote to you. I was curious to know why you gave Peter Meek only twelve months imprisonment." He snapped his fingers at a passing waiter and ordered a drink.

"'I couldn't have answered your question even if I'd felt inclined to do so," I replied. "And as you doubtless already know from the English papers, that figure has been considerably reduced by the Court of Criminal Appeal. And as you'd omitted to give your address I felt your question was purely rhetorical."

"'Very remiss of me," he chuckled throatily, "I must have been in too much of a hurry to dispatch my letter."

"'I observe you speak English fluently," I remarked. "Why write to me in Portuguese?"

"'I thought you would be more likely to pay attention to it out of sheer curiosity," he said. "The case of Major Peter Meek attracted my attention from the start. Twelve months imprisonment seemed most inadequate bearing in mind all the things suggested against him."

"'He wasn't on trial for all those things," I pointed out. "They were brought out by cross-examination when his character was put in issue. They were not proven."

"'You say that now in spite of your rather one-sided comments as the trial judge?" he riposted. "Reading between the lines of one of your more enlightened dailies I felt you thought he was more guilty of the things he wasn't being tried for than the one small thing he was. Either that, or he managed to rile you enough to upset your judgment."

"'My judgment was upset by the Appeal Court," I said.

"'The Appeal Court weren't at the trial. Their decision depended mainly on transcripts – words, printed words, dead words. You saw the man writhing under cross-examination."

"'I was never conscious that he writhed," I objected. "And anyway I don't know why I'm even discussing the case with a perfect

64

stranger – it must be the relaxing air and the fact that I'm a thousand miles from home in a strange country."

"'Come, *senhor!*" chided Toledano, "I'm not a complete stranger. Have I not written to you? Have I not introduced myself? Mere distance makes no difference. If I had not met you here, I would have called upon you in London."

"'What is it you want of me?" I asked irritably, by now more than a little puzzled.

"'I want information concerning Meek. And you have it, or are in a position to get it. Firstly, what is Meek really like? Have you a recent photograph of him? The press pictures were not good. Secondly, to what prison did they send him? And finally, when will he come out?"

'My curiosity got the better of me. "Why do you want to know all this?" I asked.

"'I have a vital, personal reason. I think your sizing up of the man in court was probably very accurate. He's a cretinous *escuma.*"

"'I'm not sure what that means," I said, "but I wouldn't give you the information even if I had it, Mr Toledano. In any event, I don't know to which prison he was sent, and it is by no means certain that he will remain there. And his release date depends to a certain extent on his behaviour. He could earn considerable remission."

'"You could nevertheless find out this information if you so desired?"

'"Perhaps. If I so desired. I can't imagine why I ever should," I replied, and Mr Toledano smiled one of his oiliest and most disturbing of smiles.

'"Perhaps I could give you the urge, the desire?" he suggested blandly. "–with just a little pressure..."

'Toledano was so charming with it all that I couldn't believe he was being serious. Seeing him sitting there beside me, paying the waiter for his drink and pushing aside the change with a flourish, beaming at passing young ladies, and at the same time smoothly suggesting he could exert the necessary pressure on me to make me obtain the information he required, was too unreal for words. I finished my drink, and got up. "Do you know, Mr Toledano," I said, "for a moment I thought you were trying to threaten me. I'm sure I must have been mistaken."

'"Do not deceive yourself," he smiled. "I will contact you again in the near future, and please have the necessary details ready. Much water has flowed along the Tagus since I last saw this man Meek, and I don't intend to let him slip through my fingers. Tell me, does he still smoke a pipe?"

'"I'm sure I haven't the faintest idea," I

said irritably, and got up to leave him. And then he said such a curious thing that I wondered if I was dealing with a mentally-deranged person. He said, "Perhaps Addendum to Sea-Lion will help you to make up your mind... I'll be seeing you... *Até logo!*""

Simon Good extended his cigarettes to the Judge, and lit one himself when the latter declined. 'I told you he was bonkers,' he said, between puffs.

'*Do* you smoke a pipe?' asked Meddlisome, at a tangent.

'I did, and I do. I wonder how he knew? Although your name doesn't have to be Peter Meek before they'll let you. And so?'

'My brief holiday in Portugal came to an end without my seeing anything more of friend Toledano. I could only assume he was mentally off-balance. Right up to the moment I stepped on to the plane I half expected him to pop up and make his outrageous demands. However, Portugal and Mario Toledano faded. On my return I was curious enough to find out where you actually were and how you were behaving, and I very nearly came to see you. At that stage of events, however, there didn't seem much point in wasting time consulting you over what might only turn out to be an old friend of yours with a similar warped sense of whimsy–'

'My dear Lordship!'

'–and once back in the sanity of the court– Did you say something?'

'Just an irritation at the back of the throat – I haven't been smoking lately.'

'–the whole jarring incident quickly diminished into something that hadn't really happened. Until one day, on H.M.S. *Discovery,* of all places…'

CHAPTER 4

Tense Past

'Have you ever been on the *Discovery*, Meek?'

'A number of times,' said Simon. 'Ships hold a fascination for me – born, I suppose, out of boyhood dreams of pirates on the Spanish Main. Indeed, was it not hinted at my trial that I had a piratical streak in me?'

'H'm, I hardly think insurance is your line,' remarked the other dryly.

'One must eat,' shrugged Simon, and Meddlisome favoured him with a sideways look which fortunately Simon didn't see.

'Insurance doesn't give much scope for being piratical,' said the Judge, and Simon nodded, although he had other ideas on the subject.

'Strange to say,' said Simon, 'the first life insurances were tied up with piracy. Sailors, afraid of being captured by Turks or Corsairs to be sold as slaves, took out a form of life insurance which lasted for one voyage only. It was intended to provide ransom money.'

'Indeed?' nodded the Judge, interested. 'Is

that so? But to revert. I was walking along the Embankment one day, when I had a desire to take another look over Captain Scott's vessel. A party was waiting to be taken around, and I hurried up the gangway with a few latecomers, and tagged on the end of the queue. Several moments later I'd stepped back half a century into the rigours of Scott's Antarctic expeditions. You will know that these fascinating little visits terminate in the wardroom, where one can see many of the personal belongings of great men like Shackleton and Evans, and my imagination never ceases to be fired. After listening to the guide, I drifted back into Scott's bunkroom to re-examine the exhibits in a glass case there. As I gazed down at these living letters from the past, a dark shadow struck across my shoulder, and a silky voice said, "Good afternoon, *senhor*, I see you are interested in the historic past." I whipped round, and there was the ominous figure of Mario Toledano.

'It took me a moment to recover. "I didn't expect to see you here," I said. He beamed benevolently.

'"I don't suppose you did, *senhor.*"

'"To what does this country owe you the honour of a visit?" I asked. "A holiday?"

'"I've come for the information I wanted about Peter Meek,' he replied genially. "And I, too, am interested in the historic past.

70

Your past."'

Simon Good's jaw swung round in sheer disbelief. '*Your* past?' he jerked. 'Don't tell me you have a past!' He grinned disarmingly. 'Mr Meddlisome, this chap's starkers.'

'We all have "pasts", Meek, whether we like it or not. "Pasts" are made up of good things and bad, but Modern English Usage prefers to think of them as being made up of bad only. One can be a saint and live for sixty years without a past, and one small indiscretion in a moment of time is sufficient to give you one. Fifty-nine-point-nine-recurring years of good counts for nothing.'

'We all make mistakes,' said Simon sympathetically. 'I've even made 'em myself. I'm not interested in your private affairs, but what was Toledano's point?'

'He said he'd detected a slight hardening of my attitude at the end of our conversation in Estoril, and felt it would be difficult to extract the information he required without applying the pressure he'd referred to. He'd subsequently tried to get the details without my help but had failed. He regretted taking the course of action he proposed, but was determined not to let you slip through his fingers. He'd go to extreme lengths to get what he wanted.'

'And what did this slug-ugly propose to do?'

'Trade certain documentary evidence concerning me for the information he wanted regarding you.'

'Seeing there was no reception committee other than you and Hammersley, I can only assume you didn't give it to him. But how could he possibly have documentary evidence of sufficient importance to intimidate one of our distinguished judges? And why hasn't he used it before?'

'You will be well aware,' said the Judge grimly, 'that during the dark days of the war Hitler planned to invade this country. The operation was to be called Operation Sea-Lion.'

'Operation Sea-Lion! That died at birth.'

Meddlisome caught the look in Simon Good's eye and rightly interpreted it. 'No, I haven't gone out of my mind, Meek. To me, Operation Sea-Lion is more alive today than it was in 1940, although it's incredible to think that something Hitler planned twenty years ago is having repercussions on me now. Years before the war German Intelligence and the Gestapo, with the aid of the fifth column in this country, prepared a list of people in all walks of life who were to be either liquidated or made use of by the occupying forces. Looked at in the cold light of day it was a terrifying document. It meant the virtual elimination of all constructive thought this heritage of ours possessed. The lucky ones on the list were the renegades, the yes-men, the office-seekers, those who – by virtue, or lack of virtue, of the skeletons in their cupboards – were likely to be blackmailed into doing whatever was required by the master race.'

'You're not telling me you were on this list?' said Simon disbelievingly.

'Yes, Meek, I was on the list,' replied the Judge, and there was a jagged edge to his voice. 'After the war I used to read with interest all about Operation Sea-Lion, but it has taken a couple of decades for me to learn with shattering dismay that I was part of Hitler's scheme, an infinitesimal part, but still a part. I could have been proud of the fact if I'd appeared as one of those to be liquidated. Unhappily, I was one of those the enemy intended to use...'

Simon Good sat in staggered silence.

'But of what use could you have been to them?' he asked at length. 'Presumably you weren't a judge then?'

'I was a rapidly rising barrister with a record of fluctuating political views which altered as often as I was burned up by some injustice or other. Perhaps they thought I'd alter my politics once more under their gentle persuasion. You see, I'd once misguidedly associated myself with the U.W.F. – United World Fascists. What they didn't realise was that my views were always dictated by a sense of righting an injustice. I was even worried over your sentence, Meek–' (the phantom smile was back on the Judge's lips) '–in spite of what the Appeal Court did, you caught me in a mellow moment when I gave you twelve months! Seriously though, the Meddlisome you see before you today is not the firebrand of a quarter of a century ago, the Meddlisome who was quick to right a wrong, quick to howl for rigorous punishment of the wrong-doer.'

'There's still quite a strong streak left, m'Lord,' suggested Simon humorously. 'But surely an advanced, progressive, extreme left or right – call it what you like – political background which burnt itself out years ago has no special significance today? There must be hundreds of people who remember you as you were, but they wouldn't hold it against you now, if, indeed they did then. And there must be millions who haven't the foggiest notion of what a United World Fascist was, and couldn't care less anyway.'

'There was more to it than just that,' said Mr Meddlisome, and Simon saw the steely eyes cloud, noted the harsh, regretful lines about the corners of the mouth. 'The document made mention of a further indiscretion, Meek, an indiscretion that's been with me for some twenty-eight years – at times mentally enlarged beyond all reason. The episode was morally indefensible, and Toledano has followed it up. It involves another person – or, rather, persons. For my own part in the sorry affair Toledano could do his worst. But I'd sooner – swing – than let these others be exposed to unhappiness.' He fell silent for a moment. 'I tell you all this, Meek, you have had command of men in difficult times, you must know their weaknesses.'

Simon was embarrassed at the Judge's outpourings. 'Show me a man without,' he said at length.

'Indeed, yes. *Your* weakness, Meek, is that you suffer from a form of inferiority complex.'

Simon Good was astonished. 'I wouldn't have said so,' he said.

'People with inferiority complex rarely do, they usually shout and scream in an attempt to prove the reverse. At one time the Army fed your insatiable need for success; subsequent years of office life should have starved you, but they haven't. It follows, therefore, that you must have been feeding on something else. Meek, I still think you deserved five years. Nevertheless, I somehow like you.' The admission came reluctantly.

'I'm glad you do,' said Simon, 'otherwise you might have condemned me to an *oubliette* like a second Count of Monte

Cristo. But what about Toledano and Operation Sea-Lion?'

'Toledano produced from a sealed envelope what purported to be a photostat copy of page twenty-two of an Addendum in the Operational Order, and laid it on top of the showcase. It was, of course, in German, which I couldn't read, but he assured me the paragraphs under Ambrose Meddlisome, K.C. related to me. He translated freely and left me in no doubt as to the truth of this, and the ugly jangling skeleton in the cupboard started its *danse macabre*. He said I could keep the copy and examine it at my leisure.'

'But how could he have got hold of a thing like that?' said Simon sceptically. 'Now you've seen him in the flesh, what nationality do you think he is? German?'

'I asked him to which country he claimed allegiance. He said any country which gave him a passport; and any country he happened to be living in or on.'

'I still don't follow how he's in possession of part of Sea-Lion after all these years.'

'Nor I. He said I could have the original page on receipt of the information he required.'

'And did you bargain with him?' asked Simon.

'I'm not very good at bargaining, Meek, but in my sudden panic the information he wanted seemed little enough, and I began to make excuses for trading with him. After all, I reasoned, with a little effort Toledano himself could doubtless find out, through ordinary official channels, in which prison you were confined. The release date would present a problem to him, though probably not to me. What still puzzled me was why he wanted your description. Although he desperately wanted to catch up with you he wasn't sure *you* were the right man. So I told him I'd get the details provided that in addition to handing over the original document he told me *why* the information was so vital to him. The data seemed poor return for what was a most embarrassing piece of paper to me.'

'So you did bargain with him?'

'To that extent, yes. It was then that he told me he would very much like to kill you. It was as important to him as that.'

'He's a psychopathic case,' said Simon.

'He says the same about you. He says he saw you kill his brother with a fanatical blood-lust in your eye.'

Simon Good was flabbergasted.

'He was *there* when I did it?'

'So he says.'

'Then why didn't he stop me?'

'I asked him the same question. He said that but for the grace of providence you would have killed him too, that you probably imagined you had in fact killed him.'

'When was I supposed to have done all this? The man wants locking up!'

'I think I'd come to the same conclusion, and then I wondered if this were all part of some complicated conspiracy to blackmail me, that *you* were involved in the scheme–'

'Me?' jerked Simon, visibly hurt. 'One of the highest-grade redbands in the prison, a Quasimodo, trusted by the vicar, revered by the inmates – young and old alike – admired by the visitors–'

The Judge ignored the build-up. 'I also began to wonder if he ever had the intention of giving me the original document, if in fact it was still in existence. I wondered if in my anxiety I had over-estimated the value of the information it contained. I wanted time to think. I had an approximate idea when you would be leaving Wormwood Scrubs, so I added on a few weeks, gave Toledano a fictitious date, explained that it might be altered according to your behaviour, and that I'd take steps to confirm which prison was holding you. If he believes the date I gave him he thinks you're still locked up. I decided I had to take you into my confidence.'

'That was nice of you,' said Simon. 'I always like to know when I'm being killed, if only to get Hammersley out of the way –

he's so sensitive about these things.'

'I wouldn't be here but for the innocent parties being involved,' said Meddlisome.

'I suppose you got your brother-in-law to translate the photostat copy?'

'Yes. And there was no doubt about it, whether or not the document was actually part of Sea-Lion, it was truthful in content.'

'So now your brother-in-law knows about your past indiscretions?' said Simon Good thoughtfully.

'Partly. I knew I could rely on his *discretion*,' said the Judge. 'He was inclined to think I'd magnified the effect any disclosure would have after all these years. He was probably trying to be kind. And in any event he doesn't know of a subsequent letter I received which implicates…'

'I don't want to know,' said Simon. 'What do the police think about all this?'

'I haven't been to the police. Wrong of me, I know, but I just can't bring myself to share my private life with any more people than necessary.'

'What about me?'

An icy glitter sparked in the Judge's eye. 'If you attempted to use any of this information, Meek, I'd see you went down for the longest stretch in history. Since you've been inside I've learned a lot about you.' (Simon Good became very alert, like an animal sensing danger.) 'At your trial I was infected with your speciousness. I'll make a bargain with you. If you get back that page of my past, the next time you come before me I'll forget what I know about yours.'

'I've never been blackmailed by a judge before, my Lord.'

'Not blackmail – a bargain.'

'I suspected you were being modest when you implied you couldn't make a bargain. How do you know there'll be a next time?'

'With men like you there always is.'

'Just how much do you know about me?'

'I'm afraid I'm not going to tell you that.'

'But I must know in order to weigh up the merits of the proposition. I appeal to your sense of equity.'

'If I told you how much or how little I know about you, you might not consider that the bargain I'm making is a bargain. I'm going to be sadistic enough to leave you in suspense, Meek.'

'I wonder if you'll tell me this, then. Who was the "alert police officer" who was instrumental in sending me down – the one you referred to in court.'

'Did you not hear me that day, Meek? I thought I made it clear that the officer would remain in the background ready to watch you in future. He may even be watching us both now.'

Simon Good restrained an impulse to look quickly around the neighbouring tables. 'He could scarcely object to my company today,' he remarked. 'What final arrangements did you make with Toledano?'

'I was to have met him a week later at the same place, on H.M.S. *Discovery,* but I received a letter cancelling the appointment. He'd found out that the ship was due for a refit and would be closed to the public until further notice. Meanwhile he had decided that to attempt to dispose of anyone in this country would be extremely foolish. Therefore I would have to induce Peter Meek to go to Portugal. If some mistake had been made and the Meek who turned up wasn't the man he was looking for, he would give him page twenty-two to bring back to me, because it was of no use to him other than as a lever to get you.'

'And if I *am* the man he's looking for?' asked Simon curiously.

'I don't like thinking about it,' said the Judge frankly. 'But he promised, on his word of honour as a gentleman, to send the page on to me by registered post.'

'I can't say I care for the arrangement,' said Simon. 'How would I identify myself – assuming I was foolish enough to go all the way to Portugal?'

'To prove that you came from me you would take the photostat, in the envelope his last letter came in. And to prove that you were the right Peter Meek – there must be others – you would take something personal, which in due course Toledano will direct.'

'If I'd known all this was going on I wouldn't have been so happy arranging the flowers for the vicar. Why didn't you warn me in jail?'

'You were safe enough in there, surely,' said Mr Meddlisome. 'Now I ask you again to think very carefully. Your case in the courts attracted the attention of Mario Toledano. He imagines – he may be right, for all I know – that you killed his brother. *Have* you a grim skeleton in your cupboard, Meek?'

'I can add nothing except that the quicker the whole Toledano family is dispatched the better.'

'Have you ever had a mental illness when you might have done something like what he suggests without being aware of it? When he said much water had flowed along the Tagus, was that merely a figure of speech or can one infer that this alleged killing actually happened in Portugal?'

'I've never been to Portugal, I told you before,' said Simon patiently.

'You didn't, Meek,' said the Judge shrewdly. 'You said you'd never been able to afford it.'

'I've never been to Portugal, then,' conceded Simon. 'So if it did happen there it can't be me he wants, can it? He's really got me confused with someone else. I don't know what he's talking about, but I'm interested enough to find out.'

'It's like this, Meek. If you secretly *know* you're the man he's after, then I can't ask you to go. The object of the exercise is Peter Meek, and if you're the right one I'm sure he will attempt to kill you. On the other hand, I'd be eternally grateful to you if you brought back that page of the Addendum.' He added hesitantly, 'I would recompense you, of course, for your services.'

'I couldn't accept payment, my Lord – that could look as if I were blackmailing you. I know just *how* circumstantial evidence can look in court. One's character is taken away before one can say Law Reform (Miscellaneous Provisions) Act.' Simon was suddenly alert. 'What does your brother-in-law think about all this?'

'First, that Toledano has obviously got a bee in his bonnet about you – which I hoped to clarify this morning. And secondly, that I'm worrying too much. Adam – my brother-in-law – like others who offer advice and comfort on such occasions, is not the one who is being blackmailed. I have always been slightly contemptuous of people who succumb to the wiles of blackmailers, but now I know how it feels; it becomes crystal clear how the blackmailer gets away with it. I only hope no more such gentlemen come up before me. Adam, of course, doesn't know the full story.'

'Has he the photostat, or have you?'

'It is deposited at my bank. Adam strongly advises me to let Toledano stew. And he doesn't trust you.'

'You're a suspicious family, my Lord. I suppose you can trust *him?*'

The question hung delicately on the air for a split second too long before the Judge answered.

'Yes,' he said. And added, 'Of course.'

'The doubt being–?'

'You're very observant, Meek. I thought I answered quickly enough. The doubt doesn't concern his loyalty to me, that goes without saying. But they tell me he's disappeared.'

'Disappeared?' jerked Simon. 'Who are *they?*'

'His employers. He's in insurance, like you. A company in St James's Street, the Goodwill – do you know it?'

'The Tyburn & New York does business with it. It's mainly a treaty reinsurance company. What happened, exactly?'

'Well, I normally see him about once a month for a lunch in the City, and I must confess that that's about the extent of our seeing each other. My ways are not particularly his ways, my time is fully occupied and our interests differ. He's spent the best part of his life in insurance on the

Continent, and since his return to this country we've maintained a vague friendship because of the past. You see, he married my youngest sister. She died in child-birth, and I don't think he ever got over the shock of losing her. And the son turned out to be a black sheep. Adam doted on the boy to keep alive her memory, but in spite of giving him an expensive schooling which Adam could ill afford, the boy turned out to be a renegade and a wastrel. He's never mentioned now, I don't even know what's happened to him. It broke Adam's heart and put years on him; and thereafter he chose to lead an isolated life. He aged terribly – and yet at times he was very young. I think a bond of sympathy joined us in a friendship which, whilst being a link with the past, never mentioned the past. I felt he didn't want it to intrude upon our private lives, and although we live fairly close to each other you could count on one hand the number of times we've been to each other's places in the last few years.

'Now I've always left it to him to ring me to fix our monthly luncheon, but as I was anxious to talk to someone I rang his office, a thing I rarely do. They told me he wasn't there, and I naturally asked when he would be back. They said they would be only too glad to know, they hadn't seen him for about three months.'

'Three months! What's he been up to? Sounds like a sentence!'

'His departmental head said that Adam had been off on sick leave, and that one or two attempts to contact him at his home had not met with success. Of course, I didn't like to say too much over the telephone because I'd actually seen him two or three times during that period, and he was as fit as a fiddle. And then they dropped the bombshell. The manager of the Goodwill, who lives near Adam, and in fact was instrumental in finding him a bungalow, thought he'd call round on an errand of mercy, and to his astonishment found the bungalow up for sale. I didn't delve too deeply into this on the telephone, and I managed to ring off without announcing my identity. You see, I was placed in an awkward position, because I know Mr Bulworthy, the manager. We're nodding acquaintances, he lives at Shere and I live at Gomshall, and we see each other at local flower shows and so on. I didn't wish to be involved in something Adam had started, about which he hadn't seen fit to inform me. I've mentioned that at times the worry lines would vanish, and the eternal boy would bubble to the surface, but I couldn't see that any joke would extend to his selling his bungalow without telling me. So I went along one evening to check up. Sure enough, the To-Be-Sold notice was up.

And unless he contacts me, I don't know how or where to get in touch with him. That's one of the reasons I've come to you.'

'You don't think he's gone to Portugal to try to get Addendum to Sea-Lion for his own ends?' suggested Simon gently.

The Judge was startled. 'What is it you're suggesting, Meek?' he snapped.

'No more than was suggested about me at my trial,' replied Simon smoothly. 'In the hands of a blackmailer the complete document might give dozens of pointers to likely victims.'

'My dear good Meek,' expostulated the other, 'if you knew Adam you'd know just how ridiculous your implication is! With all due respect to him he's settled down into one of the most inoffensive, prosaic, dull – almost, stick-in-the-muds it is possible to imagine. For a moment you had me worried!'

'Just an idea,' said Simon. 'You know, try as I will, I don't think I'm going to like this creep, Toledano. With your permission I'd like to help you.'

'I knew I could rely on you, Meek–'

'You gave me no option, my Lord.'

'–although I wish you hadn't sounded that last disquieting note.'

'You need have no doubts about *me*, my Lord. I only blackmail to strike at sanctimonious hypocrisy. I'm not interested in your private past. And now, presumably, we await the pleasure of Mario Toledano. Here is my card. Perhaps you'll be good enough to let me know as soon as you hear from him.'

'Indeed yes, and thank you. I only hope I haven't already encroached too much upon your valuable freedom.'

'Think nothing of it, my Lord,' said Simon, pushing back his chair. 'I suppose you wouldn't like to pay for the coffee – I'm right out of small change apart from the shilling you said I could keep...'

CHAPTER 5

Only a Rose

'The whole thing began with the rose,' pontificated Mr Bulworthy, putting the tips of his fingers together and pursing his lips.

'Ah,' breathed Superintendent Lingard, 'the rose.'

'I suppose you would really say the rose*bud*,' mused Mr Bulworthy, drawing a fine point on it.

'Would you now?' said Lingard, as gently as a zephyr and completely out of his depth.

Mr Bulworthy's gaze wandered ruminatively round the musty, panelled room; he appeared to be in no particular hurry to come to the point. Reflectively his eye dwelt on the shaft of sunlight which cut like a knife into the dinginess of the room, a blade of light vibrant with the dust of centuries. With interest he watched a spiral of smoke from Lingard's cigarette curl its way lazily upwards through the ever-changing pattern. A wraith from past glories seeking escape, he mused fancifully. He followed it up until the brilliant light under the edge of the ancient pelmet killed it as in a sudden darting eddy it sought final freedom through a two-inch gap in the window. Heavens, he thought, look at that bloom of dust on the pelmet, must be an eighth of an inch thick – one could grow mustard-and-cress in it! He remembered with a chuckle that once he'd seen precisely that done by a wag, along the top of a wooden partition in the washplace, as a gentle reminder to the cleaners.

'I beg your pardon,' murmured the Superintendent, scarcely louder than the smoke-wraith.

'Eh? Oh, yes, the rose. Or, shall we say, the rosebud?' (Those plush curtains could do with a clean, too. Wonder what colour they were originally? Bulworthy had seen them change from a sort of plum colour to a washed-out mauvy-purple. Still plenty of wear in them, but they could do with a re-dye. Didn't make stuff like that nowadays, been through two wars at least. Looked better in the winter, though. Sunlight was all right, but it made one conscious of unpleasant things like wear and tear and old age).

Superintendent Lingard waited patiently. If Mr Bulworthy was in no hurry, nor was he. And if the Commander (Crime) chose to send one of his superintendents to the West End office of the moribund Goodwill Insurance Company to look into the strange disappearance of one of its equally moribund clerks, then that was all right by him. It was very warm outside in the midday sun, and if he was to be a mad dog, he'd sooner be one inside in the shade taking the weight off his pins and smoking a leisurely cigarette from someone else's box. If he wasn't doing that he'd be doing something else, and sitting peacefully listening to the sleepy utterances of Mr Bulworthy suited him very well indeed.

Mr Bulworthy pulled himself together.

'And then it was that fancy waistcoat,' he said absently, brooding for a moment on the tarnished gold braid of the pelmet. 'Didn't go with the suit. Must have been purchased separately.'

'They're very popular,' whispered Lingard, feeling he ought to indicate he was still alive.

'Popular? Oh, yes. It wouldn't have been so bad if it had stopped at that.' (Yes, that braid was shocking. Funny how accustomed one became to accepting things as they *were*, never noticing the subtle changes. Like growing old together. Like always regarding old Horace Pendleton's age as being fifty-one, when by now he must be every day of seventy. Or like accepting Adam Neeve as the man he *was* rather than observing the subtle changes that had come over him before he disappeared.) 'And then those outrageous shoes with the pointed toes – I suppose I should have realised then that the man was – well, if not going off his head – was, um, well, shall we say, *queer?* Italian shoes, I think they call them.'

'Winkle-pickers,' said the Superintendent knowledgably.

'I beg your pardon?' said Mr Bulworthy, astounded.

'Italian shoes,' hastened Lingard. 'The biggest confidence trick the shoe-trade has ever perpetrated. And now they've found Spanish ones. Twinkletoes. I suppose we'll all be wearing snazzy surgical boots next to put right the damage until the manufacturers triumphantly discover brogues. Still, they're very popular with the young blades of today. And in keeping with their habit of carrying flick knives. And in not hesitating to use them. In my young day if you used anything other than your fists you were labelled a dago or a wog.'

'Quite so, why they should have to copy – dago methods – I just can't imagine.'

'Lack of education, sir. If there aren't enough public schools to go round, let's do away with them, and send everyone to the elementary. Fair shares for all, irrespective of ability. 'Strewth, what a creed! I suppose a lot of it came out of army training – one was taught that the speed of the assault was governed by the speed of the slowest man. And a lot of people found the dictum difficult to forget and carried it back into civilian life.'

'Service training *is* difficult to forget,' said the other. 'You've remembered it,' he added slyly. 'Perhaps we'd get further as a nation if we went back to the old C-A-T spells Cat methods.'

'I think we'd get further if we *used* the "cat",' growled Lingard.

Mr Bulworthy slipped back once more into the slough of despond. His eyes travelled up to the pelmet again, and the Superintendent relaxed gently so as not to disturb him. There was a nice little pub nearby in Racquet Alley, and if he could hang out the interview for a bit longer he'd follow it up with a nice, cool, sparkling pint and a cheese roll.

(Trouble was, thought Bulworthy, if you put up new braid you'd have to do the whole pelmet, have new curtains, renew the white paint – *white* paint? Or was it field-grey – and before you knew where you were there'd be eighty quid for fitted carpet. Things were bad enough under the old régime, where you had a devil you knew, where the expense ratio was pared and pared until cheese-rind was a luxury, but what would it be like under the new order, the new order of being swallowed up by a take-over bid? By reputation the Tyburn & New York were a slick company, and it wouldn't be long before their Organisation-and-Method experts would move in and have a good laugh.) He pulled himself together again.

'And then in the summer he made a practice of coming to the office without a hat. And when winter came, he dispensed with his bowler, and took to wearing, to cap it all, one of those – *caps!*'

The Superintendent laughed heartily.

'No pun was intended,' said Mr Bulworthy frostily.

'Harumph! Of course not! I was just thinking of the depths some people will sink to,' said Lingard in a heavily critical manner. (He rather liked those soft caps you could fold up and put into the pocket; must remember to get one, he thought.)

Old Bulworthy decided it was scarcely the time to ask for new fitments for a room that hadn't changed since the building went up. On the other hand, though, it might be *just* the time. Give the impression of welcoming the change so that he could get things done, the impression of being on the ball. Bit late for that, though. Anyway, he rather liked the room as it was, it was part of his life, he liked the friendly dust and dirt that hadn't been disturbed by generations of charwomen.

Superintendent Lingard looked at the presentation clock on the mantelshelf over the fireplace, and hurriedly stubbed out his

94

cigarette-end. He was cutting it rather fine if he intended to get to the Leather Bottle before the rush-hour.

'Well, Mr Bul–'

'–worthy,' supplied the other from force of habit, so many people got it wrong.

'Yes, of course, Mr Bulworthy.' (It was a good job the old boy had spoken up; he was so bird-like that Lingard had almost called him Bulfinch.) 'I was just thinking what a good old county name that was – Berkshire, isn't it?'

'Is it?' said Mr Bulworthy with interest. 'I come from Middlezoy in Somerset.'

'You do? Oh. Well, I don't want to waste your valuable time, sir,' said Lingard briskly. 'No doubt you'll be wanting your lunch shortly, and I have another pressing appointment. Suppose I take a few particulars and leave you in peace? I gather that a member of your staff is missing, that you're worried about him because he's been acting – shall we say – queerly? How long has he been missing?'

The manager of the Goodwill pondered for a moment, vaguely seeking help from the rather gloomy oil-painting of the be-whiskered founder of the company, James Mountebanke, Esquire (1843-1921. Little help was forthcoming from that vast expanse of stomach held in position by a gold chain, and Mr Bulworthy shook his head regret-

95

fully. 'I really don't know,' he said.

Lingard cocked an eyebrow in mild surprise. 'Come, sir, you must have a rough idea.'

'It's not as simple as it sounds, Superintendent.'

'Well, say within a week, then.'

'I couldn't say for certain within a couple of months.'

The other eyebrow jerked up. 'Let's start from the beginning, sir. What is this gentleman's name?'

'Adam Neeve.'

'I beg your pardon?'

'No, Superintendent,' said the other very gently, 'Not Adam and Eve. Neeve, Esquire, Adam. Adam Neeve.'

'Oh, I get you, sir,' mumbled Lingard. 'I expect many other people have made the same mistake. Yes. And how long has he been with you, sir?'

'About eight or nine years I should say.'

'So that he's comparatively young?' (The only way to deal with some of these old codgers was to put the answers in their mouths.)

'No, he's comparatively old.'

'I thought you said–'

'I said he'd been with us for eight or nine years, Superintendent, but he's by no means the young blade you pictured with a flick-knife.'

'Ah, I see, sir, he'd been employed else-where before? So he's probably nearer thirty or forty?'

'No, nearer fifty.'

'Fifty!'

'Yes, fifty, Superintendent. Strange though it may seem in this age of rockets to Venus and automobiles for the very young, people still do live to the ripe old age of fifty. Surely you've heard of the shorter working week and the longer living life of the Welfare State?'

Lingard grinned. 'Your point, sir. I'd rather assumed he was a younger man.'

'Not because of anything I've said, surely, Superintendent?'

'Possibly not, sir. I think I must have gathered the impression from the Commander back at the Yard.'

'I doubt it,' said Bulworthy, winking slyly up at James Mountebanke, Esquire. 'I think it was merely a wrong impression formed by you. It's a very warm day, isn't it?'

'The Commander gave me a sketchy outline before I came along–'

'It must have been very sketchy, because I think you will find that you've been sent along as a result of a personal call that Mr Fane made to the Commander, and he made that call because of a very brief conversation I had with him on the subject of Mr Neeve, during which I gave him only the bare bones of the situation.'

Something began to tick over in Lingard's brain. 'Mr Fane? Who's Mr Fane?'

'Mr Jullien Fane. General Manager of the Tyburn & New York.'

Lingard rocketed out of his lethargy. 'What's he got to do with it?' he said, sitting up.

'The Tyburn & New York has taken us over,' said Bulworthy regretfully. 'In order, they say, to consolidate and expand their foreign business. Everybody's doing it nowadays. Things are going full circle, we're fast coming to the day when there'll be only one butcher, one baker, one candlestick-maker. And then somebody will push a button and we'll all vanish up our own inflationary spiral.'

'There's a lot in what you say, sir.' (The Tyburn & New York! Jullien Fane! So that's why the Commander had sent him along, the sly old fox! 'Lingard,' he had said, 'someone's gone and mislaid himself at the Goodwill Insurance Company in St James's Street. Toddle along and see what's happened, will you, there's a good chap.' But no mention of the Tyburn & New York!) 'You mentioned the clothes he wore, sir – perhaps that was why I built up a picture of a younger man.'

'You weren't really listening, Superintendent. It was *because* of the clothes he

98

wore in relation to his age that made the situation so curious, even absurd.'

'Oh, I see,' said Lingard untruthfully. 'And I gather he took to wearing these – er – peculiar clothes just before he disappeared – that is,' he added quickly, 'when to the best of your knowledge he disappeared.'

'That is not precisely the case, Superintendent. Looking back carefully over the course of events, I've come to the conclusion that the – um – deterioration started every bit of two years ago.'

'Two *years!*'

'Yes, two years. With the rose.'

'Or, shall we say, with the rose*bud*.' (Lingard couldn't resist that one!)

'You have been listening after all, Superintendent, I've misjudged you.' Mr Bulworthy seemed delighted. 'Following talks with members of my staff, both male and female, I've gone back bit by bit, and I've come to the conclusion that the rot started the day he came into the office sporting a rosebud in one of those little silver holders that fit behind the lapel of one's jacket.'

'What's so strange about that to excite comment?'

'Superintendent, you evidently don't know the Goodwill Insurance Company. We're still using the same high desks and stools that went with the building in 1897 when the company was founded. It was only after the

First World War that they started to use the typewriter – everything was handwritten before then – and they didn't employ female staff to operate the machines, the male clerks were obliged to learn typing and shorthand in their spare time. Typewriters were regarded with the same suspicion that the staff of today regard the electronic computer.'

'You're trying to tell me, sir, that the Goodwill is not altogether a progressive company?' murmured Lingard.

'Not progressive? My dear Superintendent, that's the understatement of the century. The opinion has been voiced that it will be a good thing when the Industrial Revolution finally works its way round to this company. I don't want you to get the impression, though, that because the Goodwill has not progressed in certain respects with the times, that it is without funds or prestige.'

'I didn't think that for one moment, sir,' declared Lingard with undue emphasis.

'You see, ours is not primarily what the public understands by an insurance company, it deals mainly with *re*insurance business. I don't know if that expression means anything to you?'

'Indeed, it does,' said the Superintendent. 'I was once favoured with a lecture on the subject by no less a person than the

Secretary of the Tyburn & New York – a Mr Earnshaw Withers – I don't know if you know him?'

'I most certainly do. Prior to our being taken over I saw quite a lot of him. A very capable man.'

'As I remember it, if a company bites off more than it can chew on any particular risk, it lays off some of it by way of re-insurance with any company that's willing to take a chunk.'

'I wish the young people of today would remember what they're taught with the same aptitude,' said the other, in the voice of post-war experience.

'Mr Withers is a very impressive man,' replied Lingard. 'I am not likely to forget what he told me. I remember he went very high-hat because I suggested reinsurance was rather like book-making. I still think it's a good analogy.'

'It would almost seem, Superintendent, that you've been selected to come along here because of your past dealings with the Tyburn & New York. You see,' he went on, 'this company doesn't have to lure in the public with extravagantly-appointed front offices that look like coffee bars, because although we do write general business – Fire, Accident and so on – we don't rely on it for our bread and butter. In fact, we have working arrangements with other companies to relieve us of underwriting such business, although, of course, the policies are issued in our name.'

'So that leaves you up with reinsuring other companies,' said Lingard.

'Yes. By and large we are mainly what is known as a "treaty" company, that is to say, we have treaties with very many other companies under the terms of which we are given a fixed share of their surpluses. We have to pay high commission for it, but to offset this our general acquisition costs are not so high as those of the original company. And so you see, we don't require magnificent offices to create the illusion of great wealth (and in many cases these days it *is* an illusion) because we are largely a financial house tagging along on the good fortunes (or otherwise) of hundreds of insurance companies throughout the world – companies which are carrying on the real business. Not for us is the highly trained technical staff – all we need is an office, pen and ink and a few books of account, and we'll follow the fortunes of the real insurance experts. There's nothing new in Unit Trusts – virtually we've been working on the same principle for over half a century.'

'They say there's nothing new under the sun,' agreed Lingard. 'What puzzles me though, Mr Bulworthy, is why you should remember that this man Neeve wore a rosebud in his buttonhole *two years ago.* What was so special about that particular day?'

'You will have gathered, Superintendent, we're a sober-sided, strait-laced company here, and though I say it myself, even up to a few years ago our puritanical outlook was reflected in the sombre style of dress we required of our employees. Adam Neeve's rosebud stuck out like a sore thumb on a soup plate. Of course, there was nothing *wrong* in it – it was just unusual in this office, that's all. In fact, it was more than unusual, it was unique. And I happened to see it.'

'Yes, sir, quite so, but the date – why are you able to pin-point it? Two years ago is a long time.'

'Ah, yes, the date. Well, it was the Friday before the Gomshall-and-Shere joint Flower Show. Thursday night there had been a violent rainstorm which had ruined my prize roses. On the Friday morning, before coming to town, I'd looked round my garden in despair. There didn't seem to be a praiseworthy bloom left. There *was,* of course, but at first glance all seemed lost. And the first thing I saw on entering the office was the all too perfect bud which Neeve was wearing. It would have been superb for exhibiting the following day. I can feel the pang of jealousy even now – you know how it is with gardening enthusiasts.

As a matter of interest I checked up the date of that show – they hold it on the same Saturday every year – and made a note of it here. Just over two years ago, in July. So far as I can ascertain, there was nothing unusual about Neeve before that date. That was the very beginning of things.'

'Genesis,' murmured Lingard absently.

'I beg your pardon? Oh, yes, I see what you mean. Well, Neeve began to sport a rosebud almost daily, and I suppose we became accustomed to it. At that time I recollect there was a move afoot in the press urging men to – um – brighten themselves up by wearing a flower in the buttonhole. I think it was born out of that charming window-box idea which had grown up in the City business houses. Speaking as a gardener, I must say the constant display of flowers and evergreens throughout the year does cheer things up. And so it wasn't particularly noticed when Neeve's flowers got more flamboyant; and when larger varieties crept in, it was merely accepted. And then, as I say, came the fancy waistcoat and the pointed shoes, the cap. More was to follow. On Saturday mornings – we were not doing a five-day week then – I understand he actually used to wear green corduroy trousers, light brown suède shoes with thick crêpe soles, and, I understand' (Mr Bulworthy flicked his eyes upwards in despair) 'a sort of leatherette jacket.'

'Incredible,' said Lingard.

'Ghastly,' emphasised Bulworthy.

'You say you *understand?*'

'Yes, I didn't actually see him dressed thus – if you'll excuse the misuse of the word "dressed" – as I didn't come in on Saturday mornings, but his departmental head saw fit to castigate him over it. Neeve maintained it was his sports-wear. Sports-wear! He didn't play golf; in what other sports could a man of his age indulge?'

Several brilliant ideas on the subject flashed through the Superintendent's mind, but he wisely kept them to himself. 'He appears to have been making sport of the office rules,' was his only comment. 'I wonder why?'

'Of course, there always was a certain amount of latitude in the office on Saturday mornings; for example, if any of the staff slipped out for coffee, we turned a blind eye to it.'

'A very wise and enlightened attitude, I'm sure,' said Lingard. The other looked at him suspiciously, and the Superintendent wondered if he'd gone too far. 'Things have certainly changed since I was young,' he added hastily to cover up. (Lord, what it must have been like in old Bulworthy's young day!)

'And even the rules concerning dress were

relaxed a little,' went on Bulworthy. 'We didn't object to the wearing of discreet sports-wear, because most of the younger people went off on various recreational activities in the afternoon, straight from business. But I gather Adam Neeve was really carrying it too far.'

James Mountebanke, Esquire (1843–1921) frowned down at Superintendent Lingard disapprovingly, and Lingard was quite certain Adam Neeve would have got very short shrift from him. The hands of the presentation clock were creeping on.

'I was forgetting your other appointment, Superintendent, I must hurry on.'

'You'll be wanting your luncheon, sir.'

'I think I first had conscious doubts about Mr Neeve one day several months ago. I didn't have much contact with him in the normal course of events, his head of department was the natural buffer between us, but one day I was aware of being in the lift with him. I say "aware" because I *sensed* rather than saw him. I was preoccupied with a problem, and when the lift door opened I stood aside to let pass what I thought – judging by the aura of perfume – must be a woman standing behind me. Imagine my astonishment when Adam Neeve pushed boisterously by. I suppose it *could* have been after-shave lotion, or strongly perfumed hair-oil, I don't know, but to me the effect was nauseating and effeminate. And the suit! You should have seen the suit!' (Mr Bulworthy's eyes nearly rolled up under his skull in the sheer agony of the recollection.) 'It was one of those tight-trousered, chunky-looking monstrosities in striped Italian suiting – made him look like a badly-packed Christmas parcel on stilts. Perfectly ridiculous! Even then I don't think it dawned on me what a tremendous change had come over the man – it had all been so subtly spread over the best part of two years.'

'What did in fact bring it home to you, sir?'

Mr Bulworthy hedged, as though he doubted the propriety of what he was about to say. He suddenly made up his mind.

'It was when the – um – young ladies began to call for him at the office,' he said. 'Perfectly outrageous. Yes, perfectly outrageous.'

'Don't tell me you're so old-fashioned here that you don't permit the staff to have their friends call and wait for them,' said the Superintendent in amazement.

'Neither are we so modern as Adam Neeve seemed to think we were,' retorted the other acidly. He overcame his sense of delicacy. 'These young ladies were street walkers...'

CHAPTER 6

Wasting His Substance

The words came tumbling out.

'Street walkers!' ejaculated Lingard in sheer astonishment. 'How do you know?'

Mr Bulworthy shrugged his shoulders. 'You know what it was like in this district before the passing of the 1959 Street Offences Act. One was accosted at all hours of the day. One got to *know* them.'

A flicker of a smile rose unbidden to Lingard's lips, which fortunately he was able to suppress before Bulworthy could intercept it. 'What did you do about that?' he grunted.

'Well, it was a very ticklish position,' murmured Mr Bulworthy. (You bet it was, thought Lingard.) 'As you imply, Superintendent, we are not so old-fashioned as to attempt to forbid a certain amount of *social* intercourse, and if any of the staff wish to make the office a meeting place at reasonable times for after business-hours' activities, then I'm sure nobody's going to object – provided the front office isn't turned into an old-time French Music Hall lounge. And having once acceded on those lines, it is very difficult to attempt to prohibit certain people from coming in, without saying why. After all, people do have varying shades of – um – politics, and we couldn't very well put up a notice saying "No Fascists, No Streetwalkers", could we? I found myself in a very delicate position. I couldn't tackle Neeve and say, "You mustn't have your friends call for you in the office in future", because in reply to his "Why *my* friends in particular?" I could only have said, "Because we only want decent people here". And that would have been asking for an action for slander and defamation of character, and insurance companies regard their good names so highly that they will do almost anything to keep out of court – unless, of course, a real point of *principle* is involved, and then they'll fight all the way to the House of Lords. "Who steals my purse, steals trash, etc., etc.'"

'So what did you do?'

'Nothing immediately. I held my horses, and made it my business to have a good look at this changeling, Adam Neeve, to try and find out what made him tick – a regrettable modern expression, Superintendent, which sums up precisely what I sought to do. I deliberately engineered more and more contact with Neeve to see if I could detect anything from his manner or bearing which might explain the metamorphosis.'

'And did you, sir?'

'I didn't detect the reason why, I only detected further deterioration. When I saw him that day in the lift the one decent thing about him was the impeccable white shirt. But a month later, not only did he have the Italian suiting, he was favouring a French shirt.'

'French shirt?'

'Yes, one of those exquisite confections, all pleats down the front, and with frilly cuffs.'

'Good Lor',' said Lingard, amazed.

'To say nothing of cameo cuff-links to match. I also learn now he didn't confine his attentions to the ladies of the street, he'd even made advances to some of the young ladies in the office – we have to employ too many of them nowadays, Superintendent, and some aren't all they should be. I don't know why it is, they all emphasise their sex so much by the way they dress. And the result is they all look so drearily alike that if I were a young man I think I'd fall for some-one *not* trammelled by two-way stretch, uplift, knots and zips at critical points, and faces painted like wall-plaques.'

Superintendent Lingard was astonished at Mr Bulworthy's knowledge of these things, and he wondered if Mrs Bulworthy (if indeed there were such a person) suffered from any such iniquities. It may merely have been, of course, that old Bulworthy came up the escalator at Piccadilly Circus.

'Are you a married man, Superintendent? No? Then it's hardly fair of me to mention such things – you would know nothing of these female devices unless you happen to go down the escalator at Leicester Square; if you travel on that line, the only mystery that's left is what they look like with clothes on.'

(The old boy's psychic! thought Lingard.)

'And was Neeve successful, sir, with his advances?'

'The young madam of today, Superintendent, is as hard-boiled as they make them. They take all, give nothing. But one must bear in mind Adam Neeve's age; he was not a young man. That's what makes the whole thing so grotesque. Fortunately for the peace of mind of the office, I gather he was repelled with heavy losses – losses in the form of expensive lunches and odd pieces of jewellery. Though I just don't know how he could afford such peccadilloes.'

'He was not overpaid, sir?'

'He was not *under*paid,' countered Bulworthy swiftly, 'but he certainly couldn't afford his expensive tastes on what he was getting here. I discovered that most days he was indulging in lavish luncheons with the very best wines and liqueurs. And was

111

coming back to the office late and slightly the worse for drink.'

'I believe many commercial houses give luncheon vouchers. Perhaps he was using more than one at a time.'

'The sort of places he was using don't accept luncheon vouchers, Superintendent. And in any event we don't believe in them here – our feeling is that they force up the price of food.'

'Then it looks as if friend Neeve had a private income,' said Lingard thoughtfully.

Mr Bulworthy pursed his lips. 'That could be so,' he acknowledged, 'but this curious build-up – montage, if you like – goes back *before* he started to splash out. I mean, a rose wouldn't have cost much, would it? Or a cap, or a fancy breast-pocket handkerchief folded to display three points – that was another thing – but all these things were part and parcel of what I can only call his general deterioration. You see, for the first year, none of these items in itself could be called expensive, yet the overall effect in two years was one of sheer profligacy.'

'Perhaps he was banking on great expectations which took longer to bear fruit than he bargained for,' suggested the Superintendent. 'What finally brought things to a head?'

'He came in one Friday afternoon after one of his more expensive lunches, and told an important client – who wanted a motor insurance for Switzerland in a hurry – to go and take a running jump off the Matterhorn. Caused quite a stir,' said Bulworthy dryly. 'Well, I couldn't let that pass without comment, so I gave instructions for Adam Neeve to be brought up before me on Monday morning. In spite of everything, there was something about him I liked, and he was a good worker. I think I secretly hoped there would be a miraculous reformation over the week-end, that he would appear before me dressed ordinarily, like the man he was when he came to us some eight or nine years previously.'

'Ah, yes,' interposed Lingard suddenly, 'just where did he come from?'

'He came from our Lisbon office, or, rather, the head office of our Portuguese subsidiary, *Companhia portugueza de Seguros "Benevolência"*.'

'"*Benevolência*"! Portuguese for "Goodwill",' said Lingard.

'A linguist!' exclaimed Bulworthy. 'Do you know, Superintendent, you're rather cleverer than I thought you were.'

'I think we both are,' grinned Lingard. 'I was once an interpreter attached to Intelligence. And I think *you* must at least be psychic. But tell me, sir, how long was Neeve in Lisbon?'

Mr Bulworthy gazed vaguely at a bluebottle walking up Esquire's waistcoat, and wondered if it would reach the purple-veined nose which the artist had portrayed with embarrassing frankness.

'He was in Portugal from about the middle of the war onwards, I think,' he said at length. 'And before then I gather he was in Casablanca and Marseilles in another of our subsidiaries, *La Bienveillance* – and there's no need for me to tell you that that's French for "Goodwill".'

'Is there then a separate "Goodwill" company in every country, sir?'

'No, but we're well represented on the continent. For example, we have a flourishing Dutch Goodwill – *de Nederlandse Welwillendheid Verz. Mij.* – with offices in Amsterdam and Rotterdam.'

'Don't tell me he was in Holland, too!'

'Oh, but he was.'

'He was? When?'

'Just before the war, I think. And he was actually in Rotterdam during the bombing. And he stayed on for some time during the German occupation.'

'As a British National?' said Lingard incredulously.

Bulworthy looked doubtful. 'I don't know which side he was one. He could have been a collaborator. All I know is that later he was in Vichy France, and was in Casablanca when it capitulated. Of course, before the war our companies had close relations with German reinsurance companies, and it may have been that Neeve, with his wide reinsurance knowledge, was permitted to stay, under surveillance, of course, as he was of more use to the Germans in his job than in an internment camp. Has the true value of insurance in wartime ever struck you, Superintendent?'

'You mean as regards the compulsory covering of war damage?'

'No, in connection with the national economy.'

'I can't say it has.'

'Have you ever thought of how much money it earns without the use of shipping? It brings in millions of pounds annually without the use of a single ship. Nothing is sent abroad other than a "promise to pay".'

'Ah,' said Lingard, interested, 'an invisible export.'

'Precisely. I'll tell you something interesting, Superintendent. At the beginning of the war, Germany had relatively few insurance companies of sufficient standing to command or even attract the world insurance market. And yet as much money was pouring into Germany with its comparatively few large companies as was coming in to this country with its world-wide insurance reputation. And how was this achieved? I'll tell you. By hundreds and hundreds of small

115

*re*insurance companies who were quietly tagging along behind the world markets. As I've explained, no large offices were required, no specialist staff – just pen and ink, a bit in the bank, and a treaty. And when the bit in the bank was backed by the Reichsbank, it was money for old rope. That German financial wizard, Dr Shadt, plugged re-insurance business for all he was worth; how he must have laughed up his sleeve! You see, with reinsurance business, original insured are apt to get lost in a maze of cessions and retrocessions. Many a business man today would be surprised to learn that a company in say, Trieste, has helped to rebuild his factory in Wigan.'

'Surely things didn't stay like that with regard to Germany?' said Lingard, intrigued.

'Bless my soul, no. When we became fully alive to it, the Trading With the Enemy Acts began to close up the gaps, although it was a long and irksome business. We held on to premiums and froze payments of losses.'

'Very right and proper,' agreed Lingard, who had firm ideas on the conduct of total war. 'But to return to friend Neeve. What happened on the following Monday?'

'Nothing. He didn't come to the office. I rather pictured him sitting at home covered in remorse.'

'And was he, sir?'

116

'He may have been. I wouldn't know, I haven't seen him since. That was some three months ago.'

'Three months!'

'Three months, Superintendent. After a couple of days of absence, a doctor's certificate was sent in saying he was suffering from an indecipherable complaint which could have been anything from a common cold to childbirth. We suspected the former, and hoped he'd soon get better. At regular weekly intervals further medical certificates were forthcoming, all equally indecipherable, and every week we imagined he'd be back shortly, without our having to write and ask what was wrong. And then came several certificates merely saying "After effects". We could read those all right. And then a letter from Adam Neeve himself indicating he'd now gained sufficient strength to write, that the weather was rather hot for a diet of beef tea, that he hoped to be back soon. And then an unfortunate relapse necessitating a change of drugs in the hopes of alleviating the troublesome condition.'

'And just what was the condition, sir?'

'We haven't found out, yet, Superintendent. We shall be very interested to learn. I have a feeling it will be the medical discovery of the age. But first we've got to find Mr Neeve. That's where you come in.'

'We'll soon trace him, sir,' said Lingard

confidently. 'I gather from the Commander that one or two unsuccessful attempts have been made to contact Neeve at his home.'

'Yes. He lived at Westcott. As it was reasonably near to me – I live at Shere – I thought I'd drive over one fine evening and see what he had to say. I had no intention of snooping. I thought perhaps after all something really was wrong, that I'd misjudged his illegible illness. The address proved to be one of a dozen interesting-looking bungalows in a clearing – you know the sort of thing, all different, the only common factor being the price. High.'

'And you got no answer?'

'Nobody was at home. Here's the address.' Mr Bulworthy pushed over a slip of paper.

'Eden End,' grunted Lingard. 'That's the name of the bungalow, I take it? Do you think this man's a bit of a joker, sir? Adam and Eve, Eden End.'

'I wondered that myself, Superintendent. But if he is, he's the most serious and persistent joker I've ever met. In the front garden there's a beautiful apple tree – neglected, but bearing heavily – and near the bole, poised ready to strike, is a bronze serpent.'

'A real Garden of Eden,' said Lingard.

'As you say, Superintendent. Genesis.'

'I wonder if he entertained his Eves there?'

'I wouldn't know. Curiously enough, he

never struck me as being a man who would indulge in senseless whimsy – he was really very diligent, and never put a foot wrong with his work.' Mr Bulworthy glanced suddenly at the clock. 'Good heavens, Superintendent, almost lunch time. I would have asked you to stay, but I know you have another urgent appointment. I usually have something sent in, nothing much, just a light snack, some chicken and salad and an ice-cold lager to stave me over.'

Superintendent Lingard could take a hint as well as the next man, and he got up. 'I'll be on my way, sir. We'll make some inquiries down at Eden End, and let you know.'

'I think you'll be wasting your time there, Superintendent. The bungalow's been up for sale and empty for two years.'

'Empty! Two *years?*' jerked Lingard.

'Yes, almost to the very day Adam Neeve wore that rosebud. And nobody locally seems to know anything about him at all. At a neighbouring bungalow I was informed that a man occasionally calls and lets himself in with a key – it was assumed he was somebody from the house agents, although I suppose it could be someone collecting any odd bits of mail that might still be delivered there – from us, for example, or anyone else not aware of the change of address. I tell you who might be able to help you – Mr Meddlisome.'

'Who's he?'

'The Judge. You may have heard of him. Mr Justice Meddlisome.'

The gears started to mesh. 'Oh, yes. But how will he be likely to help?'

'Adam Neeve is his brother-in-law. The Judge has a cottage at Gomshall and we come into contact with each other at church fêtes and so on. When Adam Neeve returned to this country I was instrumental in finding him a bungalow, through a house agent friend of mine – you know how these things are arranged.'

'On the "old-boy net",' agreed Lingard enthusiastically.

'Er – yes, although I'm not sure I care for the *"old boy"* part of it, Superintendent. However, I see little of the Judge, and I gather he sees even less of his brother-in-law, but he may be able to help. Curiously enough, I saw Meddlisome last night.'

'Oh, yes, sir?'

'At a party at some young neighbours' of mine at Shere. An anniversary of sorts. Quite a gathering. Went on a little too long for my liking.'

'You didn't inquire after Neeve?'

'No. Old Meddlisome seemed in a very preoccupied mood. I imagined he had a legal problem on his plate and wouldn't want to be worried with trivialities. He made a show of enjoying himself when our hosts were around, but I sensed he wanted to be left very much alone. He seems to have a very soft spot for the Mendozas – our hosts – one would almost assume they were his own children. Especially young Caroline. He would rather cut off his right hand than offend her. Pity he never married. He's a lonely man. And they seem to have taken a fancy to him – I think they prevailed upon him to stay the night. His housekeeper's ill, or something. He might be able to give you a lead on Adam Neeve, Superintendent...'

As Lingard took his leave he was vaguely annoyed to feel that the jangling strings at the back of his mind wouldn't synchronise to strike a good healthy chord. The irritation was such that he almost forgot to call at the Leather Bottle. Almost.

He was glad he went. He saw Blake coming out.

CHAPTER 7

Positively Negative

'I saw Simon Good leave the Scrubs this morning, sir,' said Lingard.

The Commander cocked an eyebrow in inquiry. 'Any reception committee?'

'Hammersley was there. You remember Hammersley, sir?'

'I remember Hammersley,' said the Commander.

'And also a rather grim-looking man I couldn't place – elderly. Looked as hard as granite. Shouldn't like to cross him!'

'Probably a creditor.'

'I only got a passing glimpse of him, but I'd know him if I saw him again. I'll see if I can find his picture in the Rogues' Gallery.'

'You have a memory for faces, Lingard – you'll worry about him until you put him in the right frame. What happened?'

'Well, it seemed a bit odd. Hammersley and this other man arrived separately in the forecourt at approximately the same time, and one would have said they didn't know each other. They came together apparently casually, a brief word passed between them and they parted company again. When Good was released, the elderly man approached him, and it appeared to me that Good didn't immediately recognise him either. They had a brief discussion, Hammersley joined them, and all three drove away in Good's car. And that was that, so far as I was concerned. I went on to the insurance company.'

'H'm! As you say, odd.' The Commander reflected for a moment. 'I suppose you've really come to tell me all about your visit to the Goodwill?'

'You instructed me to report before taking any further action, sir.'

'Quite so, but before you give vent to an imaginative account of your interview, I have a piece of news for you. Simon Good called in at Richmond Police Station this afternoon to complain that his house had been broken into during his absence in jail.'

'It would have to happen to him,' said Lingard cynically. 'What jewels beyond price have been stolen?'

'Nothing beyond a small presentation case which normally contained a medal – you know the sort of thing, a small, leather-covered case lined with velvet, with a seating inside to hold the medal in place.'

'And the medal – was that stolen?'

'He's only complaining about the box – that's what makes it so curious.'

'Seems frivolous to me,' commented Lingard. 'He's probably just mislaid it – it's easy to forget where you've put things after being away for a while.'

The Commander grinned a twisted grin. 'Oh, and he did mention he thought the electricity meter had been tampered with, but not to worry, he'd contact the Electricity Board.'

'They'll be overjoyed to hear from him again,' grunted the Superintendent. 'And I suppose he blames us for not guarding his property whilst he was inside, sir.'

'He does,' agreed the Commander mildly. 'Just that. His house at Richmond has an automatic burglar alarm connected directly here. He says it was expensive to install, but that it was worth it because you couldn't trust anyone these days. It is the latest alarm with a continuous recorded tape which says in the householder's voice, "This is The Elms, High Street, China, I'm being garotted, send help at once".'

'A very good system, too, sir.'

'Yes, except that if you set the alarm and go out and forget the master key which cuts it off from the outside, you have to go back through the invisible wave, and you automatically whistle up a couple of squad cars.'

'That can be obviated if you immediately disconnect and ring up the police and tell them what's happened,' said Lingard.

'Yes,' agreed the Commander, in great good humour, 'that's what happened here.'

'But Simon Good couldn't have rung us up – he was in prison.'

'That's why he's annoyed. He appreciates there should be close co-operation with the police in these matters, and that they should be advised by the householder when there was likely to be continued absence, but he didn't think it was absolutely necessary when we ourselves had ensured his absence. He feels we had all the advice necessary. A reasonable contention, I thought.'

'What exactly happened, sir?' Lingard was perplexed.

'About a fortnight ago somebody broke in at midnight, tripped the alarm, and immediately dialled 999 and said it was all right, he was going to bed. He evidently recognised the type of alarm from the selenic cells each side of the door, and took a chance. Had some specious excuse about forgetting his pass-key, and the control room accepted it. And that's why their faces are still red. The entry is in the night-book for all to see. Heaven knows, *someone* should have remembered that Simon Good was still in prison – the case caused enough kafuffle when it came up in the courts.'

'But why go to all that trouble just to steal an empty medal box?' growled Lingard. 'You don't think it's some sort of a try-on by

Good or one of his friends?'

'I don't know what to think,' said the Commander. 'They're doing all the thinking down in the control room, and I suspect their thoughts aren't particularly worthy ones. Tell me what happened at the Goodwill office. Did you see the manager?'

'Yes, sir. He told me an incredible story about a chap called Adam Neeve who's taken two years to go to the dogs, and he's done it so gradually that nobody's noticed it, and now they suddenly realise they've got a salacious, drunken rake in their midst – or did have until he vanished about three months ago.'

The Commander listened with great attention. 'What do you think the explanation is?' he asked at length.

Lingard scratched his head. 'I hardly know what to think, sir,' he confessed. 'He could have been overworking and had a breakdown. We may find him wandering about in Newcastle. Or he could be up to his eyes in debt, and decided to clear off. Or he could be a bigamist at the end of his tether – he seems to have been a one with the girls. Or just a plain nut-case.'

'I scarcely think it would be wise to mention the alternatives to Justice Meddlisome,' said the Commander mildly.

'Oh, you know about that link, sir?' Lingard was annoyed; he had intended that titbit to be something in the nature of a surprise. 'But then you knew about the tie-up between the Goodwill and the Tyburn & New York, of course. I don't think you mentioned it yesterday.'

The Commander let that pass without comment. 'It seems strange,' he mused, 'that the man who has disappeared is the brother-in-law of the Judge who sent Simon Good down for twelve months. I can tell you this, Lingard, there's more involved here than a mere desiccated clerk being missing. On no account will you approach Mr Meddlisome.'

The Superintendent was out of his depth and he showed it. 'Then what steps do you want me to take to find Neeve, sir?'

'No steps at all, Lingard, your action must be negative. Positively negative. And don't look so huffy! You merely did what you were told.'

'I rather feel as if I've been wasting my time,' half-grumbled the Superintendent, adding a quick 'sir' as he noticed the highlights change in the Commander's eye.

'I can assure you, Lingard, you haven't been wasting your time. You've played your part according to plan, a part which couldn't have been played so well by any local station officer.'

'I don't really see why not, sir.'

'Because if any local station had charge of

the investigation into the disappearance of Adam Neeve, they would have felt obliged to try and find him.'

Lingard was startled. 'Isn't that the object?' he jerked.

'No,' replied the Commander blandly. 'The object at the moment is *not* to find him. The object is to stall off the Goodwill Insurance Company for a while. Perhaps in a few days' time I'll be able to tell you more about this man called Adam Neeve ... if I can get special dispensation from "the Pope".' (This didn't refer to the gentleman at the Vatican, but to Commander Pope, head of an obscure department at the Yard.) 'In the meantime, try and place that third man you saw outside the Scrubs.'

The Commander's cuff seemingly accidentally caught the corner of a slightly curled glossy photograph on the desk before him, and the print spun round. Lingard couldn't restrain himself.

'Why, that's the very man!' he exclaimed.

'Is it? I wondered if it might be. I got that photograph from a Press bureau in Fleet Street. Do you know who it is?'

'I can't quite place him,' grunted the Superintendent. 'The Rogues' Gallery might help.'

'Actually it's Mr Justice Meddlisome,' said the Great One gently.

'Meddlisome!' Lingard grew pink with

confusion. 'What was he up to then?'

'That's what I'd like to know. I don't suppose he was apologising to Simon Good. And I don't think he'd be flattered if he knew your line of thought.'

'He looks different without a wig,' growled Lingard, defensively.

'So would you,' said the Commander...

CHAPTER 8

No Fatted Calf

Mr Earnshaw Withers, Secretary of the Tyburn & New York Insurance Company, looked up unhappily at Simon Good. He had an unpleasant task to perform, and he wasn't one of those people who enjoyed doing unpleasant tasks. 'Oh, Good, sit down for a moment.' He put his fingertips together, and looked over the top of the desk at Simon. 'I've never before been faced with the task of having to greet a member of the staff who's just come out of prison, so I scarcely know how to welcome you, if welcome is the correct word to use.'

'I'm very glad to be back amongst friends,' said Simon. 'The prodigal son, as it were.'

Mr Withers pursed his lips. 'Er – quite. But I'm afraid there'll be no fatted calf. You will appreciate, of course, that the company has received a lot of unwelcome publicity as a result of your – misdemeanour?'

'It was much stronger than a misdemeanour, sir – they called it a crime. But surely the publicity wasn't unwelcome – it brought the name of the company before the public.

They knew that the company wasn't responsible for what I did.'

'Possibly. Unfortunately your case also brought grave doubts as to the type of staff we were employing.'

'The company gave me an excellent testimonial at the trial – and, by the way, I don't think I ever thanked you for it. I would like to take this opportunity of doing so.'

Mr Withers was not to be deflected from his task. 'Thank you,' he said shortly. 'That testimonial related to past services, as we found you, and was purely factual, without reference, of course, to all those things it was suggested you were using us for. You were sentenced to twelve months' imprisonment, that's what sticks in the public's mind.'

'It was reduced on Appeal, and the Judge was criticised by the Appeal Court. But for the "contempt" angle, nothing might have come of it.'

'Does the "contempt" angle, of which you speak so lightly, make you a worthier employee? Are the public likely to think better of the Tyburn & New York because you very nearly only went to jail for contempt? Very nearly, I say – let me remind you that part of your sentence still related to a felony under the Larceny Act.' Mr Withers appeared to make up his mind. 'The General Manager has decided to dispense with your services.'

Simon Good became very still.

'He can't do that,' he said at length.

'He has done precisely that,' said Mr Withers. 'I am instructed to give you one month's notice.'

There was an awkward pause. 'You're not getting rid of me as easily as all that,' said Simon.

'Your position is untenable here.'

'Surely the one way the management can answer public criticism is *not* to sack me, but to take me back and justify its confidence in me.'

'The management doesn't feel that way about it.' There was another awkward pause. 'I'm afraid the G.M. has made his decision, Good. Look at it from the company's point of view.'

'I'm looking at it from my point of view. I really enjoy working here.'

'Really, Mr Good, there are limits to my credulity and, I think, to your enthusiasm.'

'I shall use all means within my power to retain my job, Mr Withers – the Press, the directors, the stockholders. I shall take legal advice and sue for wrongful dismissal. There was a case in the papers–'

'I shall convey your message to the General Manager. I must remind you that you have been given one month's notice. By all means utilise whatever remaining time you have here in looking for another position.'

'Thank you. You make it sound so very reasonable. I shall also look into the victimisation angle.'

'There is no question of victimisation, Good.'

'I'm not so sure,' said Simon Good. 'I know the way these things work out. I'm almost willing to wager that before long *somebody's* going to be victimised...'

'Swithin & Matthews,' said the telephone girl.

'Mr Soames, please.'

'Hold the line.'

There was as brief pause. 'Soames,' said a voice.

'Simon Good here.'

'Simon – you old son of a what-not! You've been – away, I gather.'

'You've gathered it truly while ye may.'

'Saw it in the papers. What can we do for you?'

'I want to manipulate some shares – without interfering with Roag's.'

'You mean like spreading say seventy-five per cent of Holdings A and B over several of your other holding concerns, in unequal sums, and starting a new holding for the balance? So that *in toto* you're back where you were, the whole operation to look like genuine market dealings, and not like a dozen simple transfers.'

Simon was amazed. 'That's brilliant,' he said. 'How did you guess?'

'That's what we're here for. Swithin & Matthews, Stockbrokers to the Aristocracy. Both of them. The aristocracy, I mean, not Swithin & Matthews. It'll cost you money though, even if it is virtually out of one hand into the other.'

'It'll cost you your job, brother, if you don't do it discreetly,' warned Simon darkly.

'The scheme's already well on the way – I started on it about a month ago.'

Simon Good almost stopped breathing.

'A month ago?' he said at length.

'Yep.'

'But a month ago I was still – um – convalescing.'

'I know. That's why I'm glad to get your personal confirmation of the instructions.'

'Whose instructions?'

'A short, plumpish, mild-mannered chappy with spectacles. Met him by appointment. Seemed to know all about you. Had a mandate to act. I checked up with your office in Racquet Alley. They said it was O.K., so I went ahead. I hope I did right?'

'You couldn't have done righter. Nowadays things move faster than the quasi-optical speed of the radio wave...'

'I foresaw that the Tyburn & New York might fire you,' explained Hammersley, 'and I thought you'd need a little help from the stockholders. Certain stockholders.'

'Hammersley,' said Simon Good, 'you're a genius.'

'I am?' Hammersley was gratified. But not unduly surprised.

CHAPTER 9

Candid Views

Someone tripped the burglar alarm, and within a few minutes two squad cars converged on Simon Good's house at Richmond. There was going to be no mistake this time.

They found no one on the premises, but three doors which were normally shut were open – the front door, the back door leading down to the towpath, and the door of the refrigerator.

Simon Good was immediately informed by telephone, and, being public-spirited, he obtained permission to go home and assist the police in their investigations. It was a beautiful day.

So far as he could see nothing had been stolen, and he told the policeman who had been left on guard not to worry about the tray of spoilt ice discs as a judge had very kindly given him a real shilling. Expressing profuse thanks for the prompt action of the force, and promising to let them know if he ultimately found anything missing, he opened a bottle of beer, and settled down to read a hastily scribbled note he had noticed on the mantelshelf.

He read it through twice and reached for the telephone. He was fortunate enough to catch the Judge.

'I can only give you a couple of minutes, Meek.'

'That's better than twelve months,' said Simon. 'My place has been broken into, and whoever did it didn't get what he wanted, so he's left a note asking me to meet him in the Temple tomorrow to have a chat. I thought I'd let you know that things were moving.'

'Is the note signed?'

'Unsigned. And as a precise time, meeting place, and method of identification has been suggested, it would seem that the person who wrote it is not too sure of what I look like.'

The Judge drew a breath. 'Toledano?'

'Doesn't he think I'm still – um – convalescing? And wasn't he supposed to have gone back to Portugal?'

'He could have changed his mind. Perhaps he has discovered you are now well enough to go out.'

'We can establish nothing unless I meet him. Maybe by tomorrow evening all your worries will be over.'

'I only hope all yours won't be,' said the Judge grimly. 'Toledano's dangerous. I – I think we ought to get police protection.'

'Nothing's likely to happen in the middle of the Temple!' chaffed Simon. 'It's not Lincoln's Inn, you know.'

'Lincoln's Inn? What's dangerous about Lincoln's Inn?'

'There's a peculiar notice which says that a certain building was erected in 1774 to accommodate the Six Clerks of the King's High Court of Chancery when they moved from the old office in Chancery Lane.'

'What's peculiar about that?'

'It's the last sentence which worries me, a sort of death sentence. It says "the Six Clerks were abolished in 1842". Bit hard on them, don't you think? I suppose they took them away and had them painlessly destroyed. So far as I know the Temple hasn't a record for that sort of thing. Toledano won't attempt anything there. I expect he'll send a go-between.'

'I'm not so sure. If he's satisfied you're the man, he'll stop at nothing.'

'Perhaps you're right. I'll send Hammersley.'

'Hammersley,' said Simon over the telephone. 'I want you to do a job for me.'

'I shall be delighted to do anything for you, Mr Good. What's in it for me?'

'Just depends,' said Simon vaguely.

'There's not likely to be any rough stuff?'

'My dear chap! All I want you to do is to

meet a fellow in the Temple and have a chat with him.'

'I'm always meeting fellows in the Temple,' grumbled Hammersley. 'Can't you fix up somewhere else for a change?'

'I didn't fix the meeting place.'

'Why do you want me to do it?'

'I shan't be able to keep the appointment. And I'm no photographer.'

Hammersley became interested; he was a keen photographer, and it didn't take much to get him zooming off into the panchromatic ranges. 'Do I have to take photographs as well? It sounds as if it's to be an historic meeting.'

'Could well be,' assented Simon. 'I want you to get a picture of the man you meet – unbeknown to him, of course – so that even if you die of heart failure on the spot, I'll still know what he looks like.'

'So you don't already know him.' It was more of a statement than a question.

'I may know him. I just want to make sure. That new midget Japanese camera you were telling me about–'

'I'm dying to use it.'

'You probably will.'

'Eh?'

'You will probably get the opportunity.'

'Oh! Well, what message have I to give this chap?'

'I think he has a message for me.'

'Bit vague, isn't it?'

'Just listen and see what he says, and take his picture.'

'Where do I meet him?'

'Right in the middle of the courtyard at the side of Temple Church. There's a double circle of paving stones between two lamp-posts, and in the centre of that is an inscription on the ground about the destruction of Lamb Building in 1941. Go to that point at one p.m. tomorrow and stroll round the inner circle three times in one direction and three times in the other. Our client will then descend from cosmic space in a cloud of smoke.'

There was a doubtful pause at the other end.

'I shall feel a proper Charlie,' said Hammersley.

'Yes,' agreed Simon Good.

A few minutes to one o'clock on the following day found Hammersley drifting with utter casualness round Church Court. Pausing to read the church notices and noting that the Choir dated from A.D. 1240, he rambled on to the Master's House – climbing the few steps to peep into the garden – and thence idled back past the Library, the Treasury and Inner Temple Hall once more to the Cloisters. Slowly and thoughtfully he meandered under the arches, and one would have said that here was a dreamer of dreams, a man not of this world. One would have been mistaken.

Charles Hammersley was very much of this world, geared up to snapping point, absorbing with those deceptively mild eyes of his the details of those few people who passed by or lingered. Someone was exercising two dogs – one large and chunky, the other small and perky; Hammersley admired the way they obeyed the order to sit whilst their master strode away to the far side of the court; felt a pang of sympathy at the anxiety and agitation expressed by the animals if their master was obscured for one moment by the other passers-by; laughed at the relief displayed when the order came first to one dog, then to the other, to come and claim a reward.

He wandered over to the concentric circles between the two lamp-posts in the middle of the court, and studied the notice set in the paving in a circular stone slab some four to five feet in diameter. It informed him that Lamb Building, built in 1667, was destroyed by enemy action on the 11th May, 1941. It appeared that this historic fact was worth photographing for, fumbling at the strap of a small canvas case slung over his shoulder, he produced an old-fashioned folding camera. Opening it up, he peered down at the inscription through the ground-glass view-finder; then screwing his neck round he squinted up at the sun, made an adjustment to the lens-stop, and peered down again at the notice. Still in doubt as to the actinic value of the light, he extracted from his pocket a small object which – judging from his subsequent actions – one would have said was an exposure-meter. One would have been wrong.

He finally photographed the inscription to his satisfaction, and next devoted his attention to a long-shot of Church Court showing the Round. And then, deep in meditation, he commenced his perambulations as ordered around the inner circle of paving stones, feeling as he had forecast, a proper Charlie. Three times round seemed never-ending; he was relieved when he could reverse and unwind himself. And out of the corner of his eye he noticed a bronzed, yet very ordinary-looking man slip out of the church porch and make straight for him.

Hammersley, affecting not to see him, directed his attention to photographing the corner with the flight of steps to the Master's House.

'Good afternoon, *senhor*,' said a pleasant voice at his elbow. 'A beautiful day for taking pictures.'

'Indeed, yes,' agreed Hammersley without looking up. 'If anything, the light is a little *too* strong without a filter.' He squinted through the small object in his hand in the direction of the Master's House, adjusted his camera lens, and took another photograph, winding the film round again. 'This old camera still gives me better service than all your modern ones,' he said apologetically, glancing at the stranger for the first time, 'although I must say the modern light-meter is a boon. There are too many gadgets on the present day camera. Are you a photographer, sir?'

'I can manage a – No.2 Brownie,' smiled the other.

'Oh.' Hammersley seemed disappointed. 'I was about to ask if you'd mind taking one of me over by the steps. Souvenir of my visit to London, you know. Sounds brash, doesn't it? But you know how it is when one is alone in the world.'

'I think I could manage that – if you set up the juggernaut first,' said the other, his face crinkling in a faint smile.

Hammersley was delighted, his lonely life blossoming into gossamer happiness. He hurried over to the steps. 'This calls for the accuracy of the exposure-meter,' he said over his shoulder. 'Would you be kind enough to stand there where I'll be standing – you've no idea of the actinic variation brought about by the reflection of light from the actual object to be photographed, and film is too expensive to waste.' He shepherded the stranger into the corner by the steps, and with his tiny Japanese camera took a careful portrait of him, giving credibility to the manœuvre by first making finicky adjustment to the lens-stop of his folding camera. He screwed his eyes against the sun doubtfully. 'Better make certain,' he said, and took another careful portrait with his 'exposure-meter', transferring a mythical reading by further precise adjustment. 'I think that will do it, sir. If you will kindly get me in the view-finder and press that lever I shall be indebted to you.'

'You'll probably want to sue me when you see the result,' said the other, pressing the lever.

Hammersley wound round the film and said, 'Now I'll take one of you, sir – I'll send you a print, if you would care to leave your address.'

'Please don't – I'm afraid I'm not photogenic,' hastened the other. 'I have a thing about being photographed – reminds me of the Rogues' Gallery, I suppose.' (This was the first disquieting note.) 'I haven't had the pleasure of meeting you before, but I take it you are, or come from, Peter Meek?'

'And if I am, or do?' said Hammersley cautiously.

'Can I at least take it that you speak with the voice of Peter Meek?'

'The hand may be the hand of Esau, but the voice may well be the voice of Jacob,' said Hammersley.

'Well, actually I'm more interested in the voice of Peter Meek at the moment, but I think I see what you mean. You were destined for the Church, *senhor?*'

Hammersley ignored the natural misunderstanding. 'Have you a message for Mr Meek?' he asked.

'To the contrary, I want something *from* Mr Meek. A medal.'

Hammersley was puzzled. 'A medal? What sort of a medal? What have you done to earn it? Are you a numa – numa–'

'Pneumococcus?'

'The word I'm searching for means a coin-and-medal collector.'

'A numismatist. I am in a sense, but I am collecting only one medal. Peter Meek knows which one. Do you?'

'Ah,' said Hammersley. 'I know all the right people who know all the right things.'

'Then perhaps if you went away and had a chat with yourself, or Peter Meek, or both, and came back with the medal which fits the velvet-lined box that was stolen from Meek's house at Richmond, then we could get down to cases. It could be a matter of life or death.'

'For whom?'

'Does it matter?'

'Not if it's a matter of life. On the other hand–'

'Shall we talk about it some other time, *senhor?* You're obviously not the man I want. I'll drop Meek a line, and see who turns up next time. I'll ask him to meet me at Prince Henry's Room in Fleet Street – you know Prince Henry's Room? No. 17. It's cooler up there. I can't stand this heat.'

'You look as if you're used to a hot climate,' said Hammersley critically.

'Different sort of heat, *senhor.*'

'What name shall I tell my principal? Toledano?'

'By all means do,' nodded the other absently.

'You're sure you wouldn't care to have your picture taken?' pressed Hammersley.

'Not unless you want your camera torn apart,' smiled the other. And nodding pleasantly, he strode away towards Mitre Court.

The heat from the paving stones rose up and hit Hammersley between the eyes. He made for the chill shadows of the Cloisters, and Simon Good beat a rapid retreat into a gloomy doorway in Pump Court.

CHAPTER 10

Sense of Rumour

Jullien Fane, General Manager of the Tyburn & New York left the board-room with a face as black as thunder. The friendly air with which he handed out exceptionally large cheques in settlement of exceptionally inflated claims (whittled down by average to an indemnity) was not now in evidence. On his way to his room he said to a messenger, 'Get me Mr Rumbold,' and he waited impatiently until the Registrar appeared. 'Rumbold, here's a list of certain stock-holders – some large, some small; some, you will observe, are holding companies. Let me know their individual and total holdings. And here's a list of ex-stockholders. I want to know what they held before they sold out. I want the information right away.'

'Trouble, sir?' asked Rumbold as he took the list. He should have known better.

'Just bring me the information,' said Jullien Fane grimly. 'As soon as you like...'

Rumbold produced the information sooner than that and it didn't seem to make Jullien

147

Fane any happier.

Fane studied the statement carefully. 'It appears that taking into account these particular stockholders there's no material change in the *total* amount of stock involved? That is, by and large, the *ups* balance the *downs?*'

'That's broadly the position, sir,' agreed Rumbold, 'but surely that's not to be wondered at?'

'It is when every one of these stockholders and ex-stockholders has written in to the Chairman personally,' said Fane harshly. 'Why these in particular and nobody else?'

'There are one or two who have neither bought nor sold,' pointed out Rumbold. 'And quite a proportion of the stock put on the market was snapped up by a buyer not appearing on your lists.'

'Which buyer?'

'Roag's Syndicate.'

Jullien Fane stiffened. He rubbed his chin thoughtfully. 'Let me know who the brokers were in each of these cases,' he said.

'In two cases where the entire holding was disposed of it was Swithin & Matthews,' said Rumbold. 'I'll make a complete list.'

'Swithin & Matthews – they're Roag's brokers, aren't they?'

'I believe they are, sir.'

'You should know, Rumbold, that's what you're paid for; Roag's Syndicate isn't a two-penny-ha'penny concern. Less than a year ago they were buying up Tyburn & New York stock at an incredible rate, no matter what the price was. Have they increased their holding much lately?'

This was one question Rumbold thought he could answer. 'No, sir, apart from this recent acquisition there's been little change since that unfortunate business of the dividend warrant at St Ives.'

'What links that event in your mind with Roag's?' asked Fane curiously.

'I remember it because when Mr Withers called me in to look into the non-payment of that warrant for Mr Smith of Yeovil, Roag's had just made another large purchase, and Mr Withers commented that it was just as well the Articles of Association limited the voting power of individual stockholders, else we'd all be voted out of a job. He was implying, of course, that Roag's was beginning to acquire a very powerful financial interest in the company, and could, but for the Articles of Association, get awkward.'

'I can see very clearly what he was implying, Rumbold,' said Jullien Fane testily. 'I'm not altogether an idiot.'

'No, sir,' agreed Rumbold humbly, and wondered if it would have been better not to have said anything at all.

'Take this statement back and add the

names of the brokers involved in each case,' said Fane abruptly. 'I'm willing to wager that in the majority of cases it will be the same firm – Swithin & Matthews.'

Rumbold added the names to the list, and Jullien Fane was wrong in his surmise. Apart from the two cases Rumbold had already mentioned, the name of Swithin & Matthews didn't appear any more. Soames had done a very slick job for Simon Good, and was well worth the high rate of 'brokerage' he charged.

'Well, Withers,' said Fane, 'you were at the Board meeting and you heard what the Chairman had to say about this man Good. Because of the undesirable publicity arising out of Good's stupidity the Board were quite prepared to endorse my action in dismissing the man. But now it seems there's been a powerful wave of sympathy in favour of Good from certain stockholders. You saw the batch of letters the Chairman produced which had been sent to him personally, and I expect you were as surprised as I was at some of the extracts he read out. I had no idea the case had aroused such interest. We were told of concerns which had actually sold their holdings because of the unjust treatment we'd meted out to Good on top of an unjust sentence.

There was talk of victimisation and the "boss class". There was prattle of the first retrograde step in the history of a leading company which would mark the beginning of the company's decline before finally being taken over by a finance house. And stockholders who hadn't sold out, but had increased their holdings, only did so because they felt there'd been a misunderstanding somewhere which would be remedied immediately; that the management with the vision they thought we undoubtedly had needed men of Mr Good's calibre to back it up, and that it could only be assumed his dismissal presaged some form of promotion for him, to be announced later. There was a hint of informing the Press of our monstrous action. These are the actual letters, Withers, by all means glance through them.

'I asked Rumbold to draw up a list of the holdings of these stockholders, hoping that the analysis would show only a trivial financial interest. My hopes were sadly dashed. Take a look at that statement, Withers, we're obliged to take notice of a total interest of that size. This is real money talking.'

Withers examined the statement carefully. 'I see you've had the names of the various brokers added – had you something in mind, sir?'

'Rumbold mentioned Swithin & Matthews, and it started off something in my mind; I don't quite know what it was I hoped to prove.'

'They're brokers for Roag's Syndicate,' said Withers keenly.

'At least you're more definite than the man who's paid to know,' grunted Fane. 'What else strikes you?'

Withers pondered. 'Good is apparently a wealthy man, according to what came out at his trial. I was wondering if he has an interest in some of these concerns, and has manipulated things accordingly. Perhaps you were thinking along the same lines – that he has a link with Roag's.'

Jullien Fane sat up. 'You have indeed put into words what was half forming at the back of my mind, Withers. Curiously enough, Rumbold ties up Roag's with that St Ives business – to the extent that they were buying heavily round about that time.'

'Oh, they've purchased heavily since then,' said Withers thoughtfully.

'When?'

Withers screwed up his face in thought. 'When you last went to Holland,' he said slowly. 'Early in the year – you remember, when I remarked I thought you seemed a bit off colour and needed your holiday.'

Jullien Fane sat motionless. His mind went back to Hans Wisselink, the old jeweller in Oude Amstelweg, Amsterdam. 'The coincidence is even more curious than you can ever imagine, Withers,' he commented at length. 'However, it's not getting us anywhere. Mr Good may be a comparatively wealthy man, but he can't be as wealthy as the sum total of this stock. In any event, the greater part of the stock movement took place a month *before* he was released from jail. He couldn't have *known* we were going to fire him. No, Withers, we're barking up a gum-tree!'

'I personally wouldn't be working here if I had this wealth,' remarked Withers. 'By the way, sir, Roag's appear to have gleaned what they could in this last batch of dealings – did *they* write to the Chairman singing the praises of Mr Good?'

A weight lifted from Fane's mind. 'No, there was no letter from Roag's Syndicate,' he said. 'Well, what are we going to do with Good? The decision is ours, the Board have given us *carte blanche* to do as we think best, but any repercussions are on our heads. What's your view?'

'Basically he's a sound man, very intelligent, but I'm not so sure we want him back here – at least, not right away,' said Withers. 'It makes it very awkward in our dealings with other companies.'

'Perhaps we could find him something at one of the branches,' suggested Fane

153

thoughtfully. 'I think I'd like to give him a little rope and keep a watchful eye on him. Look round and see what you can find for him...'

Mr Withers smiled grimly to himself as he left the room. Simon Good had been very prophetic. Somebody *was* being victimised.

Jullien Fane sighed. Life was no easier since Quenella Mansfield had left with a large cheque he had since regretted signing. He wondered what she was doing now. She was so vital, the mere sound of her voice was a tonic for the tired business man; and the sound of her voice was as far as he'd ever got. His new private secretary was decorative enough – he'd seen to that – but Quenny could type too...

Simon Good had just learnt that the Tyburn & New York had taken over the Goodwill Insurance Company, when the Secretary rang for him. Mr Withers went straight to the point.

'The General Manager has reconsidered his decision regarding your dismissal,' he said, 'and has decided to give you another chance – if you feel like taking it.'

'That's very good of him,' said Simon, 'I must go and thank him personally.'

'That won't be necessary, Good,' said Withers sharply. 'I think he would prefer you not to.'

'Then I shall be grateful, sir, if you will convey my thanks. Jobs aren't easy to get. What made him change his mind?'

'I don't know,' said Mr Withers untruthfully, 'I'm merely carrying out instructions. You appreciate, of course, that you really do present a problem to us from the viewpoint of the other staff. Half of them are prepared almost to hero-worship you, and the other half regard you as a social outcast.'

'They can't all be right,' said Simon.

'We thought perhaps a move away from head office, possibly temporarily – I don't know where to quite, but that's what's envisaged.'

'I gather we've taken over the Goodwill whilst I've been away,' said Simon thoughtfully. 'Perhaps there's a job I could do there for the time being, whilst the two systems are being integrated. I may be able to put over the Tyburn & New York's methods.'

A quick gleam of hope flickered in Mr Withers' eye. The Goodwill *were* short of a man, one had disappeared following sickness – Neeve was his name, yes, that was right, Adam Neeve. Simon Good would fill the bill admirably with his knowledge of reinsurance work.

'Perhaps we could arrange something like that,' he said, almost doubtfully in his desire not to appear too eager. 'Now I come to think of it, they are a man short. I shall have to mention it to Mr Fane, of course. I'll let you know.'

'It seems a heaven-sent opportunity,' said Simon off-handedly, also not wishing to appear too eager. 'Perhaps too, sir, I might be granted a short holiday so that I can come back to the job really fit and well. The last few months have been very exacting – not at all the kind of thing I've been used to.'

'I expect it can be fitted in with other people's holiday arrangements,' conceded Withers, breathing heavily. 'So long as you're happy, Good, that's all that matters.'

Simon Good looked sharply and suspiciously at Mr Withers, but Mr Withers was as wall-eyed as a basilisk...

In the fulness of time Simon Good was instructed to report to Mr Bulworthy at the West End office of the Goodwill Insurance Company.

CHAPTER 11

A Lady of the Quality

Mr Bulworthy very quickly took to Simon Good. Simon saw to it that he was at his most charming best, he worked like a Trojan, was helpful and courteous, and Bulworthy, who had been warned by Jullien Fane that there might be a hint of trouble, found him nothing but an asset, and wondered what it was all about. He became a quick favourite with the staff, which wasn't large in comparison with that of the Tyburn & New York, and very soon he had extracted the full story of Adam Neeve as seen through the eyes of the messengers, the juniors, the typists (a wealth of information here) the desk clerks, the senior men, and even an odd word or two on the subject from Mr Bulworthy himself.

By dint of further skilful high-pressure investigation Simon unearthed some altogether curious facts about Adam Neeve, facts which in no way solved the obscure matter but merely made it more puzzling.

Everyone was agreed that Neeve was a conscientious worker. This struck some of the younger staff as being peculiar in itself. Although he was engaged on what was largely a routine job and seemed to be working out his time waiting for the years to slip by to retirement, occasionally, because of his knowledge of the Portuguese company, the *Benevolência,* he accompanied Mr Bulworthy and the Chairman on managerial visits to Lisbon, and on a number of occasions he had been entrusted with missions on his own.

It seemed that Neeve, having once got to the hub of the insurance world, was no longer interested and couldn't care less if he was spun out to the perimeter.

Simon quickly ferreted his way round the rabbit-warren of an office with all its odd-shaped cubby-holes (flatteringly called rooms) and in due course exercised his well-known charm on critical Lola Lee of the Secretarial Department. In point of fact, Lola Lee *was* the Secretarial Department, all of it. It was in despair that her parents had put her to a commercial school in Southampton Row, where she had plodded through typing, shorthand and book-keeping, and had taken some secretarial examinations which to her astonishment now put quite a premium on her services. Being endowed with certain basic good looks, she had finished things off by taking a course at a school of deportment. The result was that when she walked through the office in the spring it became obvious to the male staff why nature had provided them with necks which were made to turn. She was not liked by the female staff.

One of the junior misses was taking the Secretarial Department her morning tea when Simon kindly offered to save her a journey. A moment later, pausing only to pour back the tea from the saucer, he entered Miss Lee's tailored-to-fit cubbyhole.

'Ah, Lola, my love, your morning infusion of restorative herbs. The little wench with the El Greco look is being rushed off her feet, so I volunteered to be tea-boy.'

'Thank you. Where are the biscuits?'

'You have biscuits as well?'

'Of course I do. I pay for them.'

'I'm thinking of your figure.'

'Well, stop thinking of it.'

'To hear is to obey, moon of my delight,' said Simon, producing five wrapped Rich Tea biscuits from his pocket. Lola Lee put the packet down beside her cup with exaggerated care.

'And now, Mr Good,' she said, looking him straight in the eye, 'what exactly do you want?'

Simon Good coughed in confusion. 'When you look at me with eyes like that

159

you fill me with inevitable yearning,' he declared.

'Yes, I know, but what do you want apart from that?'

'I've been having a chat with old Bulworthy, and he's been telling me about this chap Reeves I'm replacing. Alan Reeves, I think he said – something like that, anyway.'

'Adam Neeve.'

'That's it! I was tentatively fixing up a spot of leave with him – I've been a bit off colour lately, and I need a holiday–'

'Yes, I read about the Appeal in the *Telegraph*.'

'–and somehow the talk got round to doctors' certificates, and he mentioned how indecipherable Alan Neeve's were. He seemed to think I might be able to read what the illness was. He said if I caught you in the right mood you might even let me have a peep at them. If you refused, however, he wouldn't interfere, because he believed in letting you run your own show. He thinks a lot of you.'

Lola Lee coloured slightly. 'He appears to think quite highly of you, too,' she countered. 'He doesn't confide in many people in this office.'

'Well, it's different with me,' said Simon modestly. 'I'm a man from the head office of the company which has taken you over, and as such I'm invaluable, although I says it as shouldn't. I know just what's required and what he can get away with, and old Bullo's cute enough to appreciate the position. I gather Alan Neeve was suffering from nothing more serious than child-birth.'

'We decided it was a common cold,' said Lola frostily. 'And it's Adam, not Alan. You'd better see for yourself – I suppose it's all right.'

'You're running your own show,' Simon reminded her. 'Do just what you think.'

And so Simon Good saw the file on Adam Neeve. The medical certificates were tagged neatly together, and Simon admired their utter illegibility; he couldn't have done better himself. The illness appeared to have been copied direct from the Rosetta Stone, and in each case the ink seemed to have run out just as the doctor was signing his name; and unfortunately the name-and-address stamp must have been very old and clogged-up, because all it printed was a meaningless blur. The first signs of legibility came when Neeve was suffering from 'after effects'. The courageous letters ultimately received from him seemed to have been based on the assumption that the original certificates had been decipherable, and that everyone knew what he was suffering from. Simon made a mental note of the address at the top before he pushed back the file to Miss Lee.

'Well, it's impossible to make much of

that!' he chuckled. 'I gather from Mr Bulworthy that when he called at Neeve's bungalow it was empty and up for sale. He must be a rum egg – would you say he's gone off his hinges as a result of being in insurance for so long?'

Lola thought for a moment before replying. 'He's a question mark altogether, Mr Good. We still haven't found out where he's living, and he *has* been doing strange things.'

'So I've gathered from a ready and willing staff. I decided it was grossly exaggerated.' (Simon Good was an adept at fishing.) 'After all, there's nothing very curious in brightening up one's appearance with the odd buttonhole.'

'I suppose you're right, in a way,' agreed Lola reluctantly. 'He hasn't done much wrong – other than tell a client to go and jump off the Alps, and sometimes I wish I had the nerve to tell them that myself – it's just that – just that – it doesn't add up. He was efficient, with plenty of experience, reasonably well liked, although he tended to keep himself to himself. The change in him over the past two years has been so gradual that hardly anyone gave it a thought until those – those – women started to call for him. That just about put the tin hat on it!'

'Are you sure those women *were* what everybody's telling me they were?' asked Simon.

'Mr Good. It didn't take me long to size them up – one look at their walk was enough. And eighty per cent of the staff can't be wrong, can they? If you want to see for yourself, one of them lunches most days at the Leather Bottle. She's known to her friends as Fernande – or French Fernie. Calls herself a hostess.' There was rich contempt in the last word.

'You frequent the Leather Bottle yourself?' asked Simon in surprise.

'They do a good lunch,' she said sharply. 'And at least I need a knife and fork for mine, which is more than I can say for that brassy-looking Richard.'

'You know the slang?' said Simon, raising an eyebrow. 'You've friends in Holloway? Let me take you to lunch today. At the Leather Bottle,' he added with a touch of brilliance.

'Thank you, no,' said Miss Lee. 'I'm meeting a friend at Swan & Edgar's. I'm sure you won't need me to point out French Fernie, she sticks out a mile – in more senses than one. I'll tell you something that rather intrigued me though – before you feel compelled to rush back to your work. One evening Adam Neeve was outside the office making a fool of himself with this woman, and apparently they couldn't get a taxi, so they walked up St James's Street arm in arm. I was some way behind them, making

163

for Piccadilly Circus Underground, and although I was in a hurry I didn't want the embarrassment of overtaking them. To my relief they turned off into Ryder Street, and I thought I was clear of them. When I reached Ryder Street, however, they were just round the corner, and he was in the act of slipping her what could have been a couple of pounds. Imagine my astonishment when they parted immediately and went off in different directions.'

'Odd,' agreed Simon, 'distinctly odd. And they'd only just met at the office? Perhaps things aren't what they seem. Perhaps she's blackmailing him. Or perhaps she's his wife, and he was giving her the housekeeping money.'

'It didn't seem like that.'

'I'm taking you to lunch at the Leather Bottle tomorrow,' said Simon firmly. 'Put a touch of *Utter Collapse* behind the ears. We'll have a sherry, tomato cocktail, chicken-and-ham salad, mixed fruit and cream, and coffee (black or white, as madam desires). Possibly a cigarette. In exchange for which you'll point out French Fernie to me.'

'You don't know the Leather Bottle – it'll cost you the earth.'

'It will? Then shall we say half a bitter and a meat pasty?'

Hammersley, acting on Simon Good's telephoned instructions, went to Waterloo and booked a train to Dorking North. He had a hurried snack whilst waiting for the train, and at Dorking North, sparing no expense (it was to be charged to Mr Good) hired a car from the station yard to take him out to Eden End, to see what could be learned there. As he had been told to expect, there was a TO-BE-SOLD notice nailed to one of the posts of the front gate, and he jotted down the name and address of the agent in Dorking.

The property appealed to Charles Hammersley instantly, and he would have liked to buy it. He fell in love with the ship's-wheel gate, and the poised bronze serpent at the foot of the apple tree tickled his sense of humour. He peered with interest through the grimy windows into the empty rooms.

'I could make something of this place,' he said to the driver.

'Have to spend a bit on it, I shouldn't wonder, guv,' grunted the other. 'One or two people have been after it, but they don't seem to come back. Too dear, I expect.'

'Let's go and find the agents in Dorking,' said Hammersley. 'I've got a note of the address.'

'I know it, guv. Been there several times. You're about the fifth.'

And so Charles Hammersley was taken without further ado to the bow-windowed office of Janes & Jerrold (Estd. 1880) in the High Street. He was greeted by an ancient gentleman who could have been a founder member, and who by rights should have had an ear trumpet rather than his modern transistor hearing-aid.

'I've come to make a few enquiries about a bungalow called Eden End,' said Hammersley.

The smile went from the other's face.

'I'm sorry, it's not for sale.'

'The board distinctly says it is,' persisted Hammersley genially, 'although it doesn't say when.'

'Perhaps I should say it's no longer for sale,' said the old man.

'It's just the sort of place I would like to buy,' explained Hammersley. 'Perhaps you could put me in touch with the owner.'

'That presents a difficulty. He hasn't left a forwarding address.'

'Well, if it's not being too inquisitive, how do *you* get in touch with him?'

'He calls in from time to time. He's in no hurry to sell – he's not short of money. He hasn't lived in Eden End for two years.'

'Can you give me any idea when he's likely to call in again?'

'Maybe this week. Or next year. He's like that. Unpredictable. Sorry I can't help you. Can I interest you in another bungalow in a slightly higher price range?'

'Thank you all the same, but you can't,' said Mr Hammersley, 'no matter how hard you try...'

Over the bar French Fernande was sitting by herself in all her misused glory. Simon drifted over casually.

'Miss Fernande?'

'You can say that again. Call me Fernie, dear, everybody else does. French Fernie.'

'You don't sound very French to me,' said Simon Good doubtfully. 'At a guess I would say no nearer France than Mile End Road.'

'There's no need to be rude.'

'Well, am I right?'

'As a matter of fact, you are. Bow, E.3.'

'Then I wasn't being rude. I was being perfectly correct and factual. What can you tell me about Adam Neeve?'

'Who wants to know, darling?'

'I do.'

'You a copper?'

'My dear – er – good woman. I've just come out of the Scrubs.'

'Well, for all I care, you can just go back.'

'Come, come, Fernie, that's not the way to treat a gent who's holding out a five-pound note under his newspaper.'

'Let's look at the stop press, then.'

Simon turned the paper over and exhibited the fiver. French Fernie made a tentative movement but Simon was too quick. 'Uh, uh!' he said soothingly. 'Let's get down to business first. I've been told doing business with you is a pleasure. Adam Neeve. Do you remember him? Several months back?'

'Why should I remember him, ducks? What's so special about him?'

'That's what I'm trying to find out. He may have been just another creature in trousers. The point is I've lost him, and I'm trying to find him.'

'Well, I haven't got him. Would I like another gin and lime?'

'If it will help your memory, by all means do.'

'Thank you. Although it won't help me to remember. It only helps me to forget.'

'At least that's candid.'

'French Fernie's the name.'

'The symbol of truth!'

'You're the first one who's said so apart from me.'

'There must be a first in all things. Tell me about Adam Neeve before five-pound notes go out of circulation.'

'Describe him.'

'He wore eccentric clothes – or perhaps you might not consider them so eccentric. Italian shoes, French frilly shirts with matching cameo cuff-links, striped dago suiting, a cloth cap that resembled an acorn – this was sometimes discarded in favour of a tweedy Continental trilby with a miniature shaving brush in the tartan band – age, fifty-ish.'

'That sounds like 'em all rolled into one, dear. They're all fifty-ish and slightly off-centre, else they wouldn't come to me.'

'You have few illusions,' said Simon.

'No illusions,' said French Fernie, without heat.

'You used to call for this chap in the front office of the Goodwill Insurance Company in St James's Street.'

'Oh, *him!*'

'You remember him? Excellent! I hear fivers are still in circulation. Tell me about Adam Neeve.'

'If *he's* the chap, there's not much to tell, it won't be worth a fiver. He was the queerest customer I've ever had in all my life, and believe you me I've had some queer customers. All I had to do was to call for him at his office in the evening ten minutes before closing time, hang about till he was ready, which was usually after most of the staff had had a good look at me and gone home, and then, after a boisterous greeting which I felt was not for me but for the benefit of anybody else who was still in the office, he'd take me by the arm, go out into the street, call a taxi, ask for Bond Street, pay me a fiver in the taxi, and then get out in Piccadilly and say cheerio.'

'Seems reasonable enough, and quite economic from your point of view. Didn't he ever go back to your place?'

'Never.'

'Curious.'

'Off his rocker?' ventured Fernie. 'Easiest money I've ever earned. Once he gave me a tenner.'

'How many times did he go through this routine?'

'Oh – on three or four occasions. With me, that is. He went through the same nonsense with two or three other girls – one of 'em was my friend, Virginie – that's French for Virginia.'

'Most appropriate, I'm sure,' said Simon politely.

'Anyway, her heart's nearer France than mine is.'

'She's actually French?'

'No, Barking, E.6. Just nearer France, that's all.'

'Oh. Why all the accent on France? Where does it get you?'

'It's a sort of hallmark.'

'Hallmark? Of what?'

'Well, it's a kind of guarantee of quality, I suppose,' said Miss Fernande doubtfully; she'd never really thought about it before.

'Just how silly can we get?' mused Simon in great wonderment. 'Did Adam Neeve treat Virginie in a similar way to you?'

'Exactly, except on one occasion we both had to turn up at his office within a few minutes of each other, and each ask for him separately.' French Fernie grinned at the recollection. 'Caused quite a stir, that did!' she remarked with satisfaction.

'I bet it did,' visualised Simon. 'Tell me, Fernie, was there anything in common with the other women he chose for these jobs?'

Fernande hesitated. 'I think he liked striking women,' she commented.

'I was taught never to strike a woman,' said Simon. 'At least, not without raising my hat.'

'No, darling. Striking *women,* not *striking* women.'

Mr Good looked blank, and Fernie caught the look.

'Outstanding women,' she amplified, draining her gin and lime.

Simon's eyes flickered in an ungentlemanly fashion over her form. 'Well, if you're a prototype, he wasn't disappointed. Is that *all* about him?'

'Unfortunately, yes. He faded quite suddenly from our difficult lives at a time when we were all beginning to know that the doorways and entrances of premises abutting on a street, and any ground adjoining and open to a street, would be treated as forming part of the street within the meaning of the Act.' The passage came

171

parrot fashion.

'I take it you're quoting from the Street Offences Act, 1959?'

'Yes, page 1, Section 1, paragraph 4. Price 6d at a place in Kingsway. I bought a pamphlet on the Treatment of Dry Rot at the same time.'

'You're interested in wood fungi?'

'No, but it was not so embarrassing as having to ask for the '59 Act by itself. I get easily embarrassed.'

'I bet you do, you're like me. I once went to a nudist camp and I was the only one dressed. I felt so terribly embarrassed I made them all shut their eyes. Well, I must be going now,' said Simon. 'It *was* worth a fiver. As a lady of the quality, would you care for my *Times?*' He slid the newspaper over with the five-pound note underneath.

'Thank you, *chérie*. Any time I can oblige.'

'There's probably truth in what you say,' agreed Simon Good, and took his leave.

It is to be regretted that Miss Fernande X of Bow, E.3 didn't immediately turn to the leader columns of *The Times*. The fourth leader didn't mean a thing. The five-pound note did. She was relieved to find that it hadn't been spirited away again by the gent who'd offered it.

'Men are rummy,' she ruminated through a mist of gin fumes. 'Usually want something for nothing. He's the second one

172

who's wanted nothing for something. Must be the atom bomb.'

From his corner Superintendent Lingard watched Simon Good leave the Leather Bottle. The confident set of the shoulders recalled that other day many years ago at Hondschouwen, when he'd seen him walk away from comparative safety up a battle-scarred road, Bren at the hip position, blazing away defiantly in the face of molten death until the whole landscape mush-roomed, and Major Peter Meek disappeared. Only to turn up again years later at the Tyburn & New York Insurance Company as Simon Good. Lingard remembered that hollow-eyed group at Hondschouwen – Peter Meek, Hammersley, Blake, Dutchy and Rip Strookman. There was a post-war link in that little coterie which was difficult to detect; they were clever, but Lingard was deter-mined to break the link one day, even if he had to take the bunch apart one at a time.

He finished his beef sandwich, took a final swig at his tankard. In his opinion, the whole darned human race was beyond com-prehension, and he hadn't been drinking like French Fernie...

Blake, watching Lingard watching Simon, was vaguely uneasy. He'd seen that face somewhere before, and he searched back

173

through the years for the solution. Was it at Lumm's Safes, where he worked in the old days? At Rempert's, who took them over? No, it wasn't in London. Brussels, then? He dismissed Brussels. Well, then, where? He took a good look at Lingard, and then quickly buried his head in a newspaper as the Superintendent made to move.

When he looked up again the corner seat was empty. The image of the face soon faded, for it was one which, although possessing character, was somehow characterless. It could be almost anybody's. The image faded. The disquiet lingered.

CHAPTER 12

Goes Without Saying

At Simon Good's express invitation, Mr Meddlisome had an evening meal of sorts at the former's modest bachelor establishment at Richmond, and the Judge was struck by the almost monastic frugality of Simon's standard of living.

They sat at an old-fashioned window which overlooked a long garden sloping down to the river, and whilst Simon went to the kitchen to make some coffee, the Judge dwelt on the curious mixture that was his host.

First and foremost Simon Good was Peter Meek, and nothing would alter the Judge's outlook on that point until the name was legally adopted by deed poll. The Spartan aura which pervaded the establishment, however, made him wonder if after all there was much truth in the suggestions brought out at his trial of much wealth, for the standard didn't seem very high even for an insurance clerk. Meddlisome's eye wandered away along the vista of the river, where lights on the boats were beginning to twinkle in the twilight; his thoughts wandered to deep purple night skies in Estoril, to Mario Toledano, to Adam Neeve, to the bitter-sweet sadness of long ago, to the harsh reality of the present–

'Thinking of buying the place?' asked Simon cheerily. 'Don't burn yourself on the coffee, it's hot. Help yourself to sugar.'

'Thank you.' Mr Meddlisome sipped his coffee. 'I was wondering what sort of a welcome they gave you at the Tyburn & New York?'

'Frigid. Definitely no fatted calf. In fact, they fired me.'

Mr Meddlisome was not surprised. 'I'm sorry to hear that. But you won't miss the money, will you?'

'I always miss money. However, they changed their minds, and I'm still working.'

The Judge stirred in a little more sugar. 'I'd like to know what induced them,' he said.

'I only wish I could tell you,' said Simon.

'I only wish you would.'

'Tell me,' said Simon at a tangent, 'when Adam Neeve took you out to lunch over the past two years, did he dress normally?'

'*Dress* normally?' The Judge was astonished at the question. 'Of course he dressed normally, why shouldn't he? What do you mean, exactly?'

'I've been hearing some very curious things about Adam Neeve.'

'*You* have? Where?'

'At the Goodwill in St James's Street. I work there now.'

'Bless my soul! Perhaps you'll tell me how you achieved *that*.'

'Well, the Goodwill has been taken over by the Tyburn & New York. Briefly, they didn't want me back at Head Office, there was a vacancy at the Goodwill because of Neeve, and now I'm old Bulworthy's right-hand man.'

'It sounds delightfully fortuitous,' commented the Judge dryly. 'You must tell me all about it one day when I'm no longer a judge. What have you been hearing about Adam?'

Simon told him. Mr Meddlisome was thunderstruck. He accepted another coffee without a word and drank it in silence.

'It's all so very alien to him,' he said at length. 'You say this retrogression has been developing over two *years?* I've had no inkling of it, he's always presented a normal face to me. And all this talk of loose women, it's – it's unthinkable! Before the passing of the 1959 Street Offences Act he would go a mile to avoid any street which had a reputation for that sort of thing. But if this has been going on for a couple of years, his disappearance can't have anything to do with the recent events relating to Toledano, can it?'

'Let us analyse the facts,' said Simon. 'Two years ago Neeve puts his bungalow up for sale, and goes and lives somewhere else; you don't know it, his office doesn't know it. There's nothing illegal in that, it's just strange. The sale price of the bungalow is prohibitive; perhaps he doesn't *want* to sell it. Once again, there's nothing illegal in putting it up for sale and changing his mind. The house-agents in Dorking will talk about any bungalow except Eden End. Hammersley said it was like chatting to yourself in Chinese. Now at or about the time Toledano comes into the picture, you tell Adam Neeve about it, and he is smitten with a mysterious complaint supported by highly improbable doctor's certificates; *you* know the absurdity of that part of the story, because you've seen him in the best of health. And it was only because old Bulworthy went round to see him that brought to light how completely he's vanished. It could well be that the last few months *are* tied up with Toledano, and that if your brother-in-law ultimately managed – because of his intimate knowledge of Portugal – to find Toledano and come to terms with him over that page from Sea-Lion, he would then return to the Goodwill as large as life with a final "fit-for-work" certificate. And so he goes without saying.'

'Then what would be the point of all this other nonsense that's been going on over the past two years?'

'Don't ask me, my Lord, ask your brother-in-law – when he turns up. Perhaps it's some kind of a joke – you told me he had a sense of humour.'

'Two years! Longevity is the soul of wit!'

'Times have changed,' said Simon.

The Judge gazed down at the red and green runnels of light on the slumbrous river. 'I've had a letter from Toledano,' he said abruptly.

'He wants to call the whole thing off?'

'No, he wants you. And he wants one of your medals as a means of your identification.'

'The man Hammersley met in the Temple wants one of my medals, too. They must be getting collectors' pieces. Does he say which one?'

'He says you would know which one – the one which fits a medal-box that was stolen from this house.'

'So saith the man in the Temple – who, incidentally, referred to Hammersley as *"senhor"*.'

'I'm being driven to the inevitable conclusion that the man in the Temple was Toledano after all,' commented the Judge. 'If you yourself had turned up with some positive means of identification, he would have committed mayhem in this country in spite of the risk.'

179

'He'll have an opportunity tomorrow lunch-time. He has very kindly fixed an appointment at Prince Henry's Room in Fleet Street.'

'Tomorrow! Then we can't be dealing with Toledano himself,' said the Judge, fumbling in his wallet for an airmail letter. 'This was posted two or three days ago in Oporto, and in it Toledano says he'll be there for a week or ten days.'

'And even Toledano can't be in two places at once.'

'He says he'll be at your service on September 30th at nine p.m. at a fashionable fishing village called Boa Fidelidade, which I gather is some eighty kilometres from Lisbon. If you don't see him by the first of October, he proposes to send information to the British Press, with suitable pointers as to the other persons involved. The exact rendezvous, by the way, is an inn known as the Cross-Keys.'

'How very Ruritanian!' said Simon. 'It seems then – unless the Oporto touch is a bluff – that the man I'm meeting tomorrow is a Portuguese go-between.'

'You will be able to clarify the position – if you go,' said Mr Meddlisome.

'Perhaps we can clarify the position now,' remarked Simon. 'Hammersley managed to obtain two photographs of our friend with his Mitsi candid camera. Here are the enlargements. One is very good.'

The Judge took the prints and laid them side by side on the table, and Simon switched on a reading lamp. Mr Meddlisome looked at them with keen interest, and then went rigid. For a moment he was startled into immobility. He felt for the spectacles he was now obliged to wear for close work.

'That's not Toledano,' he said. 'That's Adam Neeve...'

For a moment time stopped.

'You see the special implication of this, Meek?' said the Judge at length.

'Yes, Neeve hasn't disappeared so very far. And he doesn't trust *me* with that page of dynamite, so he's going after it himself. The one snag is that to prove his identity he must have that medal. Any old medal won't do – it must have my name on it, and it must fit the box which Toledano stole from here whilst I was arranging the Ancient and Mod. number-boards for the vicar. Adam Neeve will be unlucky.'

'You're going through with this, Meek?'

'You couldn't stop me if you tried, m'lud. I want to prove to Mr Toledano that his vendetta's without foundation. And apart from him, Adam Neeve presents an interesting problem. As I told you in court, I'm of a friendly disposition to all mankind – I've even had psychiatrists come to me with their problems. But this one baffles me.'

'I think I should warn you, Meek,' said the Judge, 'that this letter makes it abundantly clear that you are in fact the man whom Toledano wishes to kill – the Peter Meek of the "ice-shilling" trial. He found the address of this house from a report of the proceedings. Another newspaper gave your potted military history, and published the citation which went with your award for bravery in the field; and that seems to have decided Toledano. He breaks in and steals the presentation box, hides the medal in the house, and gives instructions to me in this letter to tell you where to look for it. Thus he makes doubly certain, for *I* have to inform the Peter Meek of the trial. And all that comes back to you. And now,' concluded the Judge grimly, 'he's available for interview in Portugal at the end of the month.'

'That at least gives me leeway to fix up something with old Bulworthy.'

'Can you guess where Toledano hid the medal?'

'Yes. In the refrigerator.'

The Judge was disappointed. 'How did you guess?'

'I found it. He'd strapped it with Sellotape to the roofing inside, but the frost and damp got at it, and it came adrift. When I went to use the fridge, there, hanging by only one strip of tape, was what I took to be a coin. In a moment of elation I thought the ice-box had taken to minting genuine five-shilling pieces.'

'How very disappointing it must have been!'

'It was,' said Simon sadly. Then, 'A point about the photostat.'

'I'll get it from my bank when you need it.'

'I didn't mean that. I was thinking that Adam Neeve doesn't seem worried about it, although *he* is about the medal. I suppose it *was* the photostat that you deposited at your bank?'

'Of course it was! I checked it and sealed it in an envelope myself.'

'Oh.'

'I think you still haven't appreciated the most significant thing about Hammersley's meeting with Neeve,' said the Judge, and Simon was quick to notice the frigid use of the surname. *'How does Neeve know about the medal?'*

Simon Good sat bolt upright and felt the icicles forming. He said mildly, 'I suppose you could have told him.'

There was an ugly glitter in the Judge's eye. 'The first I knew that the medal was to be the identity-disc, Meek, was when I received this letter this morning. Neeve knew of it the other day when Hammersley met him in the Temple.'

'Then if you didn't tell him, who did? You tell me.'

Mr Meddlisome's mouth hardened, and this time there was all the crackling blue ice in creation.

'Could it have been Mr Toledano?'

Simon Good considered the matter. 'Where does that get us?' he asked politely.

'Meek. There are three ways of getting a man to do a difficult or unpleasant task. The first is to *ask* him to do it. The second is to make a show of doing it *for* him. The third is to try to *prevent* him doing it. The last method produces the quickest results.'

'So?'

'I feel one sure way of getting you to Toledano is to try and stop you. I feel Toledano knows that. And I regret to feel that Neeve is an instrument in Toledano's plan.'

'But why?'

'The root of all evil – money. Have you not told me that Neeve has turned into a two-faced, drunken rake, spending more than his income? Could it be that he's working for Toledano?'

'There's only one way to find out,' said Simon, 'and that's to go and see…'

CHAPTER 13

Adam Neeve

'Shut the door, Lingard, and sit down,' said the Commander (Crime). 'I want to tell you something of the background of friend Adam Neeve of the Goodwill Insurance Company. I purposely refrained from giving you the information before you visited Bulworthy, and I'm only giving it to you now to allay your curiosity and seal your lips for all time. When you leave this room you know nothing. You may smoke if you wish, and I'll borrow one of your cigarettes, provided they aren't one of the new brands that have been filtered, dehydrated, desiccated, exsiccated, mentholated, and sealed in a box you can't open. At my age I want to enjoy the tobacco, not go through an emotional crisis with a blonde on the seashore.'

'Try one of these, sir,' grinned Lingard, offering a well-known brand much advertised on television.

'They'd better be good, Lingard, else you'll upset me for the rest of the day. Thanks. Now, Adam Neeve. Between the wars young Adam Neeve's father put him to work at a general merchandise firm in the City. The firm was a very old family business, with very old connections. It had a very old office in St Mary Axe filled with very old high stools and very old ledgers. So old, in fact, that young Neeve felt he'd be better off in a museum. It was, however, a very aristocratic firm, the board being well-larded with the aristocracy, and everyone was made to feel what a fine big family they belonged to. You know the sort of thing, Lingard.'

Lingard didn't. 'Yes,' he said.

'There was only one snag to this beautiful family picture, the firm didn't over-pay their children, whom they regarded as being little better than serfs. As for anyone ever raising the sordid question of an increase – well, it just wasn't done. But it was a very aristo-cratic firm to work for, and jobs weren't easy to come by. When young Neeve was seventeen, he had the temerity to approach the manager for an increase. The manager, an old man pushing eighty and eaten up with rheumatism, was horrified. The junior staff were only permitted to cough if they did it through the proper channels. "Do you mean an increase in salary?" he repeated dully, when he got his breath back.

'"Yes, sir, please," said Adam. "You see, if anything happens to my parents, I just couldn't live on my salary."

'"Neeve," rumbled the manager, "you mustn't worry on those lines. You won't be able to live on your salary for many years to come."

'So Adam Neeve stuck it out for a bit longer, getting more and more depressed at the desiccated, inert men around him, old young men drying up at the roots, men with responsibilities who couldn't do anything about it, and he was terrified as he pictured himself in a few years, every bit as lifeless. In a sense, from the moment we're born we're all dying, but to Adam Neeve it seemed that at that very aristocratic old firm the natural process was accelerated far too much. Now young Adam had a bit of the "old Adam" in him, and in spite of knowing that things like mentioning money were taboo, that promotion was someone else's literal funeral, he had enough guts to push his point with the management. Until one day the ancient manager called him in and told him there was an opening for a young man in their office at Liverpool.

'"Liverpool!" exclaimed young Neeve.

'"Yes, Liverpool," said the old boy. "It's quite civilised now, they accept English money, and they no longer eat missionaries. And it means more money – that's what you wanted, wasn't it?"

'And so Neeve found himself on Merseyside, in a poky office in the vicinity of the great Royal Liver Building. Here there were fewer chances of watching decay all around him, because there was one very pleasing factor about his grimy room on the third floor – it overlooked the waterfront, and he could sit at his desk and watch the never ending movement of the shipping in the fairway; ships coming from colourful places like the Americas and Cuba, Hong Kong and China – enough to fire anyone's imagination, especially if it was an imagination fully alive to the crushing, drying-up, squeezing-out processes of that out-moded family business.

'Adam used to sit and dream himself away to far-off places, until one day it occurred to him that there might be a place for him in their office in Rotterdam. The obvious first thing to do was to learn the language, so he set to work with an intensity of purpose which surprised even himself. He found an evening institute where Dutch was taught, and very soon, fired with enthusiasm, he acquired a working knowledge of the language. He picked up at a second-hand shop a Dutch course on gramophone records. The old Jew who ran the shop found Adam a battered portable gramophone and let him have it at what he called a ruinous price. Adam very soon knew every phrase and pause and inflection of that course, and it gave him a completely new slant on what he'd already learnt; and like to most of us who suddenly find we've achieved something, the world seemed a great place to be in. He sought out one or two Dutch seamen in the evenings, and to his delight they understood him, although at first he was puzzled by the sharp looks they gave him. He was talking, of course, in the refined tones of the records. But they *understood* him!

'Wasting no more time, he put in for a transfer to Rotterdam. The head man at Liverpool shook his head and said that that would be quite out of the question, as the first requisite was a sound knowledge of the language. Neeve shook him with such a fluent flow of Dutch that an immediate recommendation was sent to head office. To back up his application Adam claimed having a sound knowledge of French and German too, and it was only on reflection that he realised he'd been over-enthusiastic on this score. His French and German were of schoolboy standard only, and something would have to be done about that quickly. And so back to the evening institute. He also asked the Jewish dealer to look out for record courses in those languages. The old Jew said yes, he'd do that, but the price would be slightly higher as he forecast an immediate inflationary trend.

'In due course, Adam Neeve arrived at

Rotterdam to a brave new world, with four languages to his credit, English, Dutch, French and German, the weakest one being English. To his amazement he found he'd learned more English learning foreign languages than when he'd tried to learn it on its own. By this time Continental tongues had become an obsession with him, and spurred on by meeting Portuguese business men in the office in Coolsingel, Portuguese and Spanish were the next languages to be conquered.

'He did quite well at that office in Rotterdam, augmenting his income by teaching languages in the evenings. And then he landed a spare-time job as a courier with a travel agency at week-ends; and as his parents had died in the meantime and he had no call to return to England, in his holiday periods he conducted coach tours down into Spain and the South of France. It was on one of these tours to Spain that he met Eve and fell head over heels in love with her. She was on holiday with her parents and brother; and the brother was the man who was to become Mr Justice Meddlisome.'

The Commander stubbed out his cigarette.

'And that, Superintendent, is the link between Adam Neeve and the Judge who sent Simon Good down for twelve months.

190

There was a lightning courtship between Adam and Eve, they married in Rotterdam – rather against her parents' wishes, but they soon got over the shock – and the couple settled down in Holland, supremely happy. And then one day a young Adam was born to them, and Eve Meddlisome died of puerperal fever. Adam never recovered from the shock. He became listless, introvert, mentally ill. He doted on the boy, and when at the time of Munich he saw the embers of war being fanned up under a vow of friendship never to go to war again, he took the young boy to England, settled him in a preparatory school with Eve's parents to keep an eye on him, and then went back to Holland. And took out Dutch national papers.'

'Well, I'm a Dutchman!' exclaimed Lingard, and wished he hadn't as he caught the Commander's frigid stare. 'Why did he do that, sir?' he covered up hastily.

'He'd been back in Rotterdam for a short while when one day he was approached by an Englishman who told him he had an interesting job to offer him; a job at a Dutch insurance company a few buildings away in Coolsingel. They wanted a linguist. It meant more money. And then the bombshell. It also meant changing his nationality and becoming a Dutchman. This suggestion seemed even more strange coming from an

Englishman. Neeve thought about it, asked for more information, got it, and finally accepted the job, this time in a frightening new world filled with urgent and vain requests for war-damage insurance. When there's no stretch of sea, and your neighbour only has to climb over your back fence, you become more sensitive to the possibilities of war. To Adam the business of insurance became the ever-quickening pulse of Europe's rapidly deteriorating mood. He never again saw the Englishman who talked him into the job. War broke out.'

'And Neeve was now a Dutch national?'

'Yes. He was in Rotterdam when it was bombed.'

'He made no attempt to get back to this country, sir?'

'He became an active collaborator with the Germans.'

'A collaborator!'

'He worked with the Germans in Holland, Belgium and Occupied France, and elsewhere.'

''Strewth! I gathered from Bulworthy that Neeve had been working under surveillance of the Germans – largely because of the importance of reinsurance to the German economy, and Neeve's company, the Dutch "Goodwill", had close ties with German reinsurance companies – but I didn't think for one moment he was an active collaborator. I thought he was doing it under sufferance.'

'Oh, he was active, all right. He was given quite a free hand by the Germans, and was permitted to travel up and down Europe and into parts of Germany. They thought quite a lot of him.'

Lingard muttered something unprintable, even in these days of Anglo-Saxon licence.

'I beg your pardon?' said the Commander.

'Bulworthy mentioned Neeve was also in Vichy France and Casablanca.'

'Didn't sound like that to me,' said the Commander. 'About eight or nine years ago, Adam Neeve came back to this country.'

'Like his ruddy nerve,' snapped the Superintendent. 'I see now why Mr Meddlisome hasn't seen much of him over the years – only too glad to give him the miss, I would say.'

'When he came back, the strain of the war years was still much in evidence. He was a changed man, older than his years.'

'A lot of people went through the havoc of the war and felt the strain for years afterwards, but they didn't lose or divide their loyalties, sir.' Lingard had strong ideas on the subject of national allegiance. 'I've got no time for these people who want the best of both worlds, the people who scurry from the country when there's a smell of trouble, and then try to slink back into public favour when it's all over. And we're suckers enough to stand for it. The public has a memory like a sieve, but I'm completely unforgiving.'

'Really?' the Commander (Crime) was impressed. 'You're a hard man, Superintendent. But don't be too hasty in your judgment of Adam Neeve; he had a lot to contend with. The boy turned out to be a thoroughly bad egg–'

'Like father, like son,' snarled Lingard, '–sorry, sir.'

'Try to restrain yourself, Superintendent,' said the Commander mildly, 'you'll be getting blood pressure or something. Wait till you've heard the whole story, please. Neeve had lost his wife–'

'Yes, but that was – what? – twenty years before he slunk back here–'

'–Neeve had lost his wife, as you say, way back in the early thirties, and as a result of that shock he retrogressed into a nonentity; but like many a man who fundamentally wants to get somewhere and can't, climbing back into his shell wasn't the answer, because it only brought about a state of war within himself. But there was another war in the offing. He sends the child to England, and in order to make a clean break from his working past takes on a new job, although this actually means changing his nationality. There followed the war years with all the strain of living under the aegis of the

Germans – a lonely life because he was merely being used by his masters, and he was scorned by the Dutch who knew his background. And all the time his heart was in England.'

'It sounds like it!' grunted the Superintendent venomously.

'His son, Adam Neeve the younger, was growing up into an uncontrollable handful, and by the time his father returned to this country, had turned into a wastrel and a spendthrift, getting into all the trouble he could find or make. What with one thing and another, Neeve senior barely had the heart to apply for repatriation.'

'Cor, stone the crows!' breathed Superintendent Lingard. 'He had the nerve to apply for repatriation, sir? And I suppose we were mugs enough to grant it?'

'We were mugs enough to grant it,' admitted the Commander without heat. 'He was transferred to the West End office of the Goodwill Insurance Company. As Bulworthy may have told you, the Goodwill Insurance Company of Great Britain is the unobtrusive financial parent of a string of "Goodwills" stretching from top to bottom of Europe, and when Neeve expressed a desire to round off his insurance experience in London in the heart of the insurance world, the transfer was effected without much trouble. His boy – man now – cleared off into limbo. I can't help feeling that Neeve must have suffered from a great sense of disillusionment.'

'I can understand that,' conceded Lingard. 'It took him over twenty years to get back to where he was originally – rotting in a grimy office in London. The last few years of frustration must really have got into his bones. And finally he's gone off his nut.'

'Don't jump to conclusions, Superintendent,' said the Commander. 'Our latest information is that he's in excellent health.'

A sudden thought struck Lingard. 'Would it be indiscreet to ask how you know all this, sir.'

'I wondered when you'd get round to that question, Lingard. You'll have to forgo Rules of Evidence, and accept what the soldier said. Some of this is not even second-hand – it's what the girl's mother said her daughter said the soldier said.'

'Oh, it's like that, is it, sir? Well, whatever might be the true answer to his disappearance, I think that in his final deterioration at the Goodwill he was acting out of sheer frustration and disillusionment.'

The Commander looked steadily at Lingard for a full fifteen seconds. 'Acting, yes,' he said at length. 'He's been acting most of his life, not out of a sense of frustration, but out of a sense of loyalty. You're not frustrated if you're doing what you want to do; even in this final "deterioration" of his he's only done what he's wanted to do for some time – make a whimsical, outrageous exit which would literally rock some of the stuffed-shirts he felt he was surrounded with. But get this straight, Lingard, he was a man of fine moral fibre – perhaps even finer than that of his brother-in-law, Mr Justice Meddlisome.' (Lingard shot the Commander a look but said nothing.) 'The sense he'd always had from boyhood of being trampled on, a sense of "inwardness" if you like, turned him into – in one respect – a *little* man, and that gave him the one quality essential to his job, a never-ending job started by Pitt.'

'Pitt?' Lingard looked doubtful. 'I don't think I know him, sir.'

'Before your time,' said the Commander. 'Lived in the eighteenth century. You look puzzled, Superintendent.'

'I'm just not with you, sir,' confessed Lingard. 'What was this special quality?'

'Anonymity.'

'Perhaps I should ask, sir, what was the job?'

The Commander (Crime) looked thoughtfully out of the window, and watched for a moment the pompous struttings of a pigeon on the sill. 'He was one of our secret agents.'

CHAPTER 14

Point of No Return

Superintendent Lingard jerked upright. 'An agent!' he breathed.

'A Dutch national working in open collaboration with the Germans. And you wouldn't credit just how thorough his Dutch records were, Lingard. They showed he was born in Maastricht and brought up in the St Antonius Orphanage at Veerdijk. And the records at the orphanage prove it.'

'Then the Dutch authorities were in it with us?'

The Commander shrugged. 'Your guess is as good as mine, Lingard. He didn't use the name of Neeve, of course.' (And the Commander didn't volunteer Neeve's Dutch name-tag.) 'It was a lonely, nerve-racking life. It meant a complete break-away from his old friends in Rotterdam, and moving to a different part of the city so that his Dutch cloak could be adopted. And when war was actually upon them he was loathed by his new Dutch acquaintances, and he stood in constant danger of being liquidated by the Resistance if he hadn't been pushed on to

Amsterdam and thence to Occupied France and Vichy. And his German masters regarded him with contempt for stooping to be a willing lick-spittle lackey. And yet one false move would have sent him into a Gestapo prison never to see the light of day again.'

'I know what they're like,' said Lingard. 'I visited the notorious Gestapo prison at Breendonck in Belgium. Not at all a nice place. Run on slaughterhouse lines, with runnels to take away the blood. How did Neeve get his information over to us, sir?'

The Commander thought carefully before replying. 'You fully appreciate, Lingard, the need for not knowing a thing when you leave this room? It's all ancient stuff, but we're not supposed to know about it outside the "Vat".' (Pope, head of the obscure department previously referred to, liked his drop of Scotch, and his domain was irreverently referred to by people outside it as the 'Vat'. It had no connection with the Vatican.) The Superintendent nodded his understanding of the situation; many confidences had passed in this room. The Commander proceeded. 'You are already aware of the basic set-up, Lingard. A string of "Goodwills" throughout Europe and North Africa, each doing business with Germany and with each other; each having an entirely separate financial structure, operating under separate managements, the umbilical financial cord with its parent being so neatly tied as to defy detection; with one of the group being in neutral Portugal; with the mother company in England having broken off trading relations with the other companies in Occupied Europe – oh, yes, Lingard, the Trading With The Enemy Acts clamped down on Mum trading with the kids. The Germans for their part saw to it that the kids continued to insure and reinsure German industry, and to do business with any part of the free world which fell for it, because of the importance to Dr Schadt's economic programme. The only "Goodwill" the British company could trade with was the Portuguese one.

'You can visualise what a perfect arrangement it was for anyone with the nerve. And Adam Neeve, under the skin of his 'little-man' act, had the nerve. He moved about in the insurance world, learned all sorts of details about the industrial plant that was being insured, and with his special pass moved with a certain amount of freedom even in Germany itself – to the extent of even visiting German works and giving his expert advice on technical insurance matters such as sprinkler-installations and fire-fighting equipment. Nearly every time he went on a sprinkler inspection he stood to be shot.'

Lingard raised an eyebrow. 'How come, sir?'

'You know how a sprinkler-head works, Superintendent?'

'Roughly,' nodded Lingard. 'The water supply runs in pipes across the ceilings of the factory, and the things that hold back the water are fusible bulbs or joints in the sprinkler-heads. When the requisite temperature is reached, the bulb shatters or the joint melts, the stopper-valve drops away, and the water supply sprinkles down like mercy on the place beneath, and, it is hoped, puts out the fire. What was so dangerous about Neeve's inspections, sir?'

'He used to adjudge certain ones at vulnerable points as being unserviceable. Apparently insurance inspectors continually find that painters, in fits of enthusiasm, make a thorough job of sprinkler-heads. Instead of keeping them free of paint, they clog 'em up with enough to prevent the critical part from melting at the right temperature. Neeve, pretending to clean them, would often gum them up himself. Others, which possibly *had* been painted over, would be removed and replaced with a Neeve Special.'

'Neeve Special?'

'An explosive phosphorus-compound one. The RAF would start the fires, the working sprinklers would operate, Neeve's ones would explode in the general chaos, and apart from any immediate damage, as soon as the water drained away or the supply failed, the fires would start up again as the phosphorus-compound came into contact with the air.'

'Blimey!' said the Superintendent. 'He didn't pick that up at the evening institute!'

'You're probably right,' agreed the other. 'Now if he had any special information to pass on to us, he placed reinsurance business through Lisbon; and Lisbon, of course, was still free to trade with us.'

'And from Portugal onwards it was comparatively simple,' breathed Lingard.

'Yes. The information came through to this country to the Goodwill in St James's Street, in the ordinary monthly business returns.'

'Good lor'!'

'With a supplementary return for anything extra special,' grinned the Commander. 'And in common with business practice during the war, there was always a following-mail copy in case the first was lost through enemy action. The information was in code, of course, and there was a man planted at the Goodwill by the Labour Exchange who dealt with the returns as they came in. He retired immediately after the war, and even old Bulworthy didn't know what was going on. He thought he was very lucky in getting the services of a man who knew a bit of Portuguese – the returns had never been dealt with so quickly before, not even in peacetime. Little did he know he had a professor of languages who had been through the Admiralty Cipher Department.'

'I see now why Neeve was in all the right places at all the right times. Bulworthy was inclined to think he was a collaborator – at least, that's the impression he gave me.'

'Oh, yes, Neeve was in Casablanca, and Marseilles. He sent much valuable information about the mood of the people in North Africa, information from the Maquis in the South of France – vital knowledge when you're waiting for the right moment to jump off with Operations like Anvil and Dragoon. He moved to Portugal to get his breath, and then slipped back into Germany via Strasbourg. He continued to work as best he could, receiving encouragement from his German masters even though the whole fabric of business organisation was crumbling.

'When the Allied armies were waiting to pounce across the Rhine, Neeve was still getting word of the hinterland across the river at great personal danger. And when Germany finally collapsed, he was carrying on in Brunswick. He assisted Control Commission in the rehabilitation of the insurance industry, and they thought him a very willing collaborator. They hadn't a clue that they wouldn't even be there if it wasn't for men like him. And then he slipped quietly away and got a job at the *"Benevolência"* in Lisbon, where he was still a potential under-cover man.

'He began to feel his work was done, and he had a deep yearning to return to the country of his birth. Europe wasn't going to erupt again for a while, and even if it did, everybody would appear to be on different sides.'

'And so repatriation, and the Goodwill in St James's Street,' nodded Lingard.

'Yes, but the iron entered his soul. Although more than a lifetime had been pushed into his cloak-and-dagger activities, insurance was the bread-winning job he was familiar with; but once the dagger was buried and only the cloak left, he found himself back once more in the stuffy routine of a small peacetime office – not an office, I gather, that had even a spark of post-war drive and progress in it. He began – I think rather unreasonably – to resent every minute of what to him was now a dreary job at the British Goodwill, began to feel contemptuous of the people around him. But if anyone was at fault, it was Neeve. After all, if he didn't like it, he only had to walk out, there's no control of labour in this country yet. He was a mentally sick man, though, he took a distorted view of things. If he'd only paused to consider it, the people around him were ordinary, decent people doing an honest job within their limits, and they were only what they were because nothing in particular had ever happened to them, or the luck of the game had not been with them and there was no escape – we can't all be Adam Neeves! Small wonder that many assumed a post-war importance which wasn't warranted. We're all guilty of it, Lingard, I am, you are – don't look so self-righteous – you *are,* you know! And then he began to dwell in the realms of phantasy, and dream up how he would like to cock a snook at the world in general and the people around him in particular. I suppose we all feel like *that* in moments of depression–'

'I can't say I do,' jibbed the Superintendent.

'Lingard, you're not human, I've always suspected it.'

'Yes, but before you can start nose-thumbing in any way, shape or form, you must have some alternative security,' reasoned Lingard. 'You've got to win the Pools, for example.'

'That's just what he did,' said the Commander. 'He won seventy-five thousand pounds.'

The Superintendent sat there transfixed. 'Seventy-five thousand!' he gaped.

'Don't look so startled, Lingard. Even spies win pools – *some*body's got to win! And he didn't win right away – it wasn't till his third attempt. I think he was disappointed he had to wait so long. He tried it once or twice more after his win and then packed it up – said you couldn't rely on it for a steady income. That was over two years ago. But seventy-five thousand pounds gave him the opportunity of actually doing something a lot of people do every week, that is, walk out of whatever they want to walk out of – until they check the results on Saturday evening. You see, Lingard, Neeve was a very unhappy man. Without the excitement of his undercover work, interest in his job flagged. His home life was nothing but ashes. He'd reached the stage when he neither wanted to go to work nor stay at home, when he almost welcomed the crowded train journey between the two places, so that he could doze and relive the past, or curl up in a corner and die – he didn't care which.

'But underlying Neeve's unhappiness was an eternal sense of humour which had been stifled during the years of strain, and a spirit of devilment urged him to assume gradually, but with calculated precision, the mantle of rakishness you've just told me

206

about, becoming more and more outrageous until something had to be done
about it, finally vanishing without trace.'

'Doesn't anybody know where he is?'
asked Lingard.

'Commander Pope may know. I don't.'

'What does Commander Pope think of
Neeve's scheme for the Grand Good-bye,
sir?'

'Think of it? Strictly between you and me,
Lingard, he thought of it! And now he's
worried. You can see why we couldn't let any
station officer deal with the problem and
ferret out heaven knows what, although we
had to show willing and send *somebody*
along to the Goodwill. You know what a
jackass old Popie is after a few pints, eh?
Oh, perhaps you don't. One day, two years
ago, he and Neeve were lunching together
to discuss the inadequacies of Neeve's
annual grant-in-aid for services rendered to
a grateful nation. After several noggins of
old-and-mild, they came to the conclusion
that whilst nothing could be done about
either Neeve's grant or Popie's salary they
could at least spend the rest of the lunch-
time conjuring up various forms of soldiers'
farewells. Several interesting varieties were
discussed, and Popie (by now well under the
influence) suggested what he grandiosely
called the Progressive Retrogression
Method. This instantly appealed to Neeve,

but in a moment of clarity between pints he realised the scheme had to be backed up with money or an alternative job, neither of which was available. Popie, in a flash of alcoholic inspiration, suggested the Pools, and promptly forgot about the whole thing. Neeve went out and bought three half-crown postal orders. One a week for three weeks. The third one came up. Seventy-five thousand pounds.'

'Strewth! I've been trying for twenty years! And now he's vanished into limbo. Could he have gone back to Portugal to live?'

'I doubt it – it holds unhappy memories for him. One of the reasons he asked to come back to England was because of his son, who by then was the dissolute young man I've already painted for you. He felt he might possibly influence him away from the bad elements to which he so readily gravitated. It was a forlorn hope. The young man was mixed up in every shady racket imaginable, and he made it quite clear he wished to have nothing whatever to do with his father, and that he intended to clear out of England anyway.'

'And Neeve has seen nothing of him since?'

'He came face to face with him in Lisbon about a month ago.'

'During his "illness"!'

The Commander smiled faintly. 'Yes,

during his "illness". And what Neeve saw shook him rigid. His son, now getting on for thirty, had loose living written all over him. There were young bones covered with old flesh. Neeve even suspected him of being a junky. Imagine the meeting in Dom Pedro Square. Adam Neeve, senior, old-boned but with an essentially young outlook which broke the surface in moments of relaxation; Adam Neeve, junior, weary to death with the ravages of dissipation, looking twice his age. Poor old Adam was horror-stricken. In his anxiety to rehabilitate his son, a son conceived out of so much happiness, he made a bad mistake. He tried to induce him to go straight, to do the decent thing for once; tried to enlist his son's aid on the job he was doing in Lisbon.'

'Ah!' breathed Lingard. 'So now we're coming to it, sir! Neeve's on a job! Would it be too indelicate to ask precisely what?'

The Commander thought carefully for a moment. 'Ever hear of the Toledano Twins?' he asked.

'I don't look at the television much, sir,' confessed the Superintendent.

'They are definitely not a variety act,' said the Commander acidly. 'Before the war they were a couple of shyster lawyers, country of origin unknown, who used their knowledge of the law to prevent justice being done. They were prepared to fight any criminal's

209

case, and the number of times they secured an acquittal on a mere legal technicality was legend. Their fees were high, but who worries about cost when it's a matter of life or death?' The Commander leaned forward. 'What I'm about to tell you, Superintendent' (Lingard noted the official intonation of 'Superintendent') is Most Secret. I feel obliged to remind you of the annual declaration you sign concerning official secrets.'

'I am aware of my obligations, sir,' said the Superintendent stiffly.

'I'm sure you are – please don't take offence. Although basically what I'm going to tell you is ancient history, it may affect the lives of a number of important people living today. You've heard, of course, of Operation Sea-Lion!'

'Operation Sea-Lion!' Lingard's eyebrows crept up. 'Hitler's ill-planned scheme for invading this country?'

'Yes, although it wasn't ill-planned. It was well-planned, but Hitler was ill-advised – he relied too much on astrology. You might be wondering what Sea-Lion has to do with Adam Neeve being in Lisbon twenty years later.'

'I am extremely curious, sir,' admitted Lingard.

'The Toledano Twins were engaged by Himmler to assist in compiling an Addendum which was to contain all the gory details of leaders in all walks of life in this country, the idea being to sort out the sheep from the goats so that the sheep could be liquidated and the goats, because of the skeletons in their cupboards, used. The Addendum, of course, was commenced a long while before the war. Himmler and Goebbels had an obscure department working on it in anticipation, and the Toledano Twins, always ready to earn money of any colour, held high positions.'

'Are they still alive, sir?'

'One of them is. And unfortunately, the Addendum was never found. The T-Force, which as you know, always went in with the advance troops to salvage anything in the nature of documents, secret apparatus and what have you, did their utmost to find it. Although details of Sea-Lion were found together with directives concerning the virtual elimination of all leadership in this country, the actual department which drew up the Addendum was cloaked in so much secrecy that nothing more concrete than hints came to light out of the holocaust that was once Berlin.'

'And now the Addendum's turned up in Lisbon,' said Lingard in a heavily sardonic manner.

The Commander looked at him for a long minute, and the Superintendent wished he hadn't opened his big mouth.

'Yes, Superintendent, the Addendum's turned up in Lisbon. Or so it seems. Or part of it. And if it has, it's still dynamite. Written dynamite. And in spite of the fact that half the people mentioned in it are probably now dead, it could still blow sky-high a number of worldwide reputations – perhaps even more than it would have done twenty years ago. A minor one is Mr Justice Meddlisome.'

'Justice Meddlisome!' Lingard was staggered.

'Yes. And the surviving Toledano is blackmailing him.'

'But – but why pick on Meddlisome? Surely there must be others far more important?'

'Possibly. And perhaps he is blackmailing them, too – who knows? But he's not blackmailing the Judge for money, it's information he's after. Information concerning our old friend – Simon Good.'

'Simon Good!' Lingard sat up as the links in a chain of thought began to clank.

'Yes. Toledano wants to catch up with that gentleman and – um – kill him.'

'Good lor'!' This time the links were stretched to breaking point. 'That seems to be at least one good thing that's come out of it! But why should he want to do that?'

'Good killed his brother.'

'Killed his brother?' gaped Lingard.

'I wish you wouldn't keep on repeating

everything I say,' growled the Great One petulantly. 'Don't I speak clearly, or something?'

'But when did Good do this, sir?' pressed Lingard, anticipating action.

'Neeve's gone to find out, and, if possible, to get back any part of the Addendum that's still in existence.'

'I suppose Toledano kept a copy of the document with an eye to the future. Didn't they catch up with him after the war?'

'They did. He stood trial at Nuremburg but got away with it. He defended himself, and once again secured acquittal on technical grounds.'

'And I suppose the mistake that Neeve made in inviting his son to help him was that the young man was unscrupulous enough to see possibilities in the Addendum for his own ends?'

'Commander Pope is reticent about that angle, but there's no doubt Neeve slipped up badly there – he had no right to attempt to induce his son to help him. The job may be his swan-song, but it's still official. However, blood is thicker than water. One thing's certain, though, when this job is finished Adam Neeve won't go near Portugal again for the rest of his life. He's reached a point of no return.'

'Both as regards Portugal *and* the Goodwill Insurance Company, I suppose, sir,' said Lingard thoughtfully.

'I imagine so. He's played his little game with them, and now he'll retire in complete obscurity and try to forget. Out, brief candle. Actually Popie's a bit worried about him – even he doesn't know exactly what's happening.'

'And as Meddlisome's out of touch with his brother-in-law, it's safe to assume that the Judge went to Wormwood Scrubs to ask Good what was the strength of Toledano's allegation,' mused the Superintendent.

'Yes, or to ask him to go and prove to Toledano that he isn't the man who killed his brother, in which case presumably the information concerning the Judge wouldn't be used. What's on your mind, Lingard?'

'I was wondering, sir, what information could now be sufficiently damning to upset any of our judges today, twenty years after Sea-Lion? Does Commander Pope know what the Addendum had to say?'

'It indicated that Ambrose Meddlisome was once a member of the U.W.F – United World Fascists.'

Lingard nearly said 'So what?' but remembered where he was. He said instead, 'But so were a lot of prominent people, but when their lives were at stake they saw the error of their ways and fought with the rest of us. And anyway, the Meddlisome of yesterday is not the Meddlisome of today.

From what I've seen of these judges, the average one would tell Toledano to go and take a running jump.'

'I've no doubt Ambrose Meddlisome would say precisely that if merely he himself were involved,' agreed the Commander. 'Unfortunately the matter goes beyond that.' He relapsed into silence for a moment. 'I'm going to tell you something very private, Superintendent – it concerns an intimate detail of the Judge's early life, but it will help to clarify things for you. At the time when Eve Meddlisome first met Adam Neeve whilst she was on holiday in Spain, she was so completely occupied with Neeve that she didn't realise her brother was having a lightning affair with the daughter of a Spanish gentleman who had very strong pro-German sympathies. The affair was brief but tempestuous, a mistake, a compulsive bio-logical fusion when a man and a woman are no longer captains of their souls.' The Commander looked out of the window at the pigeons again.

'And this is the information Toledano has threatened to use?' prompted Lingard.

'Eh?' The Commander forced his attention back into the room. 'Yes, partly.'

'So if Simon Good is helping to suppress publication, it seems we've got to give him a little freedom?'

'Yes, although I can't help feeling that like

215

Neeve's son he might be tempted to use some of the information himself.'

'It might be as well to keep a fatherly eye on Mr Meddlisome, sir.'

'Better to keep an eye on Simon Good, I would have thought,' responded the Commander.

'I saw Good rubbing shoulders with French Fernie the other day,' remarked Lingard thoughtfully. 'At the Leather Bottle in Racquet Alley.'

'Ah, nearby Roag's office!'

'Yes, the Syndicate seem to use the place. The day I went to the Goodwill, I saw Blake coming out of the saloon bar.'

'Don't spend too much time of your time in public houses,' said the Great One, oozing charm.

'It appears to be a toss-up as to whether Simon Good will prevent publication of the document, or use it,' said Lingard hurriedly. 'After all, he can't feel all that well-disposed towards the Judge.'

'Those are the horns of the dilemma,' agreed the other.

'And I suppose the Spanish lady in the business could also be involved in some form of exposure, sir.'

'No, Lingard, she died in child-birth. But the illegitimate offspring, now happily married and living in this country, could be. That's the devil of it...'

CHAPTER 15

Room for Negotiation

Simon Good climbed the wooden stairs to Prince Henry's Room at No. 17, Fleet Street, that historic room without much history but with a very nice plaster ceiling. A solitary American was taking the attendant's attention, and Simon crossed over to the chairs by the leaded windows, where sat Adam Neeve.

'A delightful view of Chancery Lane,' ventured Simon by way of an opening. 'Used to be Chauncellors Lane till the middle of the sixteenth century; and before that, the Newe Street of the Templers.'

'Peter Meek?' said the other, leaning for ward keenly.

'The same.'

'You've brought the medal?'

'What do you think?'

'No.'

'Jackpot, Mr Neeve.'

Neeve looked at him thoughtfully. 'You know my name?'

'I know your name, *senhor.*'

The other grinned. 'Please sit down and

join me. Tell me how you know my name.'

'Mr Meddlisome recognised your photographs.'

'What photographs?'

'The ones my late batman took of you in the Temple with his "exposure-meter".'

'So I was sucked in by that Trojan Ass, was I?' chuckled Neeve. 'I thought he was too true to be good.' He marshalled his thoughts. 'I've located Toledano,' he said briskly, 'but locating him is not enough. I want to find out more about Addendum-to-Sea-Lion, and I don't want to scare him off. I take it Ambrose has told you all he knows?'

'I don't know about *all*.'

'The trouble is that although you can see Toledano, he's about as untouchable as a mountain king.'

'He must have an Achilles' heel.'

'He has. Women. He likes to be surrounded by them – not, I think, because of any strong biological urge, but because he loves flattery, and likes to feel he's lord of the jungle. He has a marked aversion to male companions.'

'Then send a woman.'

'That's the trouble, I don't know any.'

Simon Good's jaw swung round. 'You don't. That's not what I heard.'

Adam Neeve carefully lit a cigarette. 'And what have you heard?' he asked at length. 'And where?'

'I now do your job at the Goodwill. Need I say more?'

It was Adam Neeve's turn to look incredulous. And then the incredulity was replaced by a puckish expression which made him look like an elderly schoolboy. 'What do they really think of me?' he grinned.

'There's a marked tendency to spit after mentioning your name. But apart from that there's only a sense of outraged sanctity and shocked horror.'

'How much did they tell you?'

'Everything. More than everything. You know how it is in a smallish office. And I've had a chat with French Fernie.'

'Oh.' Neeve was silent for a moment. 'I still don't know any girl with sufficient brains, sex-appeal and courage to tackle Toledano and wheedle out of him why he so much wants to kill you. I must confess I'm interested.'

'I, too, am not without interest,' agreed Simon.

'Then do you know anyone who would take on the job? Someone with beauty and intelligence, who could look after herself in an emergency? I wouldn't let anyone go who wasn't fully aware of the odds.'

A gleam came into Simon's eyes. 'I think I do,' he said softly, 'but it would cost you money.'

'How much?'

'Depends on what the lady says, plus brokerage for me.'

'The Judge would be prepared to pay with his last drop of blood.'

'She's got plenty of that, it's money she wants. You know, I rather like old Meddlisome in spite of the generous measure of justice he weighed out for me.'

'Yes, I read the full report,' said Neeve. 'Very amusing. They tell me those scales which Justice holds over the Old Bailey have holes in them to let the rain run through – so they can't be very accurate. And I imagine Justice wears that blindfold because she can't bear to think of how much of the sentence is going to slip away through the holes at the Appeal Court.'

Simon looked thoughtful. '*You* would have to pay me,' he said. 'I couldn't accept anything for my client direct from the Judge. He's already offered me a fee for *my* services and I've turned it down – it could savour of a blackmail pay-off. And for the record, the goddess on top of the Old Bailey is *not* blindfolded. British justice sees more than you think.'

'I wonder why Ambrose came to you after all?'

'In the later stages you didn't appear to be available. You didn't tell him you'd actually decided to go after the document yourself.'

'I had my reasons.'

'Very good ones, no doubt, but how did you expect him to know that? He's a judge dealing with facts, not a clairvoyant.'

'You must take it from me, Meek, that my reasons are good reasons.'

'Why must I take it from you? Have your actions over the past two years at the Goodwill been particularly rational?'

'Have they been so terribly irrational?'

'I suppose not – if they'd taken place in a nuthouse. But they took place against the stodgy background of a somnolent insurance office.'

Neeve said abruptly, 'Find out if your female friend would be willing to act. I'll pay anything within reason.'

'It won't be within reason.'

'Let me know how much. I'll leave it entirely to you.'

'You're left in that position, I agree. Suppose she gets the facts from Toledano?'

'Yes?'

'So?'

'So what?'

'So what happens then?'

'That's when things become a bit tricky,' frowned Neeve.

'For her? For Toledano? For you? For me?'

'Not for her. Once she's found out why Toledano wants to exterminate you she can buzz off out of it. And if the reason he advances is without foundation, it won't be tricky for you either, will it? All you'll have to do will be to present yourself with the means of identification laid down, Toledano will see his mistake, and will, we hope, honour his agreement with Ambrose.'

'And if during a lapse of mental aberration I *did* murder his brother?'

'In those circumstances things would be tricky for you, yes. I would be only too happy – well, not happy – to borrow your medal and take a chance with Toledano. I would then prove that *I* was Peter Meek, he would see that I wasn't the man he had in mind, and once again, we hope, he would hand over the embarrassing document.'

'Don't you think he's already thought that someone might do just that?' said Simon.

'I think *a* Peter Meek did kill his brother, and that he'd know this man if he saw him again – after all, he says he was there when it happened. Therefore, if you didn't do it, either of us could settle the matter and get that sheet of paper without bloodshed. The crux of the business is getting page 22 for the Judge.'

'I think the crux of the business is that I want to punch Mr Toledano right on the nose,' said Simon, 'and I think I'll go and do it.'

'So you won't loan me your medal, and let me try?'

'I think not, my friend.'

Adam Neeve gazed for a moment out into Fleet Street. 'There's a wider issue at stake,' he said at length.

'And that is?'

'I can't tell you,' said the other, in some doubt.

'Well, I'll tell you something,' said Mr Good. 'You'll require something more than the medal to establish your identity.'

'You mean the photostat?'

'Yes. How did you know?'

'Ambrose told me. He showed me the letter Toledano wrote when he decided to lure you to Portugal instead of committing mayhem here. It mentioned bringing the photostat.'

'And did Ambrose show you the letter mentioning the medal?'

'I haven't seen Ambrose since he showed me the previous letter.'

'Then how did you know about the medal?'

Neeve remained silent.

'If you haven't seen the letter, how could you possibly know?' persisted Simon. He lit a cigarette. 'Did Toledano tell you?'

'Toledano?' Neeve looked genuinely shocked. 'I'm just not with you, Meek.'

'Too true you're not. Ambrose Meddlisome is inclined to think you're with Toledano.'

Neeve sat there for a moment in horrified silence. 'Poor old Ambrose,' he muttered at length. 'He thinks I'm working against him after all his family has been to me? It – it doesn't make sense.'

'The Goodwill thinks *you* didn't make sense. And now the Judge knows what went on there, knows that during the period of your "illness" you were presenting an entirely different face to him. He's entitled to doubt your integrity.'

Adam Neeve finally made up his mind. 'Listen, Meek,' he said earnestly. 'During the past few months I've tracked down Toledano. I have certain resources at my disposal, but nevertheless it's been a long and exacting task. I've chased a shadow from Portugal to Holland, from Holland to Germany, from Germany back to Portugal, and now I've located him in person. I could point him out to you and you could say whether you know him or not – even by some other name. I wish I could tell you more, but please believe me when I say there's a wider issue than just Ambrose's skeleton coming to life.'

'I'm just as anxious to have a go at Toledano as you are. After all, Ambrose did ask me to go all the way to Portugal. And as I have the medal *and* the photostat, it appears I win.'

'Ah, yes, the photostat,' smiled Neeve. 'I

could tell you something about that.'

Simon glanced at his watch. 'I'm afraid I haven't much longer,' he said politely. 'I'm a working man, you know.'

'The photostat Ambrose has been holding isn't the original one,' said Neeve. 'It's a *photostat* of the photostat. I hold the original. And it has a watermark in the paper. I suspect it's an identification mark that Toledano will look for. So the position is that you hold the medal and I hold the photostat. Stalemate, as it were.'

Simon Good said, 'Then it looks as if it's to be a joint venture.'

Adam Neeve made a wry face. 'As you wish,' he said. 'I would have preferred to have a crack at the job myself, but what is to be will be. If we go, no doubt a satisfactory solution will present itself.'

'Yes,' agreed Simon, and they each thought their own thoughts.

'By the way,' said Neeve suddenly, 'I must apologise for breaking in the other day – you can't say I haven't tried to get your medal.'

'You left the fridge door open,' reproved Simon.

'I had to get out in a hurry – the police arrived. I hope I didn't spoil any of your "shillings"?'

'A whole trayful. Fortunately I still had a shilling the Judge gave me. So your resources don't include the confidence of the police?'

'What do you think?'

'I don't know what to think, as the dumb blonde said to the obstetrician. When do we leave for Portugal?'

'As soon as we can fix it with this Mata Hari of yours – there's not much time before the end of September. If she can't extract the reason for Toledano's strange affection for you, then we'll choose the right moment and extract it ourselves. This ex-batman of yours – is he available? Can he cook?'

'Give him a few tins of stuff and he'll do something with them. Why?'

'The so-called main road into Boa Fidelidade is not at all reliable. It passes through the narrow Marcelo Gorge, and more often than not there's some sort of roadwork going on, or floods, or subsidence. Therefore the good ship *Kestrel* awaits our pleasure in Lisbon harbour. A sea-going yacht will arouse no comment in Boa Fidelidade. I've got a feeling that when we leave the place we'll be leaving in a hurry, so if we have at our disposal a car and a yacht we'll have a two-way bet.'

'You're quite a guy,' said Simon admiringly. 'You've got it all lined up. If things are being done at this level I can't see why you're dragging me in at all.'

'The medal,' said Neeve. 'I've looked it up in Whittaker's, and find it's an obscure and rarely awarded French decoration of unusual size. Only twenty were struck.'

'And your resources didn't go to making a counterfeit?'

'Not even in ice.'

'And where does Hammersley – my ex-batman – come in?'

'*Kestral* has an excellent helmsman – a Portuguese who knows the coast like the back of his hand – and a French mechanic-cum-odd-job man who cooks everything with a subtle flavour of engine oil. If your man can preserve the locked-in flavour of tinned beans I shall be eternally grateful. I like gracious living and good food.'

'That almost precludes him from the job. Can I ring you tonight?'

'No. I'll ring you. Give Ambrose my love, and tell him next time I see him his worries will be over...'

A few discreet enquiries by Superintendent Lingard revealed that Simon Good was on holiday. Portugal, they thought. Some people seemed to have time to kill.

CHAPTER 16

Toledano

Mario Toledano from time to time had pressing business to perform in Lisbon, but not so pressing as to prevent him from taking a leisurely aperitif on the hotel terrace overlooking Lisbon's famous Rocio, with its curious pebbled pavement which generations of British sailors had nick-named 'Roly-poly'. He had a reserved table for two in his own particular corner which gave a commanding view of this square officially known as Dom Pedro, for Mr Toledano was an important person, and the management cooed over him like a turtle-dove. Indeed, rumour had it that Mr Toledano *was* the management, and if there was one customer Mr Toledano looked after it was Mr Toledano.

From his seat in the corner he also had a commanding view of the terrace. And from where any companion (usually female) sat, it gave a commanding view of only Mr Toledano, and to this he was not averse for he was a vain man – if the generic term could be used without offence to the rest of mankind.

On this particular morning he was getting quite a good view of the beautiful English girl poured into the dress at the next table, who sat aloofly sipping a coffee, and who had sat thus at the same time every morning for the past few days.

The first time he had seen her he was with a bosomy, ash-blonde companion, and it was significant that the following morning and thereafter he was alone, somehow conveying the utter, abject loneliness of Mario Toledano.

Predatory Mr Toledano was about to make a killing. He imagined.

Every morning he made it his business to leave before she did, favouring her with a timid ghost of a smile which subtly suggested the tragedy of male life without the guiding hand of the tender sex, which sex someone has so wisely said is so much more dangerous than the male. And each morning, her eyes never quite meeting his, she acknowledged him with a gossamer flicker which seemed to indicate she was quite happy to leave things that way. Mario Toledano was in no sense abashed at the frigid barrier of tiny icicles; he was confident his natural charm would melt them in due course, for whilst he was used to getting his own way, he was nevertheless a patient man who knew these things couldn't be hurried. In any event, a chase like this helped to distract him from his seething hatred of Peter Meek, the man who had killed his brother; it was not good to live with this inward, boiling, bubbling negative anger. When Peter Meek turned up (Toledano had no doubts on this score) he would pay the penalty, and the inward unease which amounted to disease would be assuaged, the safety valve would operate, and all would be well again with the curious being of Mario Toledano.

He had his methods. He arrived one morning on the terrace, and to his palpable fierce displeasure, found his table occupied by two copper-bronzed girls who had every intention of staying there. This was not surprising for he had paid them a thousand escudos each for doing precisely that. The head waiter hurried forward anxiously, and what was apparently a whispered explanation and altercation took place. It appeared that the two girls had slipped through the hotel via a french window when the waiter's back was turned, and in spite of pleadings and remonstrance, they didn't seem to understand or wish to understand that the table was reserved, and short of throwing them out, there was nothing he could do about it. With a frown of annoyance, Mario looked around for somewhere else to sit, and Quenella Mansfield smiled inwardly. The betting was all Portugal to a broken shoulder-strap that the head waiter would suggest the vacant seat at her table if the *senhorita* had no objections.

Mr Toledano flattered himself that the manoeuvre was carried out with infinite finesse. With obvious reluctance on his part at having to invade the privacy of the beautiful young lady, he managed at the same time to convey faint disapproval of the head waiter for having suggested such a course. Much practice had made them quite a team. Quenella Mansfield acquiesced with a disinterested nod, and when Mr Toledano offered her a cigarette – almost by way of compensation – she graciously declined, and a moment later lit one of her own. She, too, was not without experience and technique. Mario, however, was well satisfied with progress, for nothing in life was worthwhile if it was too easy. He coughed by way of introduction.

'I am Mario Toledano,' he announced, as if that explained everything.

Quenella drew on her cigarette, and gently expelled the smoke across a shaft of brilliant sunlight. 'You make it sound important,' she smiled, and he couldn't be certain if there was a sting or not.

'It is; I am,' he replied, faintly piqued, but with considerable dignity.

She appeared to give the matter careful thought, and trickled some more smoke out through red lips contracted in a tiny circle.

She said: 'Do you mind very much if I just don't care?'

Mario managed to quell a spark of near-anger; people just didn't say things like that to Mr Toledano. But his fleshy face crinkled into a deceptively good-natured grin, spoilt only by the sensuousness of the mouth.

'I beg the *senhorita's* pardon. I merely wished to allay any fears she might have as to the propriety of this intrusion of mine. The hotels are filled with confidence tricksters.'

'Thank you for your solicitude. I have no fears. I am sure you are all you seem.'

Toledano hoped he didn't seem all he was. 'In Portugal, you understand,' he went on, 'there is a more rigid code of behaviour. Privacy is respected, casual conversation between unintroduced members of the opposite sexes is frowned upon; therefore I was anxious not to offend. I merely wished to establish my standing.'

'By sitting?' Quenella smiled at him through a spiral of blue smoke, and once again Mr Toledano wasn't sure if the conversation was going the way he wanted it to go. He forced a travesty of a chuckle from his voicebox.

'You twist my words, *senhorita,*' he said softly, his whole personality oozing gentle reproach.

'I deal in words.'

'An actress?' he inquired hopefully.

'One big act. Like you, *senhor.*'

'Very good indeed!' he chuckled. 'Very, very good. Perhaps you make a holiday?'

'Perhaps.' She blew a little more smoke in his direction so that he was obliged to sit back. 'For a countryman of Portugal, *senhor,* where privacy is so very much respected, you are asking a lot of questions.'

'A countryman of Portugal? I have no country, I merely live here at the moment. You, doubtless, have the benefit of a British passport?'

'And you, *senhor,* have the benefit of infallible charm.'

Mario Toledano was more than susceptible to flattery. 'It has been remarked upon,' he frankly admitted. He was now more than satisfied with progress. And so was Quenella Mansfield.

Mr Toledano paid attention to the glass which was placed before him, and subtly didn't press an aperitif on Quenella. He finished it rather more quickly than was his practice, and pushed back his chair. 'If you will excuse me, I have important business to attend to,' he said, as he rose regretfully to his feet. He added with caressing insinuation, 'If the gods are good to me, those young ladies will again be occupying my table tomorrow at this time.'

'They will be,' said Quenella smoothly,

and he looked at her sharply. 'The gods will be good to you, I mean,' she added, blander than ever.

'The gods were kind to you, after all,' she said the following morning. 'They have influenced the young ladies to take your table again. They appear to like it.'

'Who can blame them?' shrugged Mr Toledano. 'It is in a very good position. You permit me to join you?'

'I am using only one seat,' replied Quenella humorously. 'I hold no option on the other.'

'The gods are indeed good to me,' said the other eloquently.

'In these days of nuclear warheads one is lucky even to be alive, *senhor.*'

Mario Toledano's eyes clouded for a moment, and he controlled himself with difficulty. Yes, *he* was alive, but nothing would bring back his twin brother Emilio. That *ilegitimo,* Major Peter Meek, had seen to that. And sooner or later Major Peter Meek would pay the penalty. He dragged himself back into the present. 'Forgive me, *senhorita,* if I've been too intrusive–' He broke off suddenly, as if a sudden thought had struck him. 'I haven't yet learned your name,' he said softly.

'That's right,' agreed Quenella. 'You were saying?'

The rebuff fell on stony ears. 'Then I will call you *amiga* until our friendship blossoms.' Toledano was quite a poet in his way, and quite a philosopher, too. Her name would arrive in the fullness of time, he decided confidently – as would a hundred-and-one other intimate details, they always did. 'I was saying, *amiga*, forgive me if I've appeared too forward, but the unpredictable force of circumstance has thrown us together, and I must confess your beauty has completely carried me away.'

'I wish it would,' said Quenella lazily.

In spite of the remark he thought he detected a glint of promise in those half-veiled, provocative yes. 'Call me Mario,' he pleaded softly. 'Perhaps tomorrow you will not be playing – how do the English put it? – hard to get.'

'Don't flatter yourself,' smiled Quenella, 'I'm merely difficult to please.'

Mr Toledano laughed heartily. 'Exquisite! Allow me to buy you an aperitif.' Brushing aside a refusal, he summoned a waiter and ordered drinks which appeared with the speed of light. Waiters bent over backwards to please Mr Toledano. And Mr Toledano, breathing earnest words of fire and garlic, bent over forwards to please Quenella Mansfield. She suffered his oleaginous charm whilst they finished their drinks; and then said casually: 'Do you know the coast well, *senhor?*'

'In the immediate vicinity? Every contour, *amiga.*'

'Then perhaps you will advise me.'

'Advise you?' Mario's interest quickened, this was the thin edge of the wedge, he knew it would come sooner or later. 'Is this not what I have dreamed of?'

'I wouldn't know what you dreamed of – or perhaps I can guess. I want to see something of the picturesque fishing villages one reads about. I'm rather tired of Lisbon and Estoril. Where do you suggest?'

Mario Toledano pondered for a moment; he already knew where to suggest, but he was an artist in these matters. 'You wish to see the *people,* their quaint fishing boats with enormous eyes painted on the bows, see the men repairing their nets, their womenfolk at their embroidery and pottery–'

'Yes, with their dazzling white cottages with red-tiled roofs against a background of pine and eucalyptus trees,' nodded Quenella, who had read the guidebook. 'Tell me of such a colourful place.'

'I have one in mind, *amiga,* but I hesitate to suggest it.'

Quenella looked at him quizzically. 'Because you have a villa there?'

'Exactly. At least not a villa. I have access to an apartment in the quaintest and most rambling *pousada* imaginable. And therefore to suggest that you went to Boa Fidelidade would appear to be almost – unethical.'

'I appreciate your fine feelings in the matter,' said Quenella, 'but Boa Fidelidade sounds exciting. Surely, if I went there for a few days I wouldn't have to stay in your apartment – there must be other places, other *pousadas*.'

'*As Chaves Cruzadas* – you would say the Cross-Keys – is really the only modernised – inn? – in the place. I could perhaps speak with the owner and obtain a room for you. I am not without influence.'

'That is very kind of you, Mario. But why haven't I been taken to Boa Fidelidade? I've been on several coach tours, and I don't recollect passing through it.'

'One doesn't pass through Boa Fidelidade. There is only one very indifferent road in through the Marcelo Gorge, and the coach companies have deleted it from their itineraries ever since the road subsided and a complete coach-load tumbled into the torrent beneath. Twenty-six people perished. And that is why Boa Fidelidade has retained so much of its old-world charm, and has not become commercialised. And that is why I like it. So many places are spoilt nowadays by sordid financial interests.'

'You make it sound very attractive. Perhaps you could speak for me at the Cross-Keys.' (The room was booked before she finished speaking.) 'How can I get there – by hired car?'

'I could arrange it for you, *amiga*,' said Toledano offhandedly. 'Just as you wish.'

'Has the place a post office and telephone?'

'Oh, yes. There is also a telephone at the Cross-Keys. You wish to be able to make calls?'

'One or two. I have to meet a young female friend of mine here in Lisbon at the end of the month.'

'She is as elegant as you?'

'More so – flatterer!'

Mario Toledano nodded in pleasurable anticipation. 'Then she also must come to Boa Fidelidade.'

'She's probably far too busy. She's more successful at her job than I am.'

'Her job being?'

'She's a reporter, not just a hack like I am.'

'A hack?' said Toledano doubtfully.

'A hack writer.'

'Ah, you're seeking background, *amiga*?'

'I'm trying to forget background, Mario. I used to be a crime reporter.'

Mr Toledano froze. 'A crime reporter?'

'Yes, you know, at the Criminal Court. But I worried too much about the cases – either because the criminal got too much or too little. I had to have a complete rest. That's why I'm here.'

'So.' Toledano thrummed his fingers on the table thoughtfully. 'Tell me,' he said at length, 'do you remember the case of Peter Meek – Major Peter Meek?'

'I can't say I do. Should I?'

'It concerned a man who was nominally charged with stealing – he was making ice-"coins" for his service meter. Earlier this year. He was using the name of Simon Good.'

'Oh, yes!' exclaimed Quenella. 'I certainly remember him! I was at that trial. He was a scoundrel, if ever there was one!'

'This is very interesting,' said Mr Toledano softly.

'Is it? Why?'

'Let us talk about it some other time, *amiga.*'

'I don't particularly wish to talk about it at all,' said Quenella. 'I'm here to forget.'

'I will make the necessary inquiry for you at the Cross-Keys,' said Toledano abruptly. 'Do you like good music, *amiga?*'

'Don't tell me Boa Fidelidade has a brass band on the promenade?'

'Er – no. But I have some excellent records in my apartment. If the weather is inclement, you may come up and listen to them.'

'It used to be etchings,' said Quenella.

Mario Toledano smiled disarmingly and rose. 'Till tomorrow, *amiga.* I wonder if the girls will be at my table again?'

'I'm almost willing to wager they won't be. You know, the reason you like me is not that I'm *playing* hard to get – I *am* hard to get.'

'We shall see,' smiled Toledano confidently, and went down the steps into the brilliant sunshine...

'Who's that friendly-looking guy who's just left Quenella?' asked Simon, as they sat down at a table on the terrace.

Neeve had just met him and Hammersley at the airport, and had got down to work immediately. He grinned wolfishly. 'He's the chap who's going to kill you – Mario Toledano.'

'I don't think I like him,' said Simon critically...

CHAPTER 17

Addendum to Sea-Lion

'I hope Hammersley's cooking lives up to the general air of opulence,' said Simon later, as they looked down at the gleaming white vessel in Lisbon harbour.

'It's not mine,' apologised Neeve. 'I've only hired it.'

'That's still an achievement for an insurance clerk.'

'What's the use of saving your money?' shrugged Adam. 'You can't take it with you. Let's go aboard, and I'll introduce you to the crew.'

The helmsman was a rascally-looking Portuguese who answered to the name of Pedro; the mechanic, Pierre, was of French extraction. Both knew a smattering of English. Pedro's son, José, a lad of fourteen or fifteen, helped in the general chores.

Hammersley entered into the spirit of the thing with tremendous verve, and immediately visited a marine outfitter's and rigged himself up like a rear-admiral. It was unfortunate that a couple of hours in *Kestrel's* tiny galley took off some of the gloss, for he was wondrous to behold. By the middle of the afternoon he was talking copper-bottoms, Teredo worm, and gaff versus bermudian rig.

Neeve reported that Quenella, who had gone on ahead with him, was already going great guns with Toledano. 'She's every bit as much a psychologist as Toledano,' he said enthusiastically, 'and I'm willing to wager that with her calculated indifference she'll extract the truth from him. We contact each other in the Unifax departmental store on the Avenida da Liberdade – Hammersley can do that in future.'

One morning Adam suggested that Simon should make a flying reconnaissance of Boa Fidelidade, whilst he and Hammersley saw to things in Lisbon. 'Hammersley can see Quenella, and I have to meet a certain contact here,' he explained.

Simon readily agreed, for he was curious to see the place where he was to die. Decking himself out with panama hat, sun-glasses, camera and binoculars – so obviously a tourist – he went to a car-hire firm and was soon speeding perilously out of the town under the gentle care of a driver who spoke English. When some seventy minutes later they turned off on to the Boa Fidelidade road, Simon indicated his desire to sit with the driver. This was not so much to get the best possible view of the road as to obviate that gentleman's friendly habit of turning right round to talk.

As Neeve had already indicated, the road was indifferent, and they passed a number of indolent road-repair gangs who had every appearance of making a life work of each job. And there was one ghastly corner along the Marcelo Gorge which was taken at speed, with a sheer drop into a bubbling torrent on the right and a threatening cliff with an ugly overhang to the left.

'A dangerous corner, that, *senhor,*' said the driver. 'I'm always glad when I've got round it safely.'

'A simple philosophy, but sound,' agreed Simon.

'The *senhor* doubtless observed that outcrop of rock? It's always crumbling away and blocking the road without warning. It is inconvenient.'

Simon agreed it would bring up a nasty bruise if it fell on your thumb, and the driver laughed heartily, taking both hands off the wheel and slapping his thighs in merriment. Simon made no more jokes, and curiously enough they arrived at the outskirts of Boa Fidelidade in two complete units.

'The accident always happens to the other fellow,' said the driver philosophically. 'And now, *senhor,* what is your wish?'

'Give me an hour to look round this

charming place,' said Simon. 'Where does one eat?'

'As *Chaves Cruzadas* is the *only* place to eat in Boa Fidelidade,' insisted the driver, with much waving of the hands to indicate the appalling standards of the other *tavernas*.

'Then in one hour's time you must take me to wherever you said and join me in the best lunch they can provide.'

'The *senhor* is most generous,' said the other, delighted. 'Meanwhile I will have a little *sésta* in the back of the car to conserve my strength for the return journey.'

Simon wandered down to the crowded harbour with its gleaming yachts and brightly painted fishing boats, hypnotised by the mass of masts which moved gently to and fro like metronomes. A protective jetty arm thrust itself out to complete what was otherwise a natural harbour, and Simon ambled along to the tiny white-painted lighthouse at the end. Looking back, the town was a confusion of bright colour. Away to the left a shingle beach stretched at the foot of some cliffs, whilst to the right there were golden sands which dazzled the eye. The village itself tumbled down almost to the water's edge from half-way up the cliff, where some of the gaily-coloured villas were clinging on for dear life. The main road out of the place could be seen to climb right up through a natural declivity in the rock formation to the car-park on the outskirts, in which they had been fortunate enough to squeeze.

He spent a pleasant hour wandering around in the sunshine, occasionally taking a photograph. The shops in the narrow streets were filled with local produce, and although there was much evidence of home industry, Boa Fidelidade had not succumbed to blatant commercialism. He strolled past the rambling Cross-Keys, evincing no more than idle interest. Climbing the hill to the car-park again, he roused the driver, who straightened his clothes and slicked back his hair. 'Lead me to the *taverna*,' said Simon.

'As the *senhor* commands,' said the other happily. 'It's the big place stretching back from the quay. Did the *senhor* not notice it?'

'I probably did,' said Simon, 'but I couldn't remember the name you told me.'

'It has a swinging sign of two keys crossed,' said the driver as he urged Simon back down the hill. 'The *senhor* must have seen it.'

'Oh, that place. Yes, I did see it.'

The bar at the Cross-Keys was very much like any other bar of any other tavern designed to titillate the imaginations of the wealthy visitors it hoped to attract. There were dark green glass balls hanging in fishnet, a multitude of local curios, plenty of chromium, and tinted plate-glass mirrors behind an incredible array of strange-shaped bottles.

The driver had a thirst for the local deep-red wine, and Simon was glad when at last a girl in quaint costume informed them that their seafood luncheon was ready in the trellised garden at the back.

Everything seemed perfectly straight-forward, and Simon purposely laid off the subject of Mr Toledano.

After lunch he bought the driver a bottle of wine to take with him, and on the exciting homeward journey the car appeared to be going on something stronger than petrol.

Adam Neeve followed Simon down the hatch as he went to replace his tourist impedimenta, and Simon smiled inwardly as his eye flicked expertly over his bunk. It was a thousand pounds to a penny that during his absence his kit had been carefully searched. He hoped by now that Hammersley had searched Neeve's. But although much searching had gone on, neither the medal nor the photostat was forthcoming.

'What did you think of Boa Fidelidade, Simon?'

'Quite a pretty place to be killed in,' said Simon. 'But what's the matter with you – you look all in!'

Adam Neeve looked unutterably weary. 'I am all in,' he said. 'I've had a bit of an upset.'

'No medal?' quizzed Simon, and Adam's mood lifted a little.

'No medal,' he agreed. Then, 'No photostat?'

'No photostat,' said Simon, catching Hammersley's thumbs-down signal from the top of the hatch. 'Is that your only trouble? If it is, you're making heavy weather of it, aren't you? This is a joint venture – remember?'

'H'm, I remember.' Neeve looked very thoughtful; his mind slid into the long ago, and deep down in his eyes there was a fathomless expression. 'I have an offspring,' he said at length.

'Ambrose told me a little about him,' said Simon gently.

'I went to meet my contact this morning–'

'Your son?'

'No. An underpaid employee at the sub-post-office in Boa Fidelidade. Money talks. He has – er – advised me from time to time concerning Toledano's letters.'

'Oh. I begin to understand how you knew about the medal.'

'Yes.' Neeve thought a little more. 'This morning I sought out my son again–'

'Again?'

'Yes. A while ago I ran into him here in

Lisbon. I foolishly tried to enlist his aid to get that page from Sea-Lion. I told him a little of what was at stake. The only result was that after sponging on my hospitality for a few days he cleared off without so much as a good-bye.'

'Ambrose said he was – difficult,' said Simon sympathetically.

'Money went from my wallet. Also a notebook containing data relating to Toledano.'

Simon Good remained silent.

'After seeing my contact this morning I found my son at one of his old haunts, and tackled him with it. I told him it was essential I had the notebook back, that I might need the information to press my point with Toledano. He asked me when I was going to try.'

'What did you tell him?'

'I don't know what I told him. I was muddled, confused.'

'And did you get your notebook back?'

'He wouldn't admit to having stolen it. We parted on acrimonious terms. It – it hurts deep down, Simon, you've no idea how much it hurts. If only Eve had lived this would never have happened.'

'I don't know what to say,' growled Simon. 'It sounds trite, but I'm deeply sorry...'

'Anybody want some soup?' inquired Hammersley from the top of the hatch.

It was no surprise to Quenella when Mr Toledano grandly announced that he had prevailed upon the owner of the Cross-Keys to put a room at her disposal for the remainder of her holiday. It was a charming room overlooking the Bay of Good Faith, and, but for the circumstances, she would have enjoyed a stay there. It was also no surprise to her when Mario didn't unduly press his attentions upon her, for she realised he was a man of infinite experience. One afternoon, however, when the weather suddenly broke and much rain fell, he suggested they listened to his records; she fell in with the idea, and was soon impressed by his great knowledge of music. He had a love of Chopin and Debussy, and she spent a perfectly harmless afternoon listening to his hi-fi record player, waiting for his advances.

He said suddenly: 'Tell me about the case of Peter Meek.'

It was then that she realised how very much an obsession it was with him. 'Peter Meek?' she frowned. 'What about Peter Meek?'

'You said, *amiga,* you were at his trial. You said he was a scoundrel. Tell me about him.' His eyes were pinpoints of anticipation.

'After all this time I can scarcely remember the bare details,' she replied off-handedly.

'Then let me refresh your memory.'

From a desk in the corner Toledano produced a folder, which he thrust impatiently at her. She opened it curiously. It consisted of a number of newspaper cuttings concerning Peter Meek's trial, all from English papers. She glanced through them. 'Yes, it comes back to me now,' she said casually. 'He was a curious man.'

'Did you write any of those articles?' he demanded intently.

'Who can say? You know how editors chop things up.'

'Which paper did you work for?'

'I worked for an agency,' lied Quenella without a blush. 'At first the trial aroused little interest, and few papers sent their own reporters. I've no doubt in my own mind that if this man had been on trial for any of the other things brought out in cross-examination he would have suffered a more severe sentence. But why this collection of cuttings? Are you writing a book?'

Toledano had difficulty in controlling himself.

'He killed my brother!' he snarled.

'Oh, come, Mario,' she chided. 'Don't be absurd! Put on that E Minor Concerto again. Even though Meek was a scoundrel, he wasn't a murderer – there was no suggestion of that at the trial.'

'I didn't say he murdered him,' rasped

Toledano, 'I said he killed him. He killed him legally... But he killed him. And Emilio meant more to me than anything else in the world...'

Quenella was startled.

'Killed him *legally?*' she breathed. 'I don't follow. The only profession which comes to mind where he could have done that is that of public hangman.'

'He was a soldier,' said Toledano, getting a grip on himself.

'Oh!' Light was beginning to dawn. 'You mean this happened during the war?'

'Yes, it happened during the war,' repeated Toledano dully. 'And nothing will bring Emilio back.'

'But all that was a long time ago, Mario.'

'Nothing will bring Emilio back,' said Toledano, his eyes glazing into the past. 'He was my twin brother. Identical twin, you understand. I felt his death as much as he must have done. And it lives with me even today.'

'What do you propose to do about it now?'

'Major Peter Meek will pay the penalty.'

'How can you possibly be sure that this is the same Peter Meek, after all this time?'

'Your English papers very kindly supplied his military history. There is no doubt. The relevant cuttings are in the file. Read them.'

The warm Latin blood of Mario Toledano

oozed away, leaving nothing but refrigerated hate.

Quenella read the cuttings carefully. 'Tell me what happened that day at Hondschouwen, Mario,' she suggested very gently. 'What were *you* doing there?'

Toledano's eyes clouded reflectively.

'Just before the war Emilio and I were employed by a special branch of a German Ministry in Berlin, compiling data about certain people.'

'You are German, then?'

'I told you, *amiga*, I have no country.'

'This information you were collating – it concerned German nationals?'

'It concerned any nationals we were directed to investigate, German, English, French – what mattered it? We were being paid, and money talks more effectively than Esperanto. We were working in Paris at the time of the Invasion, and when the – liberation – of that city was imminent, we made tracks for north-west Europe on an escape route provided by the German authorities. But the Allied advance became so rapid that the only way one could ensure transport was to don the military uniforms we were provided with. All went well until we reached Hondschouwen. There we found ourselves with a unit which was to become encircled, and we had to fight with the rest.

'We occupied a factory in a commanding

position, and then got wind that an all-out attack was to be made on it to liquidate us. Fresh tank traps were hastily set up, the factory was made alive with booby-traps and primed demolition-sets, and practically all the troops were withdrawn to fortified positions on the perimeter, from which could be controlled the demolition of the factory if it were ever occupied by the enemy. Emilio and I found ourselves in one of a pair of machine-gun posts straddling the road from the factory.

'The attack came in the early hours. Best part of the Allied troops were annihilated. Only a handful got through to the factory, and we played possum all through the day and the following night. Next morning we received orders to commence demolition and eliminate any survivors. As the factory crumbled before us we kept up a withering fire, and how anyone remained alive in that holocaust I just couldn't understand, but then, I was not a soldier. The senior NCO in charge of our two posts had a spark of humanity and sent forward an emissary under a flag of truce calling on the remaining handful to surrender.'

'And did they, Mario?' smiled Quenella.

'Their officer was very rude, *amiga*. I rather gather he thought *we* were surrendering. He told us what we could do with our very efficient Spandau machine-guns. We carried on a fire of attrition.'

'And wiped them out?'

Mario Toledano was silent for a moment. 'We thought we had,' he said at length. 'I remember it as if it were yesterday. The order was given to cease fire, for we were getting no opposition. And then suddenly a Piat bomb fell just short of our command post, which was our right-hand gun-pit, in which both Emilio and I were crouching. This was followed by a welter of rifle fire which kept us down. And then out of the rubble by the factory gates stepped a British officer, smoking a pipe, Bren gun at the hip position. He walked steadily down the road towards us, withholding his fire. And then our left-hand emplacement received a direct hit with the second Piat bomb, and was knocked out. Our NCO screamed at the machine-gunners to open up, but the fools were all fingers and thumbs. They weren't able to make up their minds whether to concentrate on the solitary, relentless figure coming towards them, or on the men in the ruins by the factory gate-house. How they missed Major Peter Meek, striding it out towards them, was beyond comprehension.

'Suddenly he faltered and half spun round. I think he'd been wounded, and it stung him into fury. He covered the last bit of the journey blazing away at us like a madman. He clambered to the top of our left-hand post and wiped out the crew. Then he staggered over towards us, approaching in a blind arc where the Spandaus couldn't get him. I grabbed a stick grenade from Emilio, who was crouching there paralysed with fright, and flung it at the madman with the Bren. By some incredible fluke, he grabbed it in mid-air with his left hand and flung it back. It burst over the top of the emplacement, and killed most of us. Next I knew, he was on top of the emplacement firing burst after burst down at us. I can still see Emilio's look of sheer terror as he was killed before my very eyes.

'I managed to break cover and make for a truck parked off the road. Meek came blazing away at me like the madman he was, the lust to kill in his bloodshot eyes. I tried to back the truck in a quick turn, and must have gone over a Teller mine, for the whole countryside suddenly roared about my ears. By a miracle I was not killed, although I must have been taken for dead. When the tide of battle passed, I crawled back to the command post and found poor, dear, dead Emilio. Killed legally, according to the rules of war. I buried him.' Tears welled up in Mario's eyes, tears of emotion and affection.

Quenella sought to break the tension. 'Is it not a long while to store up so much hatred, Mario?' she said quietly.

'Emilio is dead,' said Mr Toledano. 'Nothing will bring him back. But providence has brought back Major Peter Meek. I, personally, will dispatch him.'

'What makes you so sure of that?'

'Unless he comes here to me, I intend to publish certain information I have concerning one of your English judges. Meek is coming for that information.'

'Isn't the whole thing a little unfair, Mario? You intend to kill a man you don't even know?'

'He didn't know Emilio,' said the other simply.

'Then if he doesn't turn up, isn't it a little unfair on the English judge?'

'He will turn up. And the medal he received for the action I shall get back in atonement. In any event, I am not concerned over the fate of the Judge.'

'It sounds like blackmail, to me,' said Quenella critically.

'It *is* blackmail,' said Toledano, smiling once more.

'I don't see how you could possibly have any such information about one of our judges,' objected Quenella. 'I think you have a very vivid imagination, Mario.'

Mario Toledano looked thoughtful for a moment. He went once more to his desk, and produced a wad of foolscap sheets clipped together in the corner. 'That, *amiga,*' he said, 'is part of a copy of Addendum to Sea-Lion. It was Most Secret. It bears a number in the right-hand corner. I had to sign for that copy. I managed to retain it out of the turmoil that was Germany. It contains all the necessary leads to the information I referred to about the Judge.' He replaced the document in his desk without allowing her to examine it, and she made no attempt to persuade him. Sufficient to know of its existence here in Boa Fidelidade... 'I don't normally keep this here,' he said significantly.

'And I don't think for one moment that one of our English judges would care two hoots about something that happened twenty years ago,' said Quenella. 'He'd say publish and be damned.'

'This one wouldn't,' sneered Toledano. 'It not only involves him, but also his illegitimate offspring who so far doesn't know that papa is still alive...'

'Mario, you depress me with all this talk. I still think it is ninety per cent imagination. Let us have some more music... And tomorrow, if you will lend me your car, I will go into Lisbon and see if I can prevail upon my glamorous girl friend to join me here for a few days. Do you think you could speak to the innkeeper and find her a room?'

Mr Toledano said but surely, he would do his level best.

CHAPTER 18

Desquamation of a Clerk

It was providential that Quenella managed to get back to Lisbon the following morning, because just after midday part of the outcrop of rock overhanging the dangerous bend on the Marcelo Gorge came adrift as a result of the heavy rains, effectively blocking the Boa Fidelidade road. It was the twenty-eighth of September, but Mr Toledano was not unduly perturbed. Major Meek would get there somehow.

The next day, when it became apparent that the re-opening of the road was in some doubt, Neeve suggested they made for the rendezvous by sea, and Simon fell in with the idea as it now appeared to be the easiest way into the place. Quenella insisted on coming too, although Simon was against it. Strangely, Adam Neeve thought it best that she should be with them, but Simon wasn't to know that Neeve was planning to leave them all stranded on *Kestrel* whilst he went after the Addendum himself; he wasn't to know that Neeve now had a shrewd idea where the medal was; he wasn't to know that Neeve knew a way out of Boa Fidelidade up over a mountainous goat-track. A forward bunkhouse, used for sailcloth and stores, was converted to passable quarters for Quenella, the spare stores being wrapped in a tarpaulin sheet and lashed down near the afterhatch.

They left Lisbon harbour after breakfast, and under the powerful marine engine proceeded on a sea that was like a millpond. Round about noon, the same sea took on a heavy, leaden appearance. Rain began to fall with tropical intensity and a heavy swell started. Pedro and Pierre stuck at their respective tasks, aided by young José. Quenella joined Adam and Simon in the main cabin – the forward bunkhouse was no place to rest in a heavy sea. Hammersley struggled in from his galley with a kettle of coffee, made, he assured them, from a secret formula; this they were prepared to believe.

'I wish this sea would flatten out a bit,' he grumbled. 'My glasses keep falling off into the soup.'

Adam Neeve grinned and produced a rubber band. 'Here – attach this to the frame and loop it round your ear.'

It was just as well he did, for that evening the near-hurricane Ethel-Minus swept out of the Atlantic and lambasted that part of the coast of Portugal for the next twenty-four hours before gasping for breath...

Throughout the night and the following day Pedro and Neeve took it turn and turn about in the constricted wheel-house, battling straight into the teeth of Ethel-Minus. Hammersley despaired of ever seeing Portugal again, and Quenella felt so ill she decided she just had to be alone in her forward bunk. But both Pedro and Neeve knew their job; they made a wide semi-circle out to sea, and by nightfall *Kestrel* was riding the tail-end of the tempest directly back to the Bahia de Boa Fidelidade.

'All we've got to do now is to finish the job,' said Neeve.

'That's all,' agreed Simon, casually enough.

'How about some coffee laced with rum, Ham?' suggested Neeve. Hammersley, stretched out like a dead thing, groaned. Neeve grinned sympathetically. 'All right, I'll get it,' he volunteered. 'I'll see what young José's doing.'

José, completely indifferent to the violent storm, had been left in the galley, keeping some liquid on the boil and watching the world go by.

Neeve returned with three steaming canteens. He reached for a bottle and added a noggin of rum to each. Pushing one over to Simon, he touched Hammersley's shoulder. 'Drink this up, Ham, it'll do you good.'

'Nothing will do me good,' groaned Hammersley pitifully.

'Cheers!' said Neeve, and although he and Simon gulped down the fierce concoction and felt better for it, nothing would induce Hammersley to drink the restorative products of Brazil and Jamaica.

'Did you give Quenella any?' asked Simon suddenly.

'I sent young José,' said Neeve. 'She's more likely to drink it if he takes it, so as not to offend him. It'll do her good.' He offered Simon a cigarette and they sat there smoking for a while. Neeve glanced at his watch. 'Shouldn't be long now,' he said.

'You're making for the harbour?' inquired Simon.

Neeve was non-committal. 'Pedro says it'll be the very devil to get *Kestrel* safely over the bar in this weather. Phew! It's getting hot in here, I'll be asleep in a minute. I'll see if I can give Pedro a hand.'

'I'll join you,' said Simon. 'I'm getting drowsy myself – I'd hate to be asleep when we arrive, we're late as it is.'

Neeve grinned. 'As you wish,' he said. 'But I can't run away.'

They staggered along the narrow deck to the wheelhouse, where sat Pedro at the helm, eyes glazed with strain.

'Like some coffee, Pedro?' asked Neeve.

'José already bring some.'

261

'Can we give you a hand?'

Pedro rubbed his eyes wearily and peered through the night at the dim halation that was Boa Fidelidade. 'Better I keep the helm, *senhor*. Ten, fifteen minutes – that is all.'

'I'll see how Quenella is,' said Simon, and went forward.

Adam Neeve waited a minute and returned quickly to the after-cabin. Hammersley was on his feet, his coffee untouched. He was fiddling with his spectacle case.

'Sorry to have to do this, Hammersley.'

Hammersley slipped his spectacle case in his pocket. 'Do what?' he asked curiously.

The small, compound-rubber cosh descended with scientific force – another achievement Adam Neeve hadn't learnt at night-school. 'That,' he said regretfully, and Hammersley still didn't know, he'd gone out like a light. Neeve knelt down and swiftly removed the case from Hammersley's pocket, extracting the medal which so far had eluded him.

'I should put that back, Neeve,' advised Simon, from the hatch-way.

Neeve whipped round, and where the gun came from Simon just couldn't tell. 'Keep back,' said Adam Neeve conversationally. 'I don't trust you.'

'I can see that. And you don't appear to trust Hammersley. Is he all right?'

'He'll come round. He's had a sudden black-out. I told you I had to have this medal. I've been wondering which of you had it, and it suddenly struck me that although I've seen Hammersley fiddling with his spectacle case I've never once seen him use it for his spectacles. The answer had to be that it contained what I was looking for. I intend to go after that page of Sea-Lion myself. I don't trust you, Mr Good. I fear that if you got your hands on it you would use it for your own ends.'

'Then Ambrose Meddlisome has more faith in me than you have.'

'I'm more of this world. I'm working on the assumption there are other pages of the Addendum still in existence, and that you wouldn't hesitate to use the information.'

'Or is that just what *you* have in mind, Mr Neeve? Adam Neeve, the clerk with more money than sense. Question, where does he get his money from? The scales are beginning to fall, Adam. And the man underneath is emerging.'

'I can only hope Toledano doesn't see me so clearly.'

'You seem to forget he's threatened to kill me. If you attempt to pass yourself off as me you'll probably end up horizontal.'

'That's my funeral.'

'Brother, you've said it.' Simon took a cautious step forward.

'I advise you to keep well away. I shan't hesitate to use this thing.'

'So Ambrose Meddlisome and Adam Neeve *are* on different sides of the fence! But I can't imagine you'd care to have murder on your conscience.'

'Oh, don't be melodramatic! I wouldn't kill you, I'd just wing you.'

'You've got to be accurate to do that.'

'I am accurate – if you keep still.' Neeve indicated a whisky-tot which was juddering gently back and forth along a ledged shelf. 'That glass,' he said. He shattered it with one shot.

'I see what you mean,' agreed Simon. 'I bet old Bulworthy didn't teach you *that!*'

Neeve bared his teeth in a lupine grin. 'How right you are!'

'And what do you propose to do now? Or would that be asking too much?'

'I'm going to tackle Toledano at the Cross-Keys.'

'And how do you intend to do that? Take *Kestrel* into harbour with me standing by just twiddling my thumbs?'

'No. In the first place Pedro wouldn't risk crossing the bar with this sea running and the tide on the turn – he tells me that the harbour here is one of the trickiest to enter on this stretch of the coast. Pierre and José should have organised the outboard dinghy by now. I'll run it up on the beach outside the harbour wall.'

'Assuming you reach your objective and get away from Toledano in less than two pieces, you've still got to get back to *Kestrel* with the goods. What do you think I'll be doing?'

'That brings me to the second point. Pedro will be supervising what *you'll* be doing. He's armed, well-paid and quite ruthless. And so is Pierre. As soon as I've got under way, *Kestrel* will put to sea again.'

'If you drown yourself and lose my medal, I'll never forgive you.'

'I'll never forgive myself. And you'll be in no condition to worry.'

'What do you propose to do with me, then? Lash me to the mizzen? Drop a Micky Finn in my coffee?'

Adam Neeve smiled apologetically. 'I had no Micky Finns, I had to make do with ordinary sleeping tablets. They take longer, but they get you in the end. If Hammersley had been a good boy and drunk his coffee I wouldn't have had to hit him. And I only hope Quenella's well on the way to dreamland, for I bear her no ill-will. She's told me all I want to know.'

It took several seconds for the full force of what Adam Neeve was saying to register. Simon had put down his general feeling of lassitude to the strain of the last twenty-four hours, but now the truth punched home. He stepped back quickly and slammed the hatch shut behind him, wrenching frantically at the bulky bundle of gear from the forward bunkhouse. It had nearly come adrift in the storm, and a couple of heaves completed the work. He rammed it tightly in the small space occupied by the companion-way. Flinging himself flat on the deck by the scuppers, he scooped up all the sea water he could, and drank, repeating the dose at every wave which broke. Putting a finger at the back of his throat, he was as sick as a dog. The sweat stood out on his forehead, he felt like nothing on earth, but he was confident he'd got rid of the contents of his stomach. By the time Neeve had battled his way out of the cabin, Simon was slumped by Quenella's bunkhouse. Neeve, gun in hand, looked at him suspiciously. 'Well?' he said.

'She's sleeping,' said Simon wearily, running a hand through his tousled hair. 'That was a dirty trick, Adam,' he growled, in an appropriately indistinct voice.

Pierre appeared in a hurry from his engine cubby-hole. Neeve motioned him to haul-to the dinghy whilst he executed the difficult task of clambering down into it.

'You'll never get away with it,' slurred Simon. He tensed suddenly. Hammersley, holding his head in a daze, staggered on deck.

'Stop him, Charles!' yelled Quenella from behind. She held an unlit storm-lantern in her hand. Swinging it round once, she lobbed it at Pierre. It caught him behind the ear and all but knocked him overboard. She said afterwards it was the only target she'd ever hit. And Hammersley, obeying some muzzy instinct to grab the slithering painter, missed and pitched over the side on top of Neeve. For one breathless moment Simon thought the cockleshell had capsized, but by a miracle it righted itself and disappeared from the nimbus of light around *Kestrel.*

Neeve and Hammersley were on their way...

Pierre slid his feet down into the well of the engine cockpit, nursing his head resentfully.

Simon suddenly remembered Pedro. He staggered to the wheelhouse. Pedro was slumped forward, his head lolling with the motion of the ship. Simon shook him vigorously, but Pedro's eyes remained shut and his mouth gaped in an idiotic rictus.

'He's passed out with fatigue,' yelled Quenella above the noise of the elements. 'He ought to be all right. José brought me some strong coffee but I couldn't face it. I told him to take it to his father.'

'You did what?' roared back Simon. He grabbed the canteen from a ledge and tipped it up. It was empty. He felt in Pedro's pockets and relived him of an automatic.

'I hope Hammersley's all right,' said Quenella anxiously. 'How near are we in?'

'Too near, for my liking,' jerked Simon. 'Hear the breakers? We'll run aground if we don't do something. See if you can find that Very pistol outfit in the after-cabin – watch your step, hold tight. I'll see if I can manage *Kestrel* till we can bring Pedro round. 'Strewth, what a job for a pen-pusher! The safest place for us is in the bay.' He struggled with his unaccustomed task, was glad he'd at least picked up a few tips from Pedro. Quenella returned with the Very outfit. Removing the pistol from the box he rummaged for the cartridges.

'Are you going to fire a distress signal?' asked Quenella. 'You'll bring out half the fishing fleet.'

Simon paused. 'You're right, Queen-of-the-Seas, it's merely illumination we want. Better fire a green, I suppose.' He loaded the pistol, thrust Quenella at the wheel and told her to hang on. Pointing the pistol up at arm's length, he fired. A thin trail of sparks snaked up and a green ball of fire burst in the sky, hanging there like a sinister visitor from outer space.

Boa Fidelidade was dangerously near, white horses were tumbling in over the harbour bar. He could see no sign of the dinghy. And then suddenly there was movement on the beach near the harbour wall. Two men were scuttering up the shingle. Just as the light faded there was a sudden stab of flame from the foot of the steps. Simon, all fingers and thumbs, fumbled for another cartridge, loaded again, and fired.

This time there was no discernible movement.

'Simon – I can't hold on much longer!'

Simon grabbed the wheel.

The light faded...

'Good evening, *senhor*,' said the barman, in a surprisingly gentle voice. 'What can I get you?'

'You can get me Mr Toledano,' said Adam Neeve.

...At the top of the stairs was a door from under which came a subdued line of light. Conscious that the radio down in the bar was now blaring at full strength, Neeve thrust his way into the room, kicked the door shut behind him, and stood staring at the fleshy individual manicuring his finger-nails at a desk in the corner; an individual who didn't bother to look up at the intrusion, who appeared not to have the slightest interest in anything but the all-absorbing half-moons and cuticles.

'Mr Toledano?'

'Could be,' agreed the adipose creature,

without interest, buffing his nails on his coat lapel and holding them under the desk-light to get the effect. 'And who might you be?' he added indifferently.

'If you could be Mario Toledano, I might be Simon Good.'

The oily character at the desk became very still. His eyes flicked upwards for the first time. And the olive face assumed an intelligence out of keeping with the slab of flesh. He placed the elegant little nail file on the square of green baize on the desk, and carefully lined it up beside a gold pencil. 'I've been waiting a long time for this moment, my friend,' he said, and his voice was like velvet – with a two-edged knife wrapped up in it. 'How can I be sure you are Simon Good...?'

Adam Neeve proved it. Names, addresses, an envelope with a mark under the stamp – a dicey one, that! – a photostat copy with a watermark, a medal of unusual size which fitted a presentation box, Convincing proof? Mr Toledano seemed to think so. For all Neeve's apparent casualness he was as tensed as a fully-wound main spring. He was not particularly concerned with one page of Addendum to Sea-Lion, he wanted the complete document – not to impound or destroy it, but to use it to his own advantage. Ninety per cent of the names therein would be valueless; the other ten per cent were worth their weight in gold. If he could induce Toledano to let him see the document, he would stop at nothing. He thought of the gun in his pocket, and resisted the temptation to reach for it there and then...

'...I've fulfilled my part of the bargain,' he growled, 'now fulfil yours.'

'If you say so,' agreed Toledano, and now all the sun of the Levant was in the smile. The tension in the room oozed away. He produced a gun and shot Adam Neeve dead...

CHAPTER 19

Gun of a Son

Ambrose Meddlisome waited anxiously for word from Simon Good or a letter from Toledano, and neither was forthcoming. A feeling of frustration and depression enveloped him. The blow fell one evening when a neatly dressed young man called with a small parcel and a letter which had come from consular sources via the Foreign Office.

He tore open the letter with a sense of premonition, and to his horror learnt that Adam Neeve's body had been picked up by a small Portuguese vessel on the high seas. After the last rites had been performed, it was buried at sea. The matter had in due course been reported to the nearest British Consul, etc., etc., and the young man from Commander Pope's department was now delivering the few items retrieved from Mr Neeve's body. Just like that. Cold official-dom.

Shaking like an aspen, Mr Meddlisome signed a form of receipt, and the young man withdrew discreetly. He'd seen it all before, and familiarity with the job made it no more pleasant.

Ashen-faced, the Judge examined the pitifully small parcel of Adam's belongings, a cardboard box full of dreams. Amongst the paraphernalia was a pen, a red notebook, a wallet, a key, a St Christopher on a thin silver chain, a gold ring. The Judge laid down the St Christopher gently; it had done its duty whilst Adam was alive... He examined the signet ring curiously. He recognised it as being one his younger sister Eve had given Adam a lifetime ago; *two* lifetimes ago; Eve's and Adam's. In a fit of uncontrollable anger he decided something would have to be done about Mr Toledano.

Toledano apparently had no intention of keeping his word, else surely by now the page from Sea-Lion would have come to hand. What had gone wrong? Adam *had* in some way interfered, and had paid the price with his life. That probably meant that Peter Meek was still alive. And if Toledano found that out, he might, in a fit of pique, still expose his, Meddlisome's, relationship with the Mendozas.

Mario Toledano must be silenced.

The Judge had a restless night. His active mind formulated plan after plan, and it wasn't until the early hours, after taking a couple of codeine tablets, that he dropped off into a drugged slumber. Fortunately the day before him was free, and he slept on till ten o'clock.

He washed and shaved and, scarcely touching his breakfast, made his way to town. He directed his steps to the Strand, where, if he remembered correctly, there was a gunsmith. To his dismay – or relief, he wasn't sure which – he found it was no longer there. In something of a quandary he turned back towards Trafalgar Square. He seemed to recollect there was a gunsmith in Haymarket. Or Lower Regent Street.

He found the shop. His heart started to thump heavily as he studied the racks of guns of every description in the window. In a little side window, laid out neatly on black velvet, were several revolvers and automatics, messengers of death on an appropriate pall. But how did a Judge go about *buying* a revolver? What reasons had to be advanced? What note would be taken of the purchaser? Faced with actuality, things didn't seem so easy. In the bright morning sunshine the whole business was unreal. He thought of Adam...

A car horn honked behind him from a traffic block. Turning, he saw Caroline and John Mendoza in an open sports car. Caroline was waving frantically to attract his attention. He moved over to them.

'Going to shoot someone?' asked John cheerily.

'Er – no. Just casual interest,' stammered Meddlisome.

'Shall we see you tonight, Ambrose?' asked Caroline.

Ambrose Meddlisome suddenly knew where he was going to get a gun...

'My dear, may I?' he said nervously. 'I'm at a loose end.'

'Of course you may. We won't be back till latish this afternoon. Make yourself at home.'

'Whoa back!' cried John. 'Jane's afternoon off. Give him your key, Caroline – quick – the lights are changing!'

With a wave they were gone.

The Judge put the key in his pocket, and made his way to Thos. Cook's in Piccadilly. He made some detailed inquiries regarding the journey to Portugal.

He had lunch in town to make certain he would avoid the Mendozas' maid. So far as he knew, Jane usually left the house around two o'clock to spend the rest of the day with a friend, but she might feel obliged not to go if one of her employers' close acquaintances arrived. The gun might not be where he'd seen it last, in which case he would have to search for it – for that he would obviously

275

prefer to be in the house alone.

It was with a feeling of extreme guilt that he ultimately inserted the key in the lock of the front door. He took the elementary precaution of giving a shout to make certain Jane had actually left, and after a few moments went upstairs to the guest room, with the elaborate tread of a common thief. In nervous haste he pulled open the door of the wardrobe.

As he remembered it, the gun was under some odds and ends of linen at the back of the handkerchief tray. Trembling almost beyond control, his fingers searched clumsily under the handkerchiefs and embroidered tray-cloths. He encountered cold steel. He suddenly felt unclean and miserable, a cheat abusing hospitality. He thought of Adam Neeve, and groped for the box of ammunition.

For a moment he stood there looking down at his hands, like a strangler looking at the implements of his passion. In a daze, he stared at the box in one hand, and in the other, the gun of his son...

A few moments later, he paused on the landing, deep in thought. Jane, hat and coat on ready to go out, stared up at him curiously from the hall.

'Are you all right, Mr Meddlisome?'

He didn't seem to hear her.

It was the longest afternoon and evening

he'd ever spent.

The following afternoon he sat studying a book from the Holborn Library, Tomlinson's *Use & Care of Revolvers and Automatics*. The telephone rang out stridently. He reached for the handset. 'Gomshall 31894.'

'Ambrose? Caroline here.'

'You sound distressed, my dear. What's the matter?'

'Well–' Caroline paused uncertainly. 'I hardly know how to put it – John would be furious if he knew. I've mislaid something, and I wondered if you could throw any light on it.'

The Judge's heart stood still. His eyes sought the gun on his desk. 'In what way can I help?' he said, in a voice which wasn't his own.

'When we went on holiday some weeks back, John told me to put it away somewhere safely, and to the best of my knowledge I did, and now for the life of me I can't find it. You know how careless I am about things, and now I haven't the faintest idea of what I did with it. I wondered if by the remotest chance you'd seen it about in the house anywhere. John will be livid! Are you there?'

Mr Meddlisome's throat was dry. 'I can't imagine John ever being livid with you,

Caroline,' he managed to get out at length. 'But it would help if I knew what you were talking about.'

'I'm sorry, Ambrose, I'm a wee bit het up. I know you're not going to like this, but that ring you gave me – the Spanish one – the diamond solitaire – I've lost it.'

'Ah!' breathed Mr Meddlisome thankfully.

'Ambrose? Are you all right. You sounded almost *relieved!* I thought you'd be cross.'

'Well, my dear, we can always replace a ring. I thought you were going to announce the end of the world.' He didn't say *his* world. 'It must be about somewhere. You haven't seen it since your holiday, you say?'

'I can't remember,' was the doubtful reply.

'I wondered if you could recollect seeing it. I'm frightfully sorry about it, Ambrose.'

'Don't sound so contrite, my dear. I expect you've got it insured.'

'That's not the point – I know it was of great sentimental value to you, and it was sweet of you to give it to me. I truly am sorry.'

'Don't worry. Tell John all about it, and if you still can't find it, make a claim.'

'That would mean reporting it to the police, wouldn't it? It may have been stolen, of course.'

The Judge was silent for a moment. 'Have another search, Caroline – I expect it will come to light.' He had the vaguest of recollections that recently in that house he'd subconsciously heard something small and hard drop, but, try as he would, he couldn't isolate in his mind either the time or the precise place. He had been much too occupied, of course, with the gun...

CHAPTER 20

Prodigal Joker

The Judge carefully studied Adam's personal belongings. The wallet contained nothing save a modest amount of English and Portuguese money, a book of stamps and a few bills. The notebook was practically indecipherable, having suffered from the lengthy immersion in sea-water. The St Christopher and the gold ring told him nothing more than he already knew. The key aroused his curiosity; the ring at the end was in the form of an entwined serpent, and it suddenly dawned on him that this was the key to Eden End. Poor old Adam, he certainly carried things to a logical conclusion.

Mr Meddlisome redirected his attention to the notebook. In his first turbulent spate of anger when he decided to silence Mario Toledano, he had completely overlooked how he was going to *find* that gentleman. Perhaps some of the almost illegible addresses in Adam's book might provide the answer. Under the initials 'M.T.' there was some smudgy, faded writing which looked promising. *Rotterdam, Oude Dijkstrasse, 17b. Krefeld, Johannestraat, 34.* And there was also a note of the Cross-Keys. The obvious thing seemed to be to go to the last named place first.

He picked up the key again and held it in the palm of his hand. It might be interesting to see if the bungalow held any clues, although on the face of it Eden End was empty. With a sudden shock, it occurred to him that, with Adam dead, there would be all the business of clearing up the estate, of finding the wastrel son, a most distasteful task.

His thoughts wandered back to the automatic on the desk. He had mastered the mechanism of the weapon, and all that remained now was to practise firing it. His own cottage at Gomshall was blessed with only a tiny garden, and comment would undoubtedly be aroused if an eminent judge were observed taking potshots at a tin can on a tree stump. At the bottom of Adam's garden (the Judge still found himself thinking in the present tense) there was a copse, ideal for target practice. He decided there and then to go to Eden End.

It was almost dusk when he arrived, a misty autumnal dusk with the smell of bonfires in the air. He parked his small car in the drive, and quite openly approached the front door. Although he had no proof that the key in his pocket was in fact the key to the bungalow, he was confident it would fit.

The lock turned easily, and he entered and shut the door behind him. With a feeling of intense loneliness, he wandered through the empty rooms, the bare boards echoing hollowly just like they did that day years ago when he and Adam had looked over the place for the first time. The bungalow was large and square, with a small paved well in the middle. He recalled that there was a box-room overlooking the well, and that Adam used to keep the door locked, though he made no secret of the fact that the key was on the lintel.

To Mr Meddlisome's surprise the door was still locked. Idly, his fingers reached up and there was the key. Curiously he opened the door, and stepped into a room which showed signs of habitation. There was a small bed, a table, a radio, an oil-heater capable of being used for cooking, tinned food and some old newspapers. He took a paper over to the window, and although the light was fading, he could still make out the date of issue. It was several months old. Adam had evidently used this place as an occasional *pied à terre*. What had he been up to before Toledano came over the horizon? Puzzled, Mr Meddlisome relocked the room, and went to the french windows at the rear. Outside on the sadly neglected lawn was a concrete toadstool with a gnome, and, a few yards beyond, the plantation of trees began.

The Judge unbolted the window and stepped outside. There was just about enough light for a couple of practice shots. He wandered round and found the dustbin. Inside was an empty milk tin, green with fungus. Distastefully he picked it out between thumb and forefinger, and balanced it on the garden ornament. Then he stepped back in the shadow of the room, feeling for the automatic and slipping back the safety-catch. Once or twice he took aim, raising the weapon at arm's length as per the drill book. He glanced at the gardens either side. They appeared to be empty. This was it, his first shot ever. Tensed, not knowing quite what to expect, he squeezed the trigger. He was mildly surprised to find that he scarcely felt a thing, that the noise was no more than a sharp *crack!*

The tin was still on the toadstool.

Ah, yes, aim a fraction lower than the target! He tried again, and this time the tin jumped off onto the lawn. He suddenly stiffened. A man was walking hurriedly through the trees towards the house.

Unreasonable panic seized Mr Meddlisome, but before he could take any action the man was upon him, had taken him by the arm. For a moment they stood there staring at each other in silence. The gun slid from the Judge's nerveless fingers, his jaw gaped disbelievingly. Sagging at the knees, he staggered back against the french window for support.

'What the devil are you doing with that gun, Ambrose?' said Adam Neeve petulantly. 'You nearly killed me with that first shot!'

He picked up the gun. 'What do you think you're going to do with this?' he asked curiously.

The Judge's lips scarcely moved. 'Avenge your death, Adam.'

'You need a stiff drink,' said Neeve critically. He steered the other to the inner room, and unlocking the door, made Mr Meddlisome sit on the bed. Lighting an old-fashioned oil lamp on the table, he produced from a wall cupboard some brandy and a couple of glasses. 'I'm not sure I understand you, Ambrose. Here – drink this. Now tell me all about it– *How did you get in?*' he asked suddenly.

The Judge took a gulp at his glass. Without saying a word he handed Neeve the key.

Neeve looked at it incredulously. 'Where did you get this?' he jerked.

'A man from the Foreign Office called with a small box which contained some of your personal belongings. You may be interested to learn that your body was picked up by a Portuguese vessel in the middle of the ocean. After the last rites were performed you were buried at sea.'

Neeve's glass shattered on the floor. In the subdued light of the lamp his face turned to putty. 'What items were returned?' he managed to get out.

'That key, a ring, a red notebook, a wallet, a St Christopher on a silver chain. And a pen,' said the Judge tonelessly. 'And so far, Toledano has failed to keep his promise with me. And I've had no word from Peter Meek. *Was* it Peter Meek they picked up?'

Adam Neeve turned away to hide his misery. 'No,' he said slowly, 'it wasn't Peter Meek. It was Adam Neeve. Young Adam Neeve.' He choked back his emotion. 'My ... son.'

Ambrose Meddlisome was shocked into silence. He sat there aghast, and all control seemed to have gone from his lower jaw. 'What – what happened?' he gaped at length.

Neeve took a swig from the bottle, and downed it at one go, shuddering as the raw spirit kicked back. He searched for brief words. 'When I was on Toledano's trail I came across my son in Lisbon. Ambrose, I had the shock of my life, what I saw horrified me. There was cupidity and cunning written all over him. And worse, there was the nervous twitch which even to my unpractised eye could mean nothing but drugs. I suppose I should have known better but I told him a little of Sea-Lion, and tried to enlist his help. But he was no more than a cheap crook, Ambrose – he stole money from me, and that red notebook containing addresses relating to Toledano, and cleared off into the slime again. I sought him out in one of his haunts, and tried to get that notebook back. He denied all knowledge of it, but he lied – I know he lied. He asked when I was going to call on Toledano and what my plans were. I still had a pathetic faith in him, Ambrose, and I told him.'

The Judge was distressed at his brother-in-law's anguish. 'How very sad!' he said quietly. 'I would have done the same, Adam. After all, he was your son.'

'Son!' Neeve almost spat the word. 'On the night of September the 30th we approached the harbour at Boa Fidelidade from the sea, on the tag-end of Ethel-Minus. I didn't altogether trust Meek' (the Judge shot him a swift look) 'and I decided to go after Addendum-to-Sea-Lion myself. By now I knew where it was, I wanted the complete document–'

'Why?' The word was peculiarly penetrating.

'The Foreign Office wanted it – don't look at me like that, Ambrose – and I intended to get it and give it to them, less the bit relating to you. The crew of the yacht were going to shanghai Meek and Hammersley – you know Hammersley? – and I was going ashore in the outboard dinghy. At the last minute things went wrong, Hammersley made an effort to prevent me and nearly drowned in the attempt. We landed, and I scurried up the beach to some steps leading to the harbour wall, with Hammersley in full cry. At the foot of the steps a man stepped out and attacked me. A flare suddenly lit the sky, and I recognised my attacker. It was Adam, Ambrose. My son. We grappled fiercely for a few moments, he drew a gun and shot at me twice. He got me through the arm. I don't think it would have worried him if he'd killed me. I had a gun, too, but I couldn't – wouldn't – use it against my own flesh and blood. But he had no such compunction. He knocked me unconscious and left me...' Neeve's voice trailed into a mere whisper. 'Thank God Eve didn't live to hear me say so, but it seems young Adam was more illegitimate than John Mendoza.'

'You *know?*' The Judge gaped in an agony of realisation, but his voice carried a measure of relief.

'Yes, Ambrose, I know. I knew there had to be some reason for your jitteriness other than once having been a member of the U.W.F. I followed up the same sources of information open to Toledano. The reference in the Addendum to your brief affair with the daughter of the wealthy pro-German Don Miguel Juan Mendoza carried its own implications – especially as I unearthed later the fact that Jacquenita Mendoza fled from home and sought the comfort of the Church, only to – to die in giving birth to a son. I'm sorry if I appear brutal, Ambrose.'

'Thank God somebody knows,' breathed Ambrose Meddlisome.

Neeve said gently, 'We've both been unlucky, Ambrose.'

A dozen questions jived for position in the Judge's mind. 'Why didn't you tell me *all* you discovered?'

'If I could have got that page, you could have destroyed it, and that would have been an end to the business; there was no need for me to tell you what I'd learnt. Did Toledano connect the birth of a son with John?'

'Not at first – I think. But after you'd vanished he sent me a copy of a birth registration adopting the name Mendoza, and also a copy of an entry in an old register of the church orphanage in which John was brought up. You weren't available. It was then that I went to Peter Meek. I think you can trust him in this matter.'

'Tell me about Jacquenita Mendoza,' said

Adam Neeve, 'and get it off your chest. A quarter of a century is a long time to nurse a secret.'

'There's not much to tell. I met her one evening whilst you were occupied with Eve' (the Judge smiled faintly) '–you both left me pretty much alone on that holiday, Adam – and you know how these things develop. The night before the holiday came to a close, there occurred one of those infinitesimal moments in time when the blind forces of nature combine to make one of the timeless moments in life. There was no putting the clock back, only forward. And the tragedy was that we then had an almighty row which started over literally nothing – whatever it was was so trivial that I couldn't put my finger on it later, but it blossomed into a spiteful shouting match with passions running high. Even after all these years I can still see her, eyes smouldering, as she spat out words of reproach; I can see her snatching a dress-ring from her finger and savagely thrusting it at me with a "Take this as a wedding ring, *senhor,* and don't ever come back!"

'I took her at her word, Adam, and went, although I think if I'd been in Spain a little longer we'd have ironed out that lovers' quarrel. But going back to England the next day broke the spell, the bewilderment and glamour faded, and the episode turned into something to be forgotten.' The Judge paused reflectively. 'They say it is unwise to go back. I did. Immediately before the war, I went over the old familiar places. I made a few discreet inquiries after Jacquenita Mendoza, and learned to my horror there'd been a son, learned the dismal story of Jacquenita's disgrace and death, learned of the orphan in the Santa Luzia Orfanato who had never known a father; young Juan Mendoza. He was mine all right – the circumstances and the date of birth left little room for doubt.

'I was a coward, Adam. I couldn't face adopting him. But I paid for his education, and became to him a rich uncle who ultimately sent him to school in England and secured a job for him here. He changed his nationality, and when he got married to Caroline I secured a house for them.' The Judge's eyes dimmed. 'I've since tried to do all I could for them both. Please don't think too harshly of me, Adam...'

Neeve said, 'As you've so often remarked, this is not a court of morals, Ambrose. The tragedy of life is that you can't alter what has happened.'

'Tell me what happened at Boa Fidelidade,' said the Judge.

Neeve tensed at the recollection. 'When I came round I was shivering with pain and shocked confusion. It was a wild, moonless night, and although I'd been dragged up behind some rocks, I was lucky not to have been drowned by the heavy seas. For a while I searched ineffectually for Hammersley – though I couldn't expect any sympathy from him; I'd treated him a bit roughly. And there was no trace of the dinghy. If all had gone according to my plan, *Kestrel* was away to sea again. The Cross-Keys was closed for the night, and Boa Fidelidade was as quiet as the grave. My gun was gone, so was the envelope with the photostat, and Meek's medal, too–'

'He gave it to you?' interposed the Judge.

'I took it by force from Hammersley. It wasn't till later that I discovered my signet ring and St Christopher had been wrenched from me. My son had earned himself a complete passport to oblivion. On the verge of collapse I staggered up the main road out of the village to the Marcelo Gorge, until I found a sympathetic nightwatchman guarding some road materials. He gave me a hot drink, bathed the flesh wound in my arm, and propped me up in front of his coke fire till early morning. The road had been blocked by a fall of rock, but had been cleared sufficiently for single-line traffic; he secured a lift for me on a ballast lorry going into Lisbon. In Lisbon there was no news of *Kestrel,* and later, back in Boa Fidelidade, nobody knew, wanted to know, or had even heard of Toledano. There was no trace of Quenella–'

'Who?'

'A young lady who extracted from Toledano the reason why he wanted to dispose of Peter Meek.'

'*Had* Meek killed Toledano's brother?' breathed the Judge.

'Yes – during the World War II – when he earned his "posthumous" award for wiping out two enemy machine-gun posts. Toledano and his brother were in one of them. Emilio was killed. Mario was the one who escaped. And talking of guns, where did you get this one?' asked Neeve suddenly.

'In the wardrobe in the Blue Room,' said Mr Meddlisome distantly. 'In the handkerchief tray.'

'The Blue Room?'

'Eh? Oh, the guest room at John and Caroline's house. I removed it without their permission. Adam,' said the Judge earnestly, 'they must never know about – me.'

'Don't worry, they never will. But you won't be needing this gun now – you'd better put it back.'

Mr Meddlisome became agitated. 'I – I couldn't!' he jerked. 'I feel like a thief every time I look at it. I – I–' Words failed him. 'Supposing they've missed it, and reported it?'

'Suppose they haven't,' said Neeve practically. 'Give it to me, together with any spare ammunition. Have you got a key to the place? I'll find someone who'll put it back, and nobody will ever know the difference.'

The Judge gazed up at Adam Neeve as though for the first time. 'I feel as though I've never known the *real* you,' he said.

'Is that so?' Adam Neeve seemed to have regained some of his verve. 'I'll tell you all about me one day. Meanwhile, let's go back to Gomshall and examine my remains...'

Simon Good was waiting for them on the step.

'Well?' said Simon, when mutual surprise had been overcome. 'Did you get page 22?'

'No,' said Neeve.

'Toledano wasn't satisfied you were Peter Meek?'

'I never got further than the beach. My son took over for his own ends. He got killed in the attempt.'

Simon Good remained silent for a moment. 'I'm so sorry, Adam,' he said at length. 'Things haven't worked out too well for you.'

'Nor for Ambrose. Although presumably Toledano was satisfied he got the right man, he hasn't honoured his part of the agreement. Where's Hammersley?'

'I thought he must be with you. Pedro finally got *Kestrel* into Oporto, and Quenella and I went back to Lisbon. There was no trace of you or Hammersley, either there or at Boa Fidelidade. And nobody anywhere had even heard of Toledano – it was a closed shop. I hoped Mr Meddlisome might have heard. What happened?'

Neeve told him.

'Toledano must pay,' said Simon grimly. 'Can't we cook up something and get him caught up *legally*? You know the law, Meddlisome.'

'I know English law, Meek,' said the Judge, adding with a frown, 'and we've got to find him first. And I'm very concerned about Hammersley. Are you sure he reached the beach, Adam?'

'Definitely. He started to chase me up the shingle.'

'Why didn't he come to your aid when you were attacked?' asked Simon curiously.

Neeve looked thoughtful. 'I don't really know. I suppose you couldn't really expect him to after what occurred. It all happened so quickly anyway.'

'He's not back at his flat at Mortlake,' said Simon. 'He seems to have vanished without trace.'

'I fear for his safety,' said the Judge anxiously. 'Let us come inside and talk of ways and means...'

Back at Simon Good's house at Richmond there was a cable addressed to Mr Quasi

Modo. It read:

PEPPI'S CIRCUS TWICE DAILY PON-
TEMURIO STOP GIANT'S HAMMER
INTRIGUING STOP HELICOPTER ON
TOP OF HAMMER
          CHARLES HAMMERSLEY

'What do you think it means?' asked Simon,
first thing the following morning.

'At first blush, I'd say I hit him too hard,'
grunted Adam. 'Three concrete facts
emerge, however. Hammersley's alive and
kicking. Pontemurio is one of these mush-
room holiday centres somewhere in the
mountains. And presumably there's a circus
there, performing twice daily, and it would
be to our advantage to visit it. But what
we're supposed to divine from a giant's
hammer with a helicopter on top, beats me.'

'Hammersley was in a circus once,' mused
Simon. 'Don't tell me he's got a job at last!'

By midday they were at Gatwick Airport...

They reached Pontemurio in time for the
evening performance.

The dining room of the hotel at Pontemurio
looked out across the market square towards a peculiar rock formation which stuck
up out of the houses, an inverted wedge-
shaped pinnacle some eighty feet high,

wider at the top than at the bottom.

'A curious phenomenon,' remarked Neeve to the waiter.

'*Senhor*–? Ah, yes! Many years ago the landowner built a house within the base of the rock itself. There used to be what was regarded as a right of way past it, but a couple of years ago a wealthy gentleman from Lisbon bought the property, and put a stout door at each end of the passage. It is said that he had the house modernised, but he is rarely there in spite of the costly alterations. It is known locally as the Hidden House. It was even rumoured he had a helicopter on the summit!'

'A helicopter!' exclaimed Neeve, glancing across at the jagged finger of rock. 'The top doesn't look flat enough – or large enough, for that matter.'

'It is much larger than one imagines, *senhor*. And it is said that the summit is a natural bowl which at one time collected rainwater – like a miniature lake – and served the crops. Drained, it makes an ideal landing field for a helicopter. There must be a way up through the rock. Such a machine would be very useful to hop across the valley – the only way out of the town is back along the road by which you came. To reach the other side of the valley by road one has to travel nearly ninety kilometres. I myself have never seen the machine leave the *Martello do*

Gigante – you would say Giant's Hammer – but some say they have on occasion heard it at night. In any event, the owner has evidently decided to use the Hidden House no more.'

'Indeed?' said Neeve, cocking an eyebrow.

'Yes, only this week has he had the entrances bricked up.'

Neeve and Simon Good looked at each other thoughtfully.

'There seems to be much excitement in the town,' remarked Simon at a tangent.

'The *senhor* does not know? It is always thus for the final carnival of the season. There are displays in the market place, a fair, a circus–'

'We noticed the circus, on the way in,' said Neeve.

'Every year Guido Peppi's Circus comes to town. It is very entertaining. A visit is worthwhile.'

'We must go,' said Neeve.

'The very last performance is tonight, *senhor.* If you hurry, you will just make it.'

They finished their meal and made for the outskirts of the village, guided by the growing trickle of people and the blare of the circus band.

They passed one of the freshly bricked-up entrances to the Hidden House, and Simon glanced up at the towering curiosity that was *Martello do Gigante*. 'So that's where

Hammersley's helicopter is,' he remarked. 'Toledano's, do you think?'

'Possibly – though it seems crazy to brick up the doorways if you want to use it in a hurry.'

The field with the Big Top and various booths came in view, and the bustle and excitement were infectious. A pipe-organ hammered out ancient tunes, and above the shouts of the barkers the circus band competed in noisy discord from within the tent. And with it all was the underlying thrum of the diesel generator which manufactured the electric current. They picked their way over heavily insulated cables and approached the ticket guichet. Simon pushed a treasury note through the tiny arch, and asked for two good seats.

The bespectacled clown inside the hive thrust out two numbered tickets, change to the value of twice the note, and Simon Good's medal.

'Enjoy the show, *senhor*,' said Hammersley. 'Next please...'

The performance had already started, and they picked their way to two ringside seats. Simon tripped over the feet of two gentlemen on the end seats, and was profuse in apologies.

'Don't mention it,' said Blake courteously.

'Think nothing of it,' said Rip Strookman,

and applauded vigorously as a rider fell off his horse.

Although Guido Peppi's Circus was not, as advertised, the greatest circus in the world, it was nevertheless a very good show. Just before half-time a hoard of clowns rushed into the arena in a slick welter of slapstick, followed by a very sedate gentleman pushing a refuse bin on wheels. He brought roars of delight from the children because he was so much out of place, and because they knew what to expect of him. Every now and then he paused in his perambulations to perform some astonishing contortions, carefully wiping his spectacles and slicking his clothing after each effort.

'Don't tell me,' breathed Neeve, 'it's Hammersley. Those contortions would earn him a fortune.'

'Between you and me, they have,' said Simon knowingly.

Hammersley dived both hands into the bin and produced an assortment of parcels, which he proceeded to distribute to lucky members of the audience. Small packets for the children contained sweets and cheap gifts. Enormous multi-wrapped parcels for mums and dads contained only one cigarette – to the delight of the children who got the better bargain. Simon Good's contained Addendum-to-Sea-Lion.

CHAPTER 21

Lions in Portugal

When Hammersley recovered consciousness on the beach on that storm-racked night of September the 30th he was very ill indeed. Motivated by a feeling that he ought to do something, he staggered along the shingle to the steps where he had last seen Adam Neeve, and clambered warily up to the jetty. Boa Fidelidade was on the verge of slumber, and the only signs of life came from the inn across the harbour. Picking his way along the slippery wall, he made for the Cross-Keys, not knowing what he was going to do when he got there. Nausea gripped at his stomach, and the top of his head seemed to be opening and shutting alarmingly. Perhaps a stiff drink would put things right.

By the time he reached the inn all he wanted to do was to lie down quietly and die. Vaguely he was aware of a large and ancient Citroën lorry parked near the Cross-Keys, and in spite of his misery his mind registered the giant golden lettering on the tailboard which proclaimed GUIDO PEPPI'S CIRCUS. His befuddled brain melted and swam back into the past, to the days of long ago when all was sunshine and blue skies and apple-blossom, to when he ran away and joined a travelling circus. He'd come home at last, and he didn't want to go any further.

Overcoming a queasy desire to vomit, he made a supreme effort and dragged himself up over the tailboard, crawling forward over a mass of canvas and rolled bunting. He sank down and made himself as comfortable as possible. And when he awoke the following morning he was somewhere in the middle of Portugal...

His blurry wakening had a nightmare quality. He was gradually jogged out of the twilight by the motion of the lorry as it turned off the metalled road and trundled up a rough cart-track. He was in a wringing sweat and running a slight temperature, his head throbbed like a steam engine, he was in Stygian blackness, there were loud shouts and cries in alien tongues, and above all there was the deep-throated roar of a hungry lion.

He tried to ease himself into a better position on what felt like a pile of hessian netting, and the attempt filled him with nausea. He blinked first one eye and then the other, then both, feebly waved his hand in front of them, couldn't see a thing and decided he'd lost his sight. The general racket made him wince, he wished he was in orbit away from it all. Sinking back on his hunkers he tried to fathom things out.

He was troubled by a vague familiarity with his surroundings – familiarity? How could that be? It was too dark to see a thing! And yet the sense persisted. It was like feeling he'd been here before – no, stronger than that – like coming home at last. He sat up with a jerk, and wished he hadn't. It was the smell! The smell of tentage and sawdust and animals! The bustle and excitement of the travelling circus!

The vehicle joggled lopsidedly over some ruts and came to rest with a sickening lurch that was sheer agony. There was an ever-increasing babel and bustle outside, the clatter of gear being thrown down, and a sudden heart-stopping snarl from a nearby caged tiger. Hammersley sighed, partly in weariness, partly in peace. Subsiding gently, he drifted into semi-oblivion. He couldn't care less. He had come home with a vengeance...

Guido Peppi was a vast figure of a man who had lived his life with animals and was kind to humans. When the lorry was eventually off-loaded and Hammersley was discovered, Peppi's first thought was to succour the needy. He had a place prepared in a caravan next to his own, produced blankets, dry clothing and brandy, and asked no questions.

Just after midday Hammersley was awakened from a luxurious sleep by the sound of two voices speaking in English outside the caravan. Deciding he felt better, he lit one of the black cigarettes placed by his bunk, and peered through the little lace-curtained window. All he could see from this angle was an expensive car and the back of Guido Peppi. A disembodied voice said 'I require you to look after this box till I return, Guido.'

'Would it not be safer at the Hidden House, *senhor?*'

'I have just come from the Hidden House, and I have been through the process of locking it up. I am leaving Boa Fidelidade for good, and I don't wish to be seen at Giant's Hammer more than necessary. And I'm in a hurry. To my annoyance I remembered this box as I was on my way out of the village. You will look after it until the end of the week.'

'As you say, *senhor.*'

'As I say,' agreed Toledano, coming into view as he got into his car. He drove off with no word of farewell.

Hammersley watched Guido Peppi take a small dispatch box into his caravan...

'I'm on holiday in Boa Fidelidade,' explained Hammersley. 'I went out last night to listen to the rough sea, when I slipped on the steps of the jetty and dealt myself a severe blow on the head. One can feel the bump now. What is the name of this place, by the way?'

'Pontemurio,' replied Guido, pushing over another brandy. 'By the state of your clothes, you were lucky not to be drowned, *senhor,*' he said critically.

'I could have done with this brandy last night,' said Hammersley. 'In fact I was making my way to the Cross-Keys when I suddenly felt so ill that all I wanted was somewhere to curl up and forget. And your wagon was just like home – many years ago I used to be in a circus.'

'So?' Guido Peppi's interest was aroused. 'What did you do?'

'I was in a contortionist act. But that was before World War II. One never loses the smell of the sawdust, however. In the interval we used to give out mystery packets to the children – it brought them in in their cohorts. Do you do anything like that? It costs very little.'

'No,' said Guido thoughtfully, 'but it seems a good idea.'

'Would you like me to organise a trial run?' asked Hammersley. 'I would like to repay you for your kindness, and my time is my own – if you could feed me for a day or two.'

'It shall be done,' agreed Guido. 'And you shall do it. The circus is in your veins. Show me your tricks when you feel fit.'

'I wouldn't require payment, of course,' said Hammersley grandly. 'And if in the meantime there is any other little job you'd like me to do, I shall be only too happy to oblige. A routine job like taking the money, for instance...'

He soon found out all that was to be known on the surface about Giant's Hammer, and decided quick action was required. He had no idea of what had happened to Simon Good or Neeve, and there was no time to waste. He therefore dispatched two top-rate telegrams, one to Blake and the other to Rip Strookman...

At three o'clock one morning there was a muffled bang in Pontemurio. Several people heard it, and one or two looked out of bedroom windows, but there was nothing to be seen. Ten minutes later Blake sidled along to examine his handiwork on one of the Spanish oak doors, and was pleased to find he had made a good job of the lock. He vanished silently into the covered passage. Rip Strookman and Hammersley followed like shadows.

They made their way to the Hidden

House, and discovered bricked-up windows and a heavy metal door with formidable double locks. Blake was able to devote all his skill to breaking them, as no windows from neighbouring houses overlooked the midget courtyard, and very soon they were inside. Apart from the auxiliary generator the house was linked to the public electricity supply, and soon the interior was a blaze of light. They made themselves some coffee, and while Blake and Rip attended to the safe built into virgin rock, Hammersley went on a tour of inspection.

By any standards the place was well-appointed, complete with lush bedroom, sitting rooms with illusory vistas through false windows, radio, books, records, and all the distractions without which it is impossible nowadays to live. Hammersley was experimenting with a panel of push-buttons on the wall of the bedroom, when to his astonishment a hatch in the ceiling opened and a ladder descended. Cautiously he climbed up and found himself at the foot of a shaft. The invitation was obvious, and he proceeded up a kind of iron fire-escape until he found himself looking at the night sky above the natural bowl of the summit of Giant's Hammer. And there in the middle was a helicopter.

He walked round it curiously, and then very carefully climbed to the rim of the rocky bowl and looked down at the sleeping village beneath. He went back and had another look at the helicopter...

When he returned to the others a while later, he found the room full of the heady fumes of polar-ammon gelignite. The safe door was blown, and Strookman was examining with a professional eye the diamond wealth of Mario Toledano.

'He won't miss some of these,' Rip was saying. 'They're probably ill-gotten, anyway.' He proceeded to pack them into a small handgrip.

'It looks as if he'll miss all of them,' commented Blake dryly. 'Let's look at these papers and see if we can find Simon's Addendum.'

They went through them carefully, destroying what were obviously documents and photographs which could be used for blackmailing activities. Addendum to Sea-Lion was missing.

'Toledano handed Peppi a dispatch box for safe keeping till the end of the week,' said Hammersley thoughtfully. 'That must be it.'

'Can you get hold of it?' asked Blake.

'I'll try.'

'If you describe it to me, we'll go into Lisbon and buy a substitute, and then we can examine it at leisure. But don't let Peppi see you swapping it over – else he'll twist you into contortions such as you've never known.'

'Whilst you're in Lisbon you can look for Simon,' said Hammersley. 'If you can't find him, send a cable to his home for me – I'll write one out.'

'What are we going to do about this place?' said Strookman. 'Supposing Toledano returns earlier than expected?'

'We'll have to keep him out of here as long as possible,' mused Blake. 'Some delaying action is required.'

'There was once a gentleman who dug a hole in the middle of Piccadilly for a wager,' said Hammersley thoughtfully. 'He worked on the principle that if you did it openly, nobody would object. He sat with his hole for a week before they moved him on.'

'Are you all right?' asked Rip anxiously.

'The windows here are bricked-up,' went on Hammersley. 'Can you both lay bricks?'

'I've built walls in the garden,' said Rip.

'I've done various jobs of exceptional skill on my garage and greenhouses,' confessed Blake modestly. 'So?'

'When you're in Lisbon order a load of bricks, sand and quick-drying cement, and brick up both entrances. Nobody's going to worry except Toledano, and he won't be here till the weekend – we hope. If you do the job efficiently it should delay him at least till Simon gets here to decide what to do with him.'

'Wouldn't his reaction be to clear out immediately?'

'Without his papers? Without his diamonds? Without knowing what's going on?'

'Hammersley, you're a genius,' said Blake admiringly.

'That's what everybody says,' agreed Hammersley, 'there must be something in it. And now I'd like to show you the helicopter...'

CHAPTER 22

Jokers in Jeopardy

As Hammersley forecast, little or no interest was evinced by the inhabitants of Ponte-murio when a truckload of bricks and a tip of ready-mixed cement arrived from Lisbon, and two foreigners who spoke little Portuguese commenced work on bricking up the entrances to the Hidden House. The only thing which aroused comment was the speed with which they worked; this, it was felt, was a de-restrictive practice to be deplored. In record time there appeared two brick walls, one in Flemish, and the other in English, bond. The two workmen were tidy in their work, all the surplus cement was shovelled through a gap in each wall before the last few bricks were laid, and a hundred or so bricks left over from the job were presented to an impoverished gentleman who was hanging around hopefully, in exchange for the service he rendered by sweeping clean the pavements.

Although little interest was shown in these activities, the following morning news of the job reached the ears of Guido Peppi, and

Hammersley was present when a circus hand casually mentioned the impressive speed of the workmen. Peppi's reaction was one of puzzlement. What was afoot? Had not Toledano said he would return at the end of the week? True, he had said he intended leaving the place for good, but Peppi had gathered the impression he had things to collect from the Hidden House first. Indeed, had not Toledano indicated he would have deposited therein his dispatch-box but for the fact he had already locked up?

Hammersley interrupted his train of thought. 'I, myself, had a talk with the men yesterday afternoon,' he said. 'It seems they are acting on the direct instructions of the owner – a certain wealthy gentleman named Toledano. One gathers he is leaving the district for a while, and wishes to ensure the place isn't burgled. The lengths to which some people will go are truly remarkable. A policy with a first class insurance company would more than set his mind at rest.'

Guido Peppi was to a certain extent relieved, although he doubted if any insurance company would accept Mario Toledano as a client of unimpeachable moral hazard. But if Mario had given orders for the work to be done then all was well, and if he had commanded a speedy job then the command would be obeyed to the letter.

The letter! Guido stopped in his tracks. Turning abruptly, he swung up into his caravan, pulled down the flap of his writing desk, and rummaged amongst some papers. Hammersley stood at the door, his innocent eyes noting Toledano's black dispatch-box before the desk was closed again.

'Anything the matter, Guido?' he inquired.

'I forgot to post this urgent letter,' said Guido, with a worried frown. 'It was given to me the other day in Boa Fidelidade.'

'I will attend to it immediately,' said Hammersley.

Peppi half-extended the heavily-sealed envelope and then changed his mind. 'I had better see to it myself,' he said. 'I will stroll down to the post office, and take the opportunity of seeing what sort of a job the workmen have made of these walls.'

Hammersley lit a cigarette, and sat for a moment on the caravan steps. He must have been mistaken, but he could have sworn the letter was addressed to Mr Justice Meddlisome of Gomshall, Surrey, England.

As soon as Guido was out of sight Hammersley crossed to his own quarters, and returned with a paper parcel. It was not unusual for Hammersley to be seen with paper parcels, because he packed those to be distributed during the show himself. Nevertheless, he waited for the right moment before slipping into Guido's caravan to make the exchange of dispatch-boxes.

Back in his own quarters he wrestled with Toledano's box, but he could do nothing with its double lock. He was happy, therefore, half-an-hour later, to spot two sightseers wandering round the circus site showing a keen interest in all that was to be seen. He hurried out to make their visit even more interesting, to the extent of finally showing them into his own caravan. With the aid of a pick-lock, Blake soon had the box open. They found Simon Good's medal and Addendum to Sea-Lion. Page 22 was missing.

'We'll make a fair exchange,' said Blake, producing a bulky, faded packet from his pocket. 'We'll give him back the deeds to Giant's Hammer. And a penny for luck in place of Simon's medal.'

He relocked the box, and Hammersley, making certain the coast was clear, replaced it in Guido's desk. He had just rejoined Blake and Strookman as Guido Peppi came striding back to his quarters. There was no time to dally, no time to collect the spare box and the Addendum from Hammersley's caravan. When Guido reached the trio, Blake was thanking Hammersley profusely for his kindness. 'It was most interesting,' he was saying. 'We shall certainly visit the show.'

'You will enjoy it,' promised Hammersley, and they evidently did, for they not only came to the afternoon performance but to the evening one as well, sitting in the same numbered seats.

Hammersley waited in suspense at the ticket guichet, anxiously scanning each patron. On the whole he managed the strange currency very well; in fact, on balance he seemed to have a better grip on it than most of the customers.

When the last performance started and there was still no sign of Simon Good, Hammersley's anxiety increased. True, they now had the Addendum, but tomorrow the circus would be moving on, Toledano was due to collect his dispatch-box – possibly that very night – and what would happen then was anyone's guess. Therefore Hammersley was delighted to see, at long last, Mr Good and Neeve hurrying towards the pay-box. Blake could now report to Simon as of old, and somebody else could carry the can. Hammersley was content; well done, thou good and faithful.

He was not quite so happy half an hour later when he took the cash and balance of tickets over to Peppi's caravan. This ritual was timed to coincide with one of Guido's absences from the ring, and was one to which Peppi looked forward, especially as since Hammersley had been in the pay-box the takings seemed to be in excess of the tickets issued. Hammersley arrived in time to see Toledano, dispatch-box in hand, getting into his car; things would begin to move swiftly at any moment now! Hammersley put it at half an hour at the outside, which would just about coincide with the distribution of the gift parcels to the audience. He handed over the cash to Guido, and went thoughtfully back to his own quarters, spending the next fifteen minutes stacking the assorted packets in the bin on wheels which had been left for that purpose outside his caravan. As a sudden afterthought he wrapped Addendum to Sea-Lion in easily distinguishable paper, and stowed it down amongst the others. Then ambling slowly over to the performers' entrance, he lit a cigarette and idly watched the gyrations of the Arabian steeds in the ring. These were followed by the Petrovelli Family, a trapeze act of considerable skill. A motley of clowns were beginning to gather, tall men, short men, fat men and thin men, but no normal men. It was nearly time for him to go on, on with the motley. He trod out his cigarette end, and hurried back to get his trolley.

From Guido Peppi's van there were sounds of anger.

'Just what is going on, Peppi?' snarled

Toledano. 'This is not what I left in my box!'

'Nobody has interfered with it, *senhor*,' came Peppi's voice, edged with anxiety. 'That I will swear!'

'This document was left locked up in my safe at the Hidden House,' grated the other threateningly. 'And this box contained another set of papers altogether, and a medal. And what do I find? Something completely different and an English penny. And the *senhor* says it hasn't been interfered with! And what do I find at the Hidden House? Tell me, what do I find? Both entrances bricked up. Have *they* not been interfered with either? Is the whole thing an illusion, a figment of the imagination?'

'But the *senhor* himself ordered that work to be done,' objected Peppi strongly, although there was a modulation of fear. 'It was common talk in the village. One of my men told me of it.'

'Who?'

'One of the grooms. And young Petrovelli. And *Senhor* Hammersley – yes, *Senhor* Hammersley talked with the workmen–'

'*Senhor* Hammersley?' There was a prolonged pause. Then, slowly, 'Who is this *Senhor* Hammersley?'

Guido Peppi told him, and although Hammersley couldn't divine the thought process going on in Toledano's seething brain, it was apparent that for some reason the name meant something. It seemed a good moment to beat a hasty retreat. Hammersley grabbed his trolley and took to his heels...

'Where is this man now?' said Toledano softly.

'You know him, *senhor*?'

Toledano stuffed the deeds of the Hidden House in his pocket. Deliberately, he clicked the bones in each finger on his right hand before gripping the butt of his gun. 'A week ago a man came to see me in Boa Fidelidade. He mentioned the name Hammersley. You have a *Senhor* Hammersley from Boa Fidelidade here. Where is he?'

'He is perfectly harmless, Mario, an English gentleman–'

'Where is he?' persisted Toledano menacingly.

Guido Peppi looked unhappy. 'He is due to give away his surprise packets to the children,' he said. 'He may be in his quarters. Let us look.'

He led the way to the caravan next door, climbed the steps, and turned up the calorgas lamp. 'He must be in the big top, *senhor*. See for yourself – he is not here.'

Mario Toledano gave a sudden exclamation. From his eye level he could see under the bunk in the corner. He clambered up, pushed Peppi aside, and produced a black dispatch-box. 'Not interfered with, eh, you

317

fool? There has been some sort of substitution under your very nose. I will see this man Hammersley, and he will talk. Or be silent for a very long time.'

Guido Peppi watched him striding through the gloom to the big top...

Hammersley gave Simon Good his parcel with a feeling of relief which was shortlived; he worked his way round the ring back to the performers' exit, and saw the grim figure of Toledano coming towards him, gun in hand. For a moment Hammersley was transfixed, he hated anything approaching violence.

'*Senhor* Hammersley,' said Toledano, 'I want you.'

Hammersley took to his heels and fled. And a lot of things happened in a very short while. Two circus hands made to restrain the intruder, but Toledano fired a warning shot into the roof of the tent, and with a shout started after Hammersley. Hammersley made for the gangway near Blake, scrambled over, and streaked out into the comforting night. The limelight-man in the roof reacted quickly and swung a wide-angled spot on the whole incident. Doubtless another gag of the *Senhor* Hammersley – he was unpredictable, that one!

Blake, Rip, Simon Good and Neeve, blinded by the ferocious glare, were scarcely conscious of Toledano pulling up sharply as he was about to vault the ringside. In any event, Toledano's face was in deep shadow, and they wouldn't have seen the sudden look of terror in his eyes as they lighted on Adam Neeve. He was not a superstitious man, but the likeness to the man he killed at Boa Fidelidade could have been nothing but a ghastly spectre sent to haunt him, and the yellowy-green light did nothing to allay this impression. In that staggering, geared-up, split second his eye went to the man sitting next to the apparition, a man whose eyes, staring against the glare, reminded him of eyes which had stared down at him years ago from the top of a gun-pit at Hondschouwen. Had all the devils in creation come to haunt him? The limelight flickered uncertainly, and in the brief moment before it blacked out Toledano saw the file of papers in Simon Good's hand as he held it up to shield his eyes, saw the all too familiar face-sheet of Addendum to Sea-Lion. As the spot fizzled and faded, Toledano fired a frantic shot in the direction of Good and Neeve, and leaning over as the two men automatically parted and ducked, snatched the papers and stumbled madly after Hammersley. The light spluttered on again, the quartet picked themselves up, unharmed, and raced out amidst general confusion.

The audience warmly applauded and

cheered this unusual diversion, *Senhor* Peppi could always be relied upon to think up something new!

Once out amongst the crowded side-shows, Mario Toledano made a quick decision. To attempt to find Hammersley would be to waste time. As he had discovered earlier, strange forces were at work, and much as he would like to talk with Hammersley he had no desire for the spectres at the ringside to talk with him. With surprising agility for one of his paunchiness he slid through the crowds to his car, jumped in, and joggled over the rough ground to the exit.

There were two alternatives; either to turn left along the indifferent road to Boa Fidelidade, or right to the Hidden House and the helicopter in which he could hop across the valley and over the range on the opposite side to safety. If he could only reach the helicopter! It was a chance, but he was used to taking chances. He turned right.

He was not without a certain courage, especially when primeval fear was the spur. Accelerating into the village, he took the right-hand fork, and drove furiously to the Hidden House. The street was deserted. Pulling over to the extreme right, he braced himself, wrenched the wheel over, and drove straight at the bricked-up entrance. For a moment he was stunned by the impact. But the vehicle was well-upholstered, was chassis-built, and weighed upwards of a ton. The engine was still running, the gears still worked. He reversed breakneck across the road, the one remaining headlight showing that the wall had given under the sudden blow. He came at it again like a ramrod, as hard as he could go in the short distance, and this time a positive gash appeared. He staggered out and feverishly scrabbled at the loose bricks, pushing at the door which hung drunkenly behind the gap. In a few minutes he was blundering up the passage, staring aghast at the mess Blake had made of the front door. Once inside the house it didn't take many more minutes for him to decide to cut his losses and flee. He scrambled up the iron stairway to the summit of Giant's Hammer, slammed shut an iron grille at the top, and was soon struggling to release the toggles which held the helicopter secure...

Hammersley spotted the others snaking through the crowd, and crawled out from under the hoopla stall. 'He went that way – towards the Hidden House!' he shouted. 'In his car–' But they were already in pursuit...

Simon let fly an expletive as he twisted his ankle in a rut and was forced to lag behind Neeve, who moved with relentless rhythm and purpose to the forked road. For a moment Neeve paused uncertainly, and then spotted the wrecked car. Reaching the aperture in the wall, he scrambled through and raced along the covered passageway, fumbling for the gun in his pocket. The Hidden House was a blaze of light, and he hurried from room to room like some avenging god until he came to the hatch leading to the summit. Down the shaft there came a sudden spasmodic roar as the booster mechanism kicked over the engine of the helicopter, and the giant arms started to thrash the atmosphere. Heart and lungs bursting, he clattered up the spiral stairway to the grille at the top.

Toledano was sitting at the controls of the machine, which Neeve recognised as an old German Dornski with the twin fuel tanks slung underneath. The engine seemed to die for a moment and then kicked into life again with not quite the right note.

'Toledano!' roared Neeve. 'You killed my son! I'm coming to get you!' He shook the grille, but it was self-locking and as firm as a rock. Taking aim, Neeve fired at the lock, but still it held. The helicopter started to lift gently, poised like a night-bird about to land in its eyrie. It swung on its axis and moved Toledano out of range. The engine started to cough and splutter again, and Neeve thought of the fuel tanks. Taking careful aim, he fired at the main tank, and the bullet ricocheted off into the night. The second shot buried itself in the thin metal, and as the Dornski thrashed its way to freedom over the edge of the bowl of Giant's Hammer there was an all-pervading smell of high-octane petrol...

Neeve turned and found Simon behind him.

'He's made it?' said Simon.

'Yes – and don't light a cigarette.'

'You hit his fuel tank? Then he won't get far.'

'There's a reserve tank – you can bet it's full. I didn't get time to have a shot at it...'

'Oh, dear!' said Hammersley, when they told him. 'Oh, dear, oh, dear!'

'Never mind, we'll get him somehow,' said Neeve.

'I didn't mean that,' said Hammersley, removing his spectacles and breathing on them. 'The other day my lighter was empty, and there was a little drain-tap at the base of the spare tank. I turned it on and it jammed, and I couldn't turn it off. The tank must be quite empty by now...'

The helicopter reached the low mountains the other side of the valley, gave a death rattle, and plummeted to earth like a stone.

A number of people, when they heard of Toledano's death, didn't mourn...

A little urchin named Manuel, playing near

the wreckage, picked up some papers clipped together at the corner. He didn't recognise any of the words printed thereon, he could barely speak Portuguese, let alone German. To him, stiff paper had three uses; you could scribble on it; you could make very good paper darts with it; and you could burn it. He possessed no pencil, therefore he could either make paper darts with it or burn it. He compromised by making a supply of darts and throwing them into the bonfire he made with the remainder of the sheets...

The phoenix from the holocaust that was Germany returned to the ashes on a mountainside in Portugal. All except page 22, which in due course Mr Justice Meddlisome burnt on his hearth at Gomshall, England.

'It seems,' said Neeve to Blake, 'that you have a propensity for getting into other people's houses.'

'In an emergency, yes,' agreed Blake virtuously.

'It also seems we have no further use for this gun. I wonder if you'd do me a good turn and put it back where it belongs?'

'And where's that?'

'In a house in Surrey.'

'Tell me all about it,' said Blake.

They discussed the pros and cons.

CHAPTER 23

Act with Conviction

Blake drove fast along the road out of Dorking to Shere, thankful for the powerful headlights which reached out into the darkened countryside. Turning off into Shere, he drove out past the Lavender Lady for about another half-mile, and swung off the road into a dark patch under some trees. There he extinguished the lights, and strode off up the road for a few hundred yards.

The Mendozas' house was in complete darkness. His information was that it would be empty till about one a.m. He walked cautiously round it once and decided the coast was clear. A couple of minutes and the job would be done, and Adam Neeve would be able to report to old Meddlisome that the gun was now safely back from whence he'd taken it. Rejoice, for that which was lost is found – although the chances were that the Mendozas had never missed it anyway. It was a daddle-home. The great thing was to act with conviction.

He was just inserting the key in the front

door when he suddenly froze. A high-powered car was purring its way up the road from the direction of the village. He slid behind one of the pillars of the portico, and remained motionless. It was difficult to tell if the softly-purring engine had stopped farther up the road, or whether the sounds of it had merely faded in the distance.

Blake was essentially a man of action. He turned the key and entered the house, leaving the door ajar to facilitate a speedy exit. With the aid of a pocket torch he made his way upstairs, and with a little exploration found the Blue Room. He replaced the gun and ammunition in the handkerchief tray in the wardrobe as directed, and was on his way down again when he suddenly thought it might be a better idea to leave the articles elsewhere. If the Mendozas had missed them, they would surely think it peculiar if they suddenly turned up again in the right place. If found somewhere else, it would be put down to zealous domestic reorganisation. Blake retrieved the gun and ammunition, and was on his way downstairs again to find another hiding place, when the lights suddenly snapped on, and two men were looking up at him curiously from the hall.

'Good evening, sir,' said one of them.

'Good evening,' said Blake courteously. 'May I ask what you are doing here?'

'I was about to ask you the same question, sir.'

'I'm a friend of the owner. And you?'

'We're police officers, sir. May we come in?'

'By all means do, although it seems you're already in. What appears to be the trouble?'

'We were passing by and we thought we saw someone standing in the porch. We came back to investigate.'

'Very commendable, I'm sure,' said Blake. 'The Mendozas will be gratified.'

'As a friend of the family, sir, you will know that a certain article was reported missing from this house.'

Blake stiffened. 'I did hear something of the sort,' he said casually.

'And so we've kept an eye on the place in case anybody came back for more.'

'Very wise precaution.'

'When we found the door open, we were naturally suspicious, especially when we saw you were using a torch. If the lights had gone on, we wouldn't have given it a second thought. By the way, sir, how *did* you get in?'

'With a key.'

'Oh, yes, of course, you're a friend. I was forgetting. How did you come here tonight?'

Blake paused momentarily. He sensed the question was knowledgeable, that the plain-clothes man – for all his apparent friendliness – was tensed for the reply. And he was conscious that the other man had his notebook out. 'By car,' he said.

'Ah, yes. You parked it under the trees not thirty yards from us. And what is your name, sir?'

'Bird,' said Blake, tossing caution to the wind.

'And your first name?'

'Dickie.'

'I know,' said the officer tolerantly. 'Dickie Bird, and you live up a tree. I expect your driving licence will confirm that if necessary. I think we'll take the liberty of waiting in the drawing room for the Mendozas. They told the Inspector they'd be back by one a.m. They'll be delighted to see you.' The officer was well pleased with the way things were going.

They waited in a somewhat strained atmosphere, Blake inwardly kicking himself for not having left the gun where he'd put it at first. He wondered if he could slip it somewhere in the large drawing room, but it was furnished in the modern style, all spindly legs and very hygienic, but useless for hiding places. Apart from which he was conscious of the all too casual indifference of the policemen.

After an eternity, a car drew up outside, and the policeman who had done most of the talking went out to the front door to greet a puzzled trio.

Blake tensed as he heard John Mendoza's voice raised in a note of inquiry. 'Hullo, officer, what brings you here? Brought back our diamond ring? – But how in the name of thunder did you get in? Don't tell me we left the door open?'

'The door was open, sir. We were invited in by an old friend of yours who'd let himself in with a key. I expect you'll be pleased to see him.'

John Mendoza hurried into the room followed by Caroline and Ambrose Meddlisome, looking from Blake to the other plainclothes man, who had risen immediately. Blake remained seated, taking it easy while he could.

'Don't know him from Adam!' growled John Mendoza.

'No?' said the first officer, delighted. 'Then doubtless a friend of Mrs Mendoza's?'

'Never seen him before in my life,' declared Caroline.

'I must have misunderstood him,' said the other, pleased as Punch. 'Do you know him, Mr Meddlisome?'

Blake became alert. Meddlisome! So this was the old boy for whom he was doing a good deed. From the way things were going it looked as if he'd also be the old boy who'd send him down for six months – or probably life, considering that Simon got twelve months for fiddling a bob's worth of electricity! He was aware that Mr Justice Meddlisome was gazing down at him dispassionately. He wondered what he looked like with a wig. Perhaps he'd find out.

'I don't know this man,' said Ambrose Meddlisome.

'He's right, you know, he doesn't,' declared Blake, playing for time. Now would be the moment to declare the purpose of his visit. Now or never. Tell them how the old boy had borrowed the gun to avenge the death of someone who wasn't dead, and how he, Blake, had volunteered to put it back because he was skilled at such operations. Didn't sound too good. There'd be questions and embarrassment all round. Now or never. It looked like never. Anyway, perhaps he'd get away with it. After all, he'd done nothing really wrong. Not like when he'd done that Reigate job at van Meyer's mansion. Nominally forty thousand pounds' worth of loot, there. It was *most* annoying! Old Meddlisome could have put the gun back himself tonight without all this complication. But could he though? He couldn't possibly know the purpose of Blake's nocturnal visit to the Mendozas' house, and yet he looked as ill at ease and guilty in the presence of the two officers as if he'd actually shot Toledano. Blake grinned to himself.

'Something amusing, sir?' asked the senior officer.

'In a way,' said Blake.

'Perhaps you'll tell us about it on the way to the station. We can do with cheering up.'

'Can I give anyone a lift?' asked John Mendoza. 'I'm running Mr Meddlisome back into Gomshall in a minute – we've only dragged him in for a nightcap. What about you?'

'Not for me,' said Blake.

'No, not for you, sir,' agreed the senior man. 'Thank you all the same, Mr Mendoza, but we'll be on our way. Some other time, perhaps. Our own vehicle is up the road.'

Blake was taken into Dorking for further questioning. He was on his own, and he knew it.

The following morning they gave him another grilling, and this time there was another man in the room. Blake was dismayed to see that it was the character he couldn't place that day in the Leather Bottle. The irritating thing was he still couldn't place him.

'First there's breaking and entering,' said Superintendent Lingard.

'I didn't break anything,' protested Blake virtuously. 'I used a key.'

'Oh, yes, the key. Where did you get it?'

'It was in the lock when I turned it,' said Blake with great exactitude.

'And before then?'

'That's a different question.'

'It's part of the same question.'

'Arising out of breaking and entering?'

'Arising out of that, yes,' sighed Lingard.

'I merely turned the lock. I didn't break it.'

'No? Just as well – that would have been malicious damage, and the punishment may be heavier if the offence is committed by night. And for your information, the turning of a lock for the purpose of unlawful entry is considered breaking. So is drawing a bolt or opening a closed window. And even coming down a chimney.'

'You don't say!' said Blake, fascinated.

'I do say,' said Lingard firmly. 'And then there's your pretending to be a friend of the Mendozas.'

'Is that criminal?'

'If it's tied up with intent to commit a felony, yes.'

'What felony?' said Blake, interested.

Lingard was very patient. '*Intent* to commit a felony was the phrase I used,' he said cautiously.

'How could you possibly know my intentions?'

'They were becoming fairly obvious, weren't they, bearing in mind the circumstances, coupled with behaviour which amounted to wilful obstruction of the police in the course of their duty.'

'And I tried to be so helpful,' said Blake

sadly. 'These circumstances – doubtless you could summarise?'

'By all means. You were in a strange house – it *was* a strange house, wasn't it? You hadn't been there before, had you? Then you wouldn't know that a valuable solitaire diamond ring was missing. Oh, but of course, you're a friend of the family, you must have been there before! You would know all about the ring! You weren't by any chance looking for another?'

'Whoa back! This is like "Have you stopped beating your wife"!'

'It seems then you were making a friendly call on people you don't know, to enter a house you've never been in before with a key that wasn't yours, and with a gun and ammunition for which you hold no licence or certificate, and which you admit isn't yours anyway. And you enter at a little after midnight on the one night your friends aren't there.'

'Oh, I agree, it is all very circumstantial,' said Blake.

'I can't wait to hear the judge chuckle when you tell him that,' said Lingard. 'By the way, you weren't wearing a disguise, were you? An improvised mask? They tell me you had a knotted cravat, with the knot at the back – wearing it back to front, as it were.'

'I always wear it like that,' said Blake.

'Why do you ask?'

'Being disguised at night carries with it an implication of terrorism, and is quite an offence. Coupled with burglary you might just as well make your funeral arrangements. You ought to read the Larceny Act some time. It's most interesting.'

'I must get a copy.'

'They'll probably have one in the prison library.'

'I'm sorry there was nothing unusual in the way I was wearing my scarf,' apologised Blake.

'So am I. Tell me about the gun.'

'It fires bullets.'

Lingard swore he'd get this smart Aleck if it was the last thing he did. 'So I gather,' he said with considerable restraint. 'Several are missing from the clip. I suppose you wouldn't know where they are?'

'I haven't a clue,' confessed Blake. 'Probably just missing. The gun isn't mine, remember? Has it been fired recently?'

'I'm asking the questions. But in case you don't know, the weapon has been thoroughly cleaned and oiled – even the rounds have been wiped.'

'Care of small arms – almost the first thing they taught us in the army.' Blake stared thoughtfully at the Superintendent. 'I know your face,' he said frowning. 'We've met before, somewhere.'

'Monte Carlo?'

'It goes back a long way. It worries me.'

'Perhaps we were at the same school.'

'I doubt it. I came up the hard way.'

'So did I. Depends which side of the fence you picked. Or which fence. I came from an L.C.C. Central School with an academic bias. Yours was probably more technical. Taught you metal-work, and all about locks and safes.'

'Funny you should say that. Do you know what I did before the war?'

'You mean your job at Lumm's Safes?'

'You know about that?' said Blake in considerable surprise.

'Oh, yes, we know all about that,' said Lingard affably.

'Why should you?'

'Not so very long ago there was a burglary at Reigate.' (Blake almost stopped breathing.) 'Forty thousand pounds' worth of diamonds were stolen and were never recovered. And a wing of Mr van Meyer's mansion was burned down either as a result of the use of polar-ammon gelignite, or as a clumsy attempt to cover up traces of the burglary. The diamonds were in a Lumm safe.'

'So?'

'We checked up on all the old Lumm employees, particularly those who were dismissed as a result of the Rempert's take-over. We never got the culprit.'

'Surely the fire didn't destroy *all* the clues?'

'I said it was a clumsy attempt, sir. You wouldn't know, of course, but polar-ammon gelignite is a paste form of explosive. After the lock had been packed, a wedge of putty was used to seal the keyhole. The force of the explosion blew the putty out into a cranny untouched by fire. Perfect shape of the keyhole.'

'Interesting.'

'More than that, sir – damning. You see, where it had been pressed home into the lock, it retained a thumbprint. Not a complete print, or a perfect print, but nevertheless, a print.'

Blake's world suddenly junketed crazily around him on a broken axis. He strove to place this smooth individual before him.

'Where were you on the night of the Reigate burglary?' asked Lingard suddenly.

'I haven't the faintest idea, officer,' said the other. He glanced at his finger-nails. 'When exactly was it?'

Lingard gazed speculatively at him for a long moment before handing over a newspaper cutting. 'This might refresh your memory,' he said sardonically.

Blake skimmed through the cutting. 'I was out of the country,' he said. 'Holland, I think.'

'Can you prove it?' asked Lingard quickly.

'Passport?' suggested Blake confidently. 'I usually like to be out of the country on these occasions.'

Superintendent Lingard rose with a sigh and lit a cigarette. 'I think we can find a bit more to charge him with, Sergeant,' he said, between puffs. 'And if you haven't already done so, take his dabs. And please, please be careful with his right thumb. I don't want the print to be smudged...'

Blake came up and got two months. To the amazement of the court he asked if, in the light of all the offences listed, this were adequate. For this impertinence, Judge Knott co-operated quickly and gave him an extra month. For some reason Blake seemed pleased.

'What went wrong?' asked Simon on visiting day. They were seated opposite each other in a little booth in a room near the prison gate, precisely twenty-eight days later.

'I did a good turn,' said Blake, 'and whenever I do a good turn it never works out. The only time I helped an old lady across the road she didn't want to go.'

'That's life,' agreed Simon. 'Tell me about it.'

'Well, this old lady–'

'The gun.'

'Meddlisome hooked it from the Mendozas' home at Shere—'

'What on earth for?'

'To avenge what he thought was his brother-in-law's death. Fortunately Neeve turned up and relieved him of it, but felt he couldn't leave it to Meddlisome to replace it. It seems that the old boy, having taken it surreptitiously, was as shaky as a willow every time he faced the Mendozas. Adam figured he would more than likely confess his misdemeanour to them, and start off a whole train of explanation leading to heaven knows where, involving us all. But if Adam could suddenly tell Ambrose the gun was back in place with nobody the wiser, then all would be well. The mere presence of the police that night at Shere shook the old boy rigid. He'd have probably had kittens if he'd known why I was in the house. I've never seen a law dispenser so ill-at-ease in the presence of law enforcers.'

'And yet he was prepared to commit mayhem to avenge Adam Neeve's death,' pointed out Simon.

'From what Neeve tells me he'd have probably shot the wrong one! And would then have sentenced himself to death with the last round. I think that having had time to work out all the implications of what might have happened if he'd actually embarked on whatever plan he had, he just

338

couldn't face even *thinking* about the gun. What the psychologists call a traumatic bloc.'

'If you say so. So you volunteered to replace it?'

'I came to an arrangement with Adam.'

Simon looked thoughtful. 'I can't help wondering why they didn't make more of that gun. What did you tell the police?'

'That it was a war souvenir I should have handed in long ago, and that, strange though it might seem, I was going to dump it in a river. They didn't believe me, of course.'

'They proved otherwise?'

'Yes, but not that I *wasn't* going to dump it in a river. They proved it was a Russian gun, a relic of the Korean War. Not my war. And it wouldn't fire.'

Simon's jaw swung up. 'Wouldn't fire? But we know it would. We know it *did.*'

'Not when Adam handed it over to me. The firing-pin had been filed short. It wouldn't reach the base of the rounds. He made a good job of it.'

'So it seems you're in here for sweet Fanny Adams.'

'Caught in the web of destiny,' said Blake tragically. 'They suspect I stole a ring or something and was going back for more. That's almost an insult after the van Meyer diamonds. There's one thing that worries me though – they've got a line on that Reigate job. A thumb-print on a lump of putty blown from the keyhole of the safe. In the hurry we had to make two attempts. It could either be mine or Rip Strookman's.'

'If they didn't charge you, it looks like Rip's.'

'They may be saving it up for later – that Superintendent looked very determined. I wish I could place him.'

'You didn't get his name?'

'There were no formal introductions,' said Blake sadly.

Simon Good looked gloomy. 'Quenella's been well paid, Rip has some more diamonds to play with, Hammersley's had his fun, but it looks as if we've worked hard for nothing.'

Blake grinned. 'Not entirely. I said I came to an arrangement with Adam. The arrangement was that if anything went wrong he'd compensate me for loss of earnings. I worked that out at a modest two hundred pounds a week. He was confident nothing would go wrong, and agreed enthusiastically. We shook on it. Twelve weeks at two hundred a week is two thousand four hundred.'

'I hope he doesn't forget to pay you. That leaves me. Talk about the Welfare State!'

'You haven't done so badly – you've not been killed.'

A prison officer glanced at the clock on the wall, and rang a bell. 'Time's up!' he said sharply. There was a shuffle of chairs at the booths, and the visitors prepared to return to the freedom of being away from their loved ones.

'See if you can get a look at the Governor's safe while you're here,' said Simon.

'I'll do that,' said Blake.

'I'll be seeing you,' said Simon.

'I won't go away,' promised Blake...

The Commander (Crime) buzzed for Lingard. 'I thought you'd like to know, Superintendent, that Adam Neeve is no longer missing. He's turned up again at the Goodwill.'

'Has he, by George! I wonder what he had to say.'

'He's been suffering from a breakdown due to overwork, and amnesia, and has asked the directors to consider his early retirement. Wonderful thing, amnesia – can't remember a thing. He has a doctor's certificate to prove it.'

'Did he write it himself?'

'Oh, no, it's genuine enough.' The Commander coughed discreetly. 'It was signed by a Foreign Office doctor – Commander Pope swears by him... Tell me, Lingard, something puzzles me. Meddlisome went to Simon Good for assistance. Blake's a friend of Simon Good's. Meddlisome's a – friend of the Mendozas. And yet the Mendozas and Meddlisome deny knowing Blake – to the extent of letting him go to jail on what amounts to a series of technicalities. It's doubtful if he'd have been caught at all but for the fact the locals were keeping an eye on the place because of that missing diamond ring. Just what *was* he doing in the Mendozas' house?'

'Could have been after more jewellery, sir.'

'*More?* That Reigate thumb-print wasn't his, you know, in spite of our suspicions. It only wants Mrs Mendoza to find her ring in the bathroom, and our suspicions even in this case seem groundless.'

'Well, Blake doesn't seem to mind going to prison. There's Simon Good complaining because his sentence was too long, and Blake because his wasn't long enough. The whole mob is plumb crazy!' snorted the Superintendent. 'They should all be in a nuthouse!'

CHAPTER 24

A Question of Outlook

Caroline greeted her husband excitedly. 'John! I've found the ring! Guess where!'

'Where you put it?' suggested John indulgently.

'Meeow! I had a sudden brainwave. I seemed to remember putting it amongst some linens, and I had another look in the wardrobe in the Blue Room.'

'And there it was?'

'Not immediately. I'd looked there before, but I had all the trays out today to see if it had either fallen out into the bottom of the wardrobe, or perhaps got lodged on one of the runners.'

'And there it was?'

'No, there it wasn't. Don't be impatient! As I was replacing the trays I noticed that the bottoms project about an inch where they ride against the back-stops. And *there* it was, wedged firmly in between the back of a tray and one of those little glued-in blocks of wood. Must have been there all the time! Ambrose will be delighted!'

'You'd better ring up the Inspector and tell

him you're ever so sorry he's been troubled.'

'I'll leave that to you, darling. If I tell him, he'll only say "Just like a woman."'

'It occurs to me,' said John, 'that if they hadn't been keeping an eye on the place they wouldn't have caught that chap with the gun.'

Caroline looked thoughtful. 'John. When I was searching through the trays, one thing puzzled me. I thought that old army gun of yours should have been there.'

'Well, wasn't it?'

'No.'

'Didn't I leave it at the back of the odd-ment drawer in the sideboard?' said John, screwing up his face in thought.

'No, we've moved it since then – was it when Jane came?' Caroline had a sudden thought. 'Perhaps that man, Blake, stole it – he had a gun.'

'Couldn't have been mine – the police said his wouldn't fire.' John suddenly grinned. 'I expect Ambrose was trying to sell mine that day in Haymarket!'

'John–' Caroline hesitated. '–He *was* a bit strange that day. Do you remember what he said when you asked him if he was going to shoot someone? He said *"No!"*'

'What's strange about that?'

'Well – surely the normal answer in such circumstances would be "Yes". A funny question calls for a funny answer. "Yes, I'm going to shoot the Income Tax man." You caught him on the hop – it was as though the real answer should have been "yes" but he was impelled to say "no". As though he had something to hide.'

'You're imagining things, Caroline.'

'And that was the day we gave him the key. Jane said he looked – queer.'

'Jane said? I thought it was her afternoon off?'

'She was late going out. She crossed the hall, and he was standing at the top of the stairs – in a trance, she said. She spoke to him, and he didn't answer, so she crept out and left him to it.'

'So?'

'Well, why was he *up*stairs?'

'Bathroom?'

'There's the downstairs cloakroom.'

'Perhaps Jane was there. Anyway, if you give someone the freedom of the house you must expect a little curiosity to be displayed. You're not suggesting that Ambrose, of all people, was rifling our private belongings, or planning an armed robbery? You're quite sure the gun isn't there?'

'Yes. I noticed it had gone when I first looked for the ring. I thought perhaps you'd shifted it, I meant to have mentioned it to you at the time.'

'I wonder if I put it up in the loft with all that other Army junk? I really can't remember – I'll check next time I look at the tank. I wish I'd handed it in years ago when they called for souvenirs to be surrendered. I can't report it now. Still, not to worry.' He was silent for a moment, and a faraway look crept into his eyes. He said softly, 'Ambrose will be pleased we've found the ring.'

Caroline nodded mute assent. 'Do you really think it belonged to your...' Her voice trailed off.

'Yes, Caroline, I'm pretty certain it was my mother's. Why else was it of such sentimental value to an old man? *His* mother's? No. Too far back, I imagine, for the sentiment to be alive. And why bestow it on us, of all people? Besides, apart from the Spanish government mark, there's the peculiar claw setting of the Mendoza family. Without a doubt it once belonged to the Jacquenita Mendoza who ran away from her family in disgrace, who died giving birth to me. And without a doubt it is the counterpart of the ear-rings in her possession when she died. The Mother Superior was very kind to let me have them – that woman had a wealth of gentle compassion, I've often thought of her. Compassion breeds compassion, hate breeds hate. There was a time when I swore I'd never forgive Ambrose Meddlisome, but compassion and tolerance won.'

'Knowing him for the kindly man he is

today,' said Caroline, 'I feel there must have been mitigating circumstances which we'll probably never know.'

'Like he didn't want a scandal because he was about to be called to the Bar?' said John lightly. 'The *bar sinister*. I suppose he's subsequently tried to make amends in a roundabout sort of way, what with getting us this house, and his various kindnesses. I think I feel rather sorry for him.'

'Shouldn't we let *him* know *we* know?'

'He's an old man, Caroline. For years he's been living with his dreams in a castle of cards. Why should we jog it or blow it down? I'm sure that his legal mind has weighed up the pros and cons, and that he feels exposure would harm us more than him. He's living in the idiom of another age, when such things meant so much more than they do today. No, Caroline, if there's any telling to be done, it must come from him, not from us.'

Caroline bestowed a light kiss on his forehead. 'You're very sweet,' she said.

'If we told him, he'd die of shock. Let him live out the rest of his life with the grand illusion.'

'You have your good points,' said Caroline critically.

'*Are* there any others?' he asked in faint surprise.

'Not that you'd notice,' she agreed fondly.

'It's a good job we're both sensible about this sort of thing, John. Still, I suppose there must be a lot of fathers who want to keep quiet about their illegitimate sons.'

'It's a question of outlook,' said John. 'I think there must be a lot of sons who want to keep quiet about their illegitimate fathers...'

The publishers hope that this book has given you enjoyable reading. Large Print Books are especially designed to be as easy to see and hold as possible. If you wish a complete list of our books please ask at your local library or write directly to:

Dales Large Print Books
Magna House, Long Preston,
Skipton, North Yorkshire.
BD23 4ND

This Large Print Book, for people
who cannot read normal print,
is published under the auspices of

THE ULVERSCROFT FOUNDATION